The Drop-Dead Temple of Doom

Book Eight
of the
Alvarez Family Murder Mysteries

by
Heather Haven

i

The Drop-Dead Temple of Doom © 2021 by Heather Haven

The Wives of Bath Press
5512 Cribari Bend
San Jose, Ca 95135

http:// www.heatherhavenstories.com

Praise For The Series

♥ "Heather Haven makes a stellar debut in *Murder is a Family Business.* With an engaging protagonist and a colorful cast, Haven provides a fresh voice in a crowded genre. We will be hearing more from this talented newcomer. Highly recommended." **Sheldon Siegel, *New York Times* Best-Selling Author of *Perfect Alibi***

♥ *A Wedding to Die For* "Wonderfully fresh and funny!" **Meg Waite Clayton, Author of *The Race For Paris***

♥ "I Just finished *Death Runs in the Family* and I loved it! This has turned out to be one of my favorite series and I sure hope there will be another installment in the near future!" **Becky Carbone, Global Ebook Awards**

♥ *DEAD...If Only* "A must-read 5-star series!" **Cindy Sample, National Best-Selling Author**

♥ *The CEO Came DOA* "This is a strong work in the genre of the mystery/thriller!" ***San Francisco Book Review***

♥ *The Culinary Art of Murder* "This latest installment of Haven's murder mystery series offers a twisty whodunit laced with a healthy dose of suspense. A solidly entertaining mystery" ***Kirkus Reviews***

♥ *Casting Call for a Corpse* "There was never a dull moment in this entertaining cozy mystery, which includes plenty of action, a well balanced range of twists and turns, and even a few laugh out loud moments." **Cassidy's Bookshelves**

Acknowledgments

A special thanks to Josie Thompson, Director of Planning for the Foundation For Anthropological Research & Environmental Studies Inc (FARES), whose life's work served as inspiration for the book. She has left me with these words:

> *Nothing can take the place of visiting the ancient preclassic Mayan site of El Mirador! All five senses come alive in the jungle and one's feeling of connection with nature and culture is solidified. Thanks to Mother Nature for creating this ancient Karst Basin where the muddy muck keeps developers at bay. The FARES foundation has championed cultural and environmental conservation in this region for over thirty years. By using advanced mapping technologies (LIDAR) we are able to prove to the world that there once existed a truly immense empire nestled in tandem with natural forces, only found in the Guatemalan jungle.*
> *The best way to understand and get to know Mirador is to visit. Once you visit, I am sure you will fall in love with it and want to protect this global environmental and cultural treasure. KNOW, LOVE, PROTECT*

Using my writer's imagination, I took my perception of the important work being done in Guatemala's Mirador Basin and spun it into a wild tale. That stated, I did try to keep the underlying facts correct. However, any untruth or misinformation is totally the fault of this author.

Thanks to Beta readers Mary Wollesen, Roseanne Dowell, and Grace DeLuca. Each of them has made wonderful suggestions throughout the years and have helped me turn out a better book every time.

More thanks to friend and editor, Baird Nuckolls. Her insight is amazing. Also thanks to editor/proofreading team, Paula and Terrance Grundy.

https://paulaproofreader.wixsite.com/home or https://editerry.wixsite.com/proofreader

There is nothing too small for these three to catch! However, any imperfections within this book are solely my responsibility.

Dedication

This book is dedicated to my mother, Mary Lee. I miss her terribly. She was a one-of-a-kind person and the world became a slightly colder place with her passing in 2014. It is also dedicated to long-time friend, Paula Winters Fields, who passed several months ago. These women will never be forgotten as long as those of us who loved them still breathe.

I would also like to dedicate this book to my husband, Norman Meister. Funny, loving, and romantic men like him are rare. And I got me one! Thank you, darling, for just being you.

And lastly, I dedicate it to first responders and all frontline people who devote their lives to the care and betterment of those around them. Also to all the organizations that help protect the plants, animals, people, and history of this ever-increasingly fragile planet.

God bless you all.

Table of Contents

Chapter One... 2

Chapter Two 9

Chapter Three 13

Chapter Four 22

Chapter Five.. 27

Chapter Six.. 33

Chapter Seven... 39

Chapter Eight.. 44

Chapter Nine 48

Chapter Ten 51

Chapter Eleven 61

Chapter Twelve 70

Chapter Thirteen 75

Chapter Fourteen 85

Chapter Fifteen... 89

Chapter Sixteen 93

Chapter Seventeen 99

Chapter Eighteen.. 108

Chapter Nineteen.. 117

Chapter Twenty... 123

Chapter Twenty-One... 128

Chapter Twenty-Two 136

Chapter Twenty-Three.. 142

Chapter Twenty-Four.................................. 147

Chapter Twenty-Five................................. 155

Chapter Twenty-Six.................................. 159

Chapter Twenty-Seven............................... 167

Chapter Twenty-Eight................................ 174

Chapter Twenty-Nine................................ 181

Chapter Thirty 184

Chapter Thirty-One 196

Chapter Thirty-Two 199

Chapter Thirty-Three................................ 203

Chapter Thirty-Four 208

Chapter Thirty-Five 214

Chapter Thirty-Six 217

Chapter Thirty-Seven 221

Chapter Thirty-Eight 229

Chapter Thirty-Nine 235

Chapter Forty.. 239

Chapter Forty-One 244

Chapter Forty-Two 249

Chapter Forty-Three 255

Chapter Forty-Four 259

Chapter Forty-Five................................... 264

Chapter Forty-Six 275

Chapter Forty-Seven................................. 281

Chapter Forty-Eight.................................. 286

Chapter Forty-Nine.. 293

Chapter Fifty 300

Chapter Fifty-One 310

Afterword by Josie Thompson............................... 317

Books by Heather Haven 319

About Heather Haven 320

Connect with Heather at the following sites:........ 321

The Drop-Dead Temple
of Doom

Chapter One

"JJ's in trouble," a familiar voice said.

I put down my e-reader and focused on my husband of nearly a year, six-foot-two Gurn Hanson, a honey of a man with sun-streaked brown hair and a square jawline. My own personal Adonis looked worried. This was surprising. It takes a lot to rattle my man.

JJ is Gurn's cousin. Only a few months younger, she's in nearly every childhood picture I'd seen of him. Adult life may have sent them their separate ways, but when growing up, they were practically joined at the hip.

Hubby continued to stare at me. Uh-oh. I took a deep breath. This was not going to be the relaxing Sunday morning I'd hoped for. Or, truth be told, felt I deserved.

I am the in-house investigator for the family-owned, Silicon Valley-based detective agency, Discretionary Inquiries. The aforementioned is called D. I. by everyone except my mother and CEO, Lila Hamilton-Alvarez. She doesn't like abbreviations, nicknames, or salty language. It can be a challenge.

D. I. is known far and wide for taking on the who, what, where, and how of stolen computer software, hardware, and

2

intellectual property. Then we help bring the villains to justice. Just like our business card says.

But we sure got fooled on the last case. Under the guise of being about bad business practices, this job could have been labeled Cain Clobbers Abel. One brother coveted the other brother's wife. And scored. It was worse than any soap opera I've ever seen because I wound up being one of the cast members.

Just to make it clear, we don't usually deal with this type of case. Volatile and distasteful. But we were committed. Or should have been.

It took three hideous weeks of twelve-hour days to prove there was no business malfeasance on either brother's part, much to each one's dismay. Following this revelation, Lila Hamilton-Alvarez suggested—in the nicest possible way—they get over themselves and seek therapy. But not before apologizing to their own mother for causing her such heartache.

Then the lovely Lila presented them with a bill large enough to buy a small Greek island. After she cashed their check, she sent them on their way.

My mother survived this odious event with barely a mascaraed eyelash out of place. Not so with me. I looked like something Tugger, My Son the Cat, decided not to drag in because he has standards.

At thirty-four years old, my eyes had bags under bags. My long brunette hair exploded with a sudden case of split ends. I needed an emergency facial, done by either Heavenly Skin Beckons or Roto Rooter. I wasn't fussy.

After we closed the case, I spent the next day in bed trying to recover. I wore a garden's worth of sliced cucumbers on puffy eyes, took scissors to split ends, and then binge-watched *All Creatures Great and Small*. I began to heal.

3

Come Sunday, I was in a laid-back, love-the-morning mood, relaxing outside on the deck in one of our comfy lounge chairs. The sun was shining, birds were singing, and a soft breeze was blowing. Both cats, Tugger and Baba, snoozed at my feet. Baba Ganoush, having come into my life with Gurn, was this darling long-haired, gray-and-white girl kitty, the textbook complement to the lean orange-and-white Tugger. They worshiped one another.

The day stretched out before me. I was especially looking forward to the end of this perfect day. Tío, my uncle, is a retired chef and had invited us for dinner. And I would be able to eat my head off, as I was four pounds under goal.

In short, all was right with the world. Naturally, that was about to change. I steeled myself and repeated hubby's words back to him.

"JJ's in trouble? If memory serves me, she couldn't come to our wedding because she'd been sideswiped by a jaguar. And I don't mean the car."

"She would have been there if she could." His tone was just a tad defensive. Once again, very unlike him. "And she did send us that temple rubbing."

"Absolutely, darling, and it hangs in our hallway with pride. Just a little attempt at humor," I said.

"Of course it was, sweetheart. Sorry, I didn't mean to snap." There was the man I loved and adored. Welcome back. Shaking his head, he went on, "I know I don't see JJ a lot these days. But we grew up together."

"And you're close. I get it."

"I just got off the phone with her." He took a breath to go on, but I interrupted before he could speak.

"JJ called you from the jungles of Guatemala?"

"She called to tell me Martín is missing. Missing! He disappeared yesterday."

4

"Her husband's missing?" Goodbye laid-back mood. I swung my legs to the floor and sat upright. "Oh my God! What do the police say?"

"There seems to be a delay in alerting them. Her boss, a Dr. Joan Lancaster, has pressured her not to. JJ says there has been some trouble on the site, and the police have been out there a few times already. One more visit, and Dr. Lancaster is afraid the Ministry of Justice will shut the site down. JJ agreed to wait a day or two if she could call me instead."

"This Dr. Lancaster is in charge of the whole project?"

"Yes." Gurn came around to the lounge chair opposite me and sat down on the edge of it, tense, tense, tense. "You know Martín is a paramedic, right?"

I nodded. "I remember. Something about there being a lot of people living around ancient cities in the Mirador Basin. Doesn't he run a nonprofit clinic to take care of their basic health needs?"

"Yes, an offshoot of the dig, but privately funded. He's doing good work in places where they're short on doctors and long on snakebites."

"You make the jungle sound so inviting. Go on."

"Three days ago, there was a cave-in at a nearby site. Probably due to recent rains. Some men were hurt, just scrapes and bruises. They sent for Martín to help patch them up."

"Wait a minute. Isn't there an on-site doctor?"

"Took the day off and went to Antigua. Martín and his assistant were covering. I think the doctor is due back later today. Anyway, Martín left immediately. It's only a few miles away, but it can take several hours to walk that far through the jungle."

"No cars or jeeps?"

5

"No taxis, either." He smiled briefly, then sobered. "That part of the rainforest is too dense and is only reachable by foot. He and his assistant were supposed to be gone for a day, two days tops. On the morning of the day he was due back, Martín called JJ, who was in Flores at the time—"

"What is Flores? The closest town?"

"Yes. Martín told JJ they were leaving and on their way back. He said they would be there before she returned. That's the last she heard from him."

"Maybe one of his patients needed them to stay longer, and he didn't or couldn't let JJ know."

Gurn shook his head. "In that type of setting, you don't change plans and not let people know. Not done. Besides, they have satellite phones, shortwave radios, cell phones—when they work—and walkie-talkies. When it got dark, and they still hadn't arrived, she talked to someone at the cave-in site. Martín left in the morning, as planned. Even though you try not to be in the jungle at night, she and a team set off from their end, hoping to meet up with them. They got all the way to the other site without a trace of either man. Both vanished."

"Oh my God. And she can't go to the police?"

"Not at this point. JJ promised to wait. From what she says, Dr. Lancaster is coercing her to at least give them a chance to find him on their own. Otherwise, the entire project might be shut down. One hundred jobs at stake. JJ doesn't want the site closed any more than Dr. Lancaster does. Anyway, she called me for help."

I leaned forward and touched his hand with my own. "Oh darling, I am so sorry. I'm not surprised she's turning to you."

My voice was calm and knowing. When I met Gurn, he'd hit the ripe old age of thirty-six, a little long in the tooth for a Navy SEAL. He'd recently stepped down from active duty and now taught Naval Reserve Officers Training Corps or

NROTC, did occasional work for some bigwigs at the Pentagon, and ran his own CPA business. But before that, he'd been on missions in Iraq and Afghanistan, performing the usual feats of heroism these incredible people perform.

Even in military retirement, this side of my man was never far away, his need to serve, to help, to right the wrong. I was used to it. Or as used to it as one can get before she has to start coloring her hair to get rid of all the gray. Even though Clairol and I are best friends, I am proud of him.

"Of course, she'd want your help," I continued, with a smile. "Part of your SEAL training was to fell a tree with a pocketknife, swim with it underwater for six or seven miles, surface, and use the branches to build a bridge. All before lunch."

"Not quite," he said with a slight smile. "That's more along the lines of Paul Bunyan. Although basic training often felt like that."

"Wait a minute," I said. "Isn't the terrain of Afghanistan and Iraq completely different than the Guatemalan jungle?"

"Yes, but remember when I was part of a volunteer team helping to put out the Amazon fires? We didn't get them all, but every fire we extinguished helped."

"That's right! You were there for over two weeks. I couldn't wait for you to come home, but you were doing something important."

I smiled. He shot me another fleeting smile, then the worried look returned to his face.

"There has to be a reason why those two men haven't returned. Whatever it is, it's not good."

"Don't go to the dark side yet," I said. "It's only been a day."

7

"Even with their knowledge of the jungle, they won't last long out there if one or both are hurt and can't reach anyone. I've never heard JJ as upset as this. Or as scared."

"Well, I know I would be beside myself if you were missing. You should go, darling, of course. After all, she's family. Blood is thicker and all that. I'll be worried about you trekking through the jungles of Guatemala, but I understand you have to go."

"Maybe you'll be too busy to be worried. JJ and I want you to come with me."

Chapter Two

I was so startled, the e-reader flew out of my hand, twirling in an arc through the air. It landed with a thud at the end of the chaise lounge next to Tugger. His naps being sacrosanct, he got up in a huff and gave me the old evil eye. Tugs turned around twice and plopped down once more beside Baba.

The two-footed took a moment to watch the four-footed display. Then I spread my hands, palms up in an open gesture, trying to be the voice of reason.

"Darling, you can't be serious. Why would you want to take me with you? I would just be in the way. You and JJ have the skills for running around a jungle. I don't."

"You've got a black belt in karate."

"I don't think that would work on a jaguar."

"You've got a sharp, adapting mind. You do a ballet barre every day. You're in great shape, agile, and flexible. I can personally attest to that."

"Let's not bring our sex life into this."

"I would be with you every step of the way. Actually, I'll follow you wherever your nose takes you."

"But—"

"Nobody does after-the-fact investigation like you."

"But—"

"You have the reputation as one of the world's greatest ferrets."

"But—"

"Sweetheart, if anyone can find Martín, it's you."

"Now you sound like Tío." My uncle thinks I can do anything and everything. Apparently, my husband does, too. All this supergirl press can give one a headache. I rubbed my forehead while Gurn went on.

"Sweetheart, I know you like to say you won't go anywhere you can't plug in your hot rollers."

"Or where they don't have a Starbucks."

"Sweetheart, you're tougher than you think."

"You've called me sweetheart three times, but that still isn't going to win me over."

He studied me for a moment, then let out a huge sigh. "There's one more thing you should know. JJ's pregnant. Almost three months. She just had it confirmed by a doctor. That's why she went to Flores."

"Pregnant!"

"She says she and Martín have been trying for five years, ever since they got married." He paused again. "I don't want to see her widowed in her first trimester. Not if we can do anything to prevent it."

I looked at him and he looked at me. The birds continued to sing; the breeze continued to blow; the sun continued to shine. But a black cloud hung over my man and, therefore, me.

I stood up. "Okay, I'm in."

Relief flooded his face. "Thank you, sweetheart."

"That's four sweethearts, but that doesn't make me any more jungle ready. Nonetheless, I'll try not to embarrass you. If I do, I told you so. So, when do we leave? Tomorrow morning?"

"One hour."

"One hour!"

"We need to try to get to the site before nightfall. Like I said, you don't move in the jungle during the night if you can help it." He looked at his watch. "It's oh-eight-hundred hours now. We don't have a lot of daylight. Even taking off in an hour is cutting it close. We'll fly the new plane."

He'd recently traded in his Cessna Skyhawk for a Citation M2 jet. Gurn was thrilled because the jet was faster than the Skyhawk and could travel farther without refueling. What I appreciated was the jet was quieter and had a larger bathroom. Gurn raced ahead with more thoughts on preparation.

"The flight should take roughly eight hours, building in time for refueling. We'll park the plane at the Flores airfield. There's no place to land any nearer. The M2 needs at least three thousand feet of landing strip, you know."

"I didn't, but nobody tells me anything."

He went on as if I hadn't spoken. "JJ's arranged for a thirty-minute helicopter ride from the airport to the drop-off point. She'll meet us there for the short hike to the site. We should just make it before dark. Bring your hiking boots."

"You worked all this out on your way from your office to the back deck?"

He grinned at me. "I've done a lot of this kind of thing before. Let's get moving. We need to file a flight plan, have the jet fueled up, and get to the airfield. JJ's got all the supplies we'll need once we get there."

Then, with his green-gray eyes burning into my dark-blue ones, he pulled me into a hug. "Thank you," he whispered. "I know I've pressed you into doing this, but you're good with it, hon, aren't you?"

"I'm good with it." And I was.

We broke free and kissed lightly. "You're right. I was selling myself short. I'll pack everything I bought for our

11

camping trip last month. Although I don't think Yosemite is anything like the jungle. And we did stay at the Ahwahnee."

"True, but we went hiking every day and camped overnight at the lake."

Panic hit me. "Yes, but you did everything. You got us lakeside, set up the tent, caught the fish, cooked the dinner — " I broke off. "Remind me. What did I do?"

"You found a lost dog and reunited it with its family. Took you a couple of hours."

"Oh, that." My tone was dismissive. "It was simple. I tracked them down from the dog's tags. The vet to the family to the neighbors and then their campsite at Yosemite. I just followed the trail. They were only a few miles away."

"You would have found them if they were in New Zealand."

He stared at me hard, pride and love softening the expression on his face. Then he grinned. I grinned back.

"And I'm going to need about a gallon of insect repellent."

"I'll get you two."

I sat down again on the chaise, mind racing. "I'll have to arrange for Tío to take care of the cats while we're gone and cancel tonight's dinner with him. Too bad, he's making chiles en nogada. Nobody makes a walnut sauce like he does. I'm in between assignments now, so I'll let Lila know I won't be coming into the office for — how long do you think we'll be gone?"

"Two or three days. No more than five. If we don't find Martín by then, he may never be found."

Chapter Three

The phone call to Lila did not go the way I hoped. My mother listened in silence, and at the end of my spiel, said these terrifying words:

"I'll get back to you." Then she hung up.

As I sat on my end of the line listening to dead air, I tried to stay calm. Lila Hamilton-Alvarez is a force to be reckoned with at the best of times. I don't even like to think about the worst. I took a deep breath and went about the business of letting other people know of the new plans.

"Good morning, Richard," I said to my kid brother and the IT guru of D. I. "What are you doing?"

"I am feeding your niece her morning Pablum, which means I'm wearing more of it than is getting into her mouth."

"Where's Steffi's mommy?"

"Vicki's having a morning sleep-in, courtesy of a husband who knows how to make points with his wife."

"Well, smart you. Listen, Richard," I said, getting right to it. "Gurn's having a family crisis. Remember hearing about JJ, the archaeologist working in Guatemala? She's his cousin."

"Of course I do. But JJ isn't an archaeologist. She's the director of planning for the El Mirador Basin Antiquities."

"So, she's what? A city planner?"

"*Exactamente.* Most city planners will have an undergraduate major in urban planning or geography, with an additional major or a minor in political science, history,

13

public policy and administration, economics, sociology, architecture, environmental science, or civil engineering."

"How come you know this?"

"Huckster called me ten minutes ago, so I looked her up on the internet. He wants to borrow some equipment from D. I.'s stash. Sat phones, nighttime goggles, things like that."

Huckster is Gurn's nickname given to him when he was a kid by friends and family. When you're saddled with a name like Gurn, it's only right.

Richard went on, "While I have you on the line, tell him I'll messenger them to the hangar to save you guys from having to stop off at the office."

"Wait a minute. How did you know I was going, too?"

"He made a wish and I knew you would grant it. Moving on, as I'd mentioned to him—so I say unto you—the communication satellite D. I. rents time from is orbiting over Mexico. The reception might be a little sketchier as far south as Guatemala. However, we'll buy time in Guatemala. It should be up and running by the time you get there."

"Thanks, Richard. As usual, you're the best. I didn't know D. I. had nighttime-vision goggles."

"Lee, we have the most up-to-date surveillance equipment on the market. Our Lady insists on it."

While I call our mother She-Who-Must-Be-Obeyed, Richard calls her Our-Lady-of-Perpetual-Motion, sometimes shortened to Our Lady. This is all behind her back, of course. To her face it's yes, ma'am, yes, ma'am, three bags full, just like the nursery rhyme.

"I had no idea. Well, good for Mom."

"Getting back to JJ, she also heads a ten-year project plan for donors."

"Richard, you are just a fount of information. A ten-year donor deal sounds like it means money."

14

"Of course. What is any field study without it?"

"Doomed?"

"A bit dramatic but apt. Having read JJ's bio—which you might do—she's raised all the money for LIDAR so far."

"LIDAR. That would be...?" My voice dropped off because I had no idea. "Never mind. I don't have the time to learn. But as usual, I'm impressed with your knowledge."

"Don't be. I have the site up on my screen and I'm reading from the opening page while I'm feeding Steffi. I guess you could say I'm multitasking. Want to hear more about the Mayans?" He went on without waiting for an answer. "They were master engineers. Since ancient times, they have celebrated the arrival of spring or fall at the equinox."

"The equinox happens when?"

"Every six months, once in March and again in September. It splits Earth's day almost in half, giving us about twelve hours of daylight and twelve of night."

"Well, now you're just showing off."

"My daughter is mesmerized. She's staring at me openmouthed."

"That's because you're the man with the food."

"Don't destroy my illusion. To continue, an e-group is a civic center for visualization of the two equinoxes. They—"

I let out a laugh. "Enough! I'm on overload. But please send me the URL for that site."

"Will do."

"Maybe after more coffee I'll read it on the plane. I need to go. More calls to make. Kiss that cutie patootie for me."

"I'll wait until I wash the Pablum off her," he joked. Then his tone became more serious. "Sister mine, I know how you feel about jungles and other remote places in the world. Out of your comfort zone. But Huckster will be with you. You're the best there is, and if anyone can find the guy, it's you."

15

"Thank you, brother mine. More to the point, I will be with Gurn. I didn't want to say anything to him — he's got enough on his plate — but I have a bad feeling about this."

"Uh-oh."

"Dr. Lancaster's reaction, JJ's boss. Not wanting to call the police. Doesn't sound right. Something else must be going on if she's willing to risk the safety of one of her people rather than call in the police."

"I hadn't thought about it that way. Be careful, Lee."

"I can be pretty nimble on my feet when I have to be."

"Of course you can." He went on in a rush. "Okay, I'm not worried about you."

"Liar, liar, pants on fire. And I love you for it."

"Now you're being maudlin. Wear a large brimmed hat. Things tend to fall from trees onto people's head."

"Are you kidding me? On top of everything else, I have to watch out for things falling on my head? Like what?"

"It says right here on the site, and I quote, 'wear a large brimmed hat for things falling out of trees.' They're pretty vague about what will be falling out of trees, but I would err on the side of caution. Hanging up now."

Next, I phoned Stanley. He's our office manager and general factotum. Phoning on a Sunday is something you don't do with most employees. But not so with Stanley. He thinks, breathes, and lives D. I.

In between bites of a crab omelet, Stanley told me that, come Monday, he would alert the staff on a need-to-know basis of my latest adventure. He would take care of everything, he said, including watering my plants. I didn't remind him he does that, anyway. Then he told me to be sure to take an anti-snake-venom kit with me. He could have gone all day without saying that.

16

The last phone call was to my uncle. "Tío, there's been a change of plans."

"Oh? It is not something bad, *espero*."

The word espero means *I hope* in Spanish. Tío came to this country from Mexico when he was a young man, so his accent is heavy. But his voice is a rich baritone filled with intelligence, sincerity, and kindness. Listening to him talk is almost a musical experience. I took a deep breath and explained the situation.

"Then you must go," he said without a moment's pause. "We will celebrate another time."

Of course! In all the excitement, I had forgotten. We were to celebrate his new volunteer job taking him out of retirement. A string of local animal shelters put him in charge of creating specialty meals for health-challenged animals, making them well enough for forever homes.

Regarding my pampered pets, he was completely on board with taking care of them, as I knew he would be. He didn't even try to make me feel guilty about dinner, either, even though he'd been cooking for a couple of days for the feast. But that's Tío. You can't rise from picking strawberries in the fields of Salinas to becoming the executive chef at one of the top restaurants in San Jose and not be an extraordinary man.

After my phone call to him, I concentrated on packing. There is nothing like trying to put eight pounds of potatoes into a five-pound bag or cramming everything I needed into my knapsack. And I still had to save room for shampoo, deodorant, and a small, hand-held fan. The battery-operated fan was de rigueur as far as I was concerned. Steamy jungle. So not me.

The front doorbell rang while I huffed and puffed. I hesitated and stood listening to the drone of the bell.

17

It's barely eight thirty on a Sunday morning, I thought. *Whoever you are, go away.*

The bell rang again, more insistently this time. I rethought my hesitation. One of us had to answer the door in case it was Instacart with my Sunday delivery of cinnamon buns. Gurn was dealing with the ground crew and filling out the necessary online paperwork for carrying extra fuel in the cabin of the jet. That left me. I dropped the knapsack, ran to the front door, and flung it open.

If I hadn't already been out of breath from tearing across the apartment, the woman standing in the doorway would have taken it away. There, in all her glory, was the star of *Mogambo,* the 1953 box-office hit, actress Grace Kelly.

Okay, not really. I was face-to-face with my own mother, the incomparable Lila Hamilton-Alvarez. But Lila sure could have been Grace Kelly's stand-in. I'm an old-movie buff and *Mogambo* happens to be one of my personal favorites. The movie, shot in Africa, also stars Clark Gable and Ava Garner. At the time, Ava Gardner's jungle shower scene went down in song and legend. Hubba hubba.

But I digress. Back to Lila. There she was head to toe in a beige safari ensemble. This included a long-sleeved bush jacket and laced-up knee-high boots. She even carried a pith helmet tucked under one arm. A matching knapsack dangled from the other hand.

Let's face facts. Nobody can wear boring beige like my mother except the aforementioned Grace Kelly. These two can take a shade that drains the color from the faces of 99.9 percent of the women across the land and make it pop.

"Mom! Why are you dressed like you're going to a costume party?"

"Are you going to let me *in,* dear, or *not*?"

18

In a daze, I stepped aside. Lila Hamilton-Alvarez strode inside, in a very ladylike but determined way.

"Mom, what's going on?"

"I *just* got off the *phone* with Ida."

I faltered. "Who's Ida?"

"Who is *Ida*? Jacqueline's *mother*. Try to pay *attention*, Liana."

"Who's Jacqueline?"

"*Who* is Jacqueline? Who is *Jacqueline*?"

In case it's not clear, my mother is a woman who likes to stress certain words when she speaks, just in case a moron—that would be me—can't get her meaning any other way. I have decided not to be insulted.

"Wait a minute. Jacqueline. As in Jacqueline Jeanette. That's JJ. Of course. So, you spoke with JJ's mother? Wait a minute. You phoned JJ's mother?" My tone turned accusatory at the last question. It was wasted on her.

"I didn't phone *her,* she phoned *me. Ida* and I have *been* on the phone with each other *all* morning," Lila said, dropping the knapsack to the floor and placing the helmet on the coffee table. "Ever *since* Jacqueline phoned to tell her about *Martín.*"

"Wow! JJ sure has sure been burning the jungle wires. And can't you just call her JJ or Jackie? It would sound less like a first lady."

"No."

"Okay then."

"What Jacqueline is *not* privy to is her father is in the *hospital* having heart bypass surgery this afternoon."

"Oh, no! When it rains, it pours. That's too bad. I'll bet JJ wouldn't take it well on top of her husband being missing."

"The bypass surgery is *news* Ida is keeping from her daughter until the *operation* is over. A *thoughtful* mother, a woman after my *own* heart. *Conversely,* Ida wants to keep the news of *Martín's* disappearance from her *husband* until his health is cleared up."

"This Ida likes to keep a lid on things," I put in.

"*Poor* thing, she has to talk to *someone*," Lila said as if I hadn't spoken.

"JJ or Ida?"

"*Ida.* Please try to *concentrate*, Liana."

"Concentrating."

"When *Ida* told me what was going *on* in Guatemala, she was in quite a state. I *assured* her I would do *right* by the situation."

I was at a total loss. "Wait a minute. Back up. How do you two even know each other?"

"Why, Liana, *shame* on you. Are you so *caught* up in your own day-to-day existence that you don't *remember* Gurn's family at your *wedding*?"

"Of course I do." My false bravado filled the room. "Ida and…" I drew a blank.

Frankly, even if I hadn't remembered Gurn's family at the wedding, very few people, besides my mother, would have blamed me. The event took a back seat to a lot of other things going on at the time. The day before the nuptials, the church burned down. Then a banged-up-and-bruised Gurn, who'd been MIA for a couple of days, showed up in the middle of the night straight from a secret mission. Then right before the ceremony, I was held at gunpoint by a villainess who'd murdered four other people and wanted to take me hostage in order to leave the country. It was only with a lot of fancy footwork I managed to stay alive and keep my wedding gown from being ruined. You could say, at the time, the guest list was not my number-one priority. I tuned back to my mother's dulcet, if reprimanding, tones.

"*Samuel.* Samuel Hanson. Ida and Samuel Hanson. They are Jacqueline's *parents. Honestly,* Liana."

"Of course, of course. Their names just slipped my mind… for the moment."

"To *reiterate,* even though Jacqueline and Martín were *unable* to attend the wedding, that did *not* stop the *rest* of Gurn's family."

"And that would include Aunt Ida and Uncle Samuel. Got it."

"*Lovely* people."

"Absolutely. Lovely people." I squeezed my eyes shut and went back to our reception. "She was the skinny woman in the corner dressed in a gray Chanel suit, and he had a big nose."

"Not a *flattering* description but appropriate. To get back to the *subject* at hand, Ida wants to *spare* her daughter any *excessive* worry and assures me that Samuel will be *fine* in a few days. The *miracle* of modern medicine. But there is *still* the trial of Martín's disappearance. Where is *Gurn,* by the way?"

I tried to keep up with her, often a losing proposition. "Uh… in his office finding out how much extra fuel he can legally carry in the cabin of the jet. Wait a minute. What did you mean when you told Aunt Ida, you 'would do right by the situation'? You said that a moment ago."

"Why, I should have *thought* it was evident. I am going *with* you, my dear. Ida was *so* relieved."

If there'd been a Linus blanket I could have pulled out from under a piano and thrown over my head, I would have done it. And sucked my thumb.

Am I really going to the deep, dark jungles of Guatemala with my mommy?

21

Chapter Four

"No, no, no, no," I said, shaking my head and fighting back hysteria. "You don't want to go. No, no, no, no, no. Absolutely not. No way. No, no, no, no, no."

"Stop being so *negative*, Liana. Of course I want to *go*. Otherwise, I *wouldn't*. You are being *most* annoying."

"Mom, let's be reasonable. Your idea of roughing it is shopping at Saks instead of Neiman Marcus."

"You *forget* yourself, Liana."

"I do?"

"You do. *Your* mother—"

"That would be you," I interrupted. "I remember you at the wedding. Lovely in lavender."

I winked at her good humoredly. Lila shot me a dirty look. I backed off immediately.

"Sorry. A little attempt at humor. Hasn't really been working for me today."

Lila closed her eyes for a moment before going on. Apparently, I continued to be the most annoying person in the world.

"I will *elucidate*," she said.

Uh-oh. When Lila elucidates, we're all in big trouble. My heart in my mouth, I listened.

"You seem to have *forgotten* I took a *double* major at Stanford, Liana," Lila said. "Business administration *and* anthropology. Business to help your *father* make a success of Discretionary Inquiries. Anthropology for the pure *love* of it." She took a deep breath and went on. "There are many *similarities* between archaeology and anthropology. They both focus on *understanding* human culture from the *deepest* history up to the *recent* past. Archaeology *differs* from anthropology in that it focuses *specifically* on analyzing material remains *such* as artifact and architectural remnants."

"Sorry, Mom, I had forgotten. My bad."

But she was not done. "And I would like to remind you that your *mother* has completed two *weeks* of survival training in the *wilds* of Washington State while *you* were staying at the very *luxurious* Ahwahnee." Her tone was accusatory, to say the least.

"I wasn't luxuriating all the time. We went camping." My voice was loud and defensive. I added in a softer tone, "Overnight. Once."

"And *Gurn* did everything."

"I found the dog!"

Lila smiled at me, suddenly relaxing. "I remember. Liana, *dear* child, you are the *cleverest* person I know."

"Uh-oh. This is worse than your elucidations, Mom. When you start complimenting me, I am about to get walloped over the head by something."

"There's that *razor*-sharp, *suspicious* mind that serves you *so* well."

"Now you're just plain scaring me."

"Liana, you have your *skills*, my dear, but you are *still* going to need some *assistance* in the jungle. *Ida* knows that. *I* know that. *Gurn* knows that but is probably *loath* to say so. *Husbands* will be *husbands*. But not to fear. I will be your *trusted* assistant while we are there."

"Excuse me?" I felt like I'd been zapped by a cattle prod. "My... uh... what?"

"I shall *cling* to you like..." Here she paused.

With dread in my heart, I filled in the rest of the sentence. "Like Saran Wrap on a turkey leg?"

"I was *going* to say, like a *new*born babe."

"Uh…" And then I froze. The simplest of words would not come to me. Lila took my silence to mean compliance.

"It's *settled*. Let's have some *coffee* before we depart, shall we? I am in need of *additional* caffeine."

"Coffee?" I barely got out the one word. This was because I almost swallowed my tongue.

"It sounds to me as if *you* could use a *strong* cup *yourself*, Liana."

Lila grabbed my arm and dragged me off to the kitchen, chatting as we walked down the hall to the kitchen.

"Ida is *aware* of my survival training. I *apprised* her of my advancing skills in our *many* email exchanges during my training in the wild. I'm sure I mentioned to *you*, as well, that I maintained the number-*two* position for excellence, only *surpassed* in scores by Mr. Dirk Goodman."

She hadn't. But then she'd never mentioned her friendship with Gurn's aunt, either. She gave me one of her rare smiles tinged with something I didn't want to know about.

"Dirk Goodman," she repeated softly. "A *very* apt name for the gentleman."

Now not even able to stutter, I stood wordless for a moment, then glanced around me.

"*What* are you looking for, Liana?"

"Uh, let me think. Got it! The coffeepot."

"It's on the counter *right* in *front* of you, Liana, in its *usual* place."

And if it were a snake, it would have… Stop thinking about snakes. I also decided not to delve further into the Dirk Goodman topic. I can handle only so much at one time.

24

"You seem to have developed quite a friendship with JJ's mother," I said, pouring the dark brew into two cups, with a shaky hand.

"Possibly I *haven't* mentioned to you that Ida and I initially bonded due to our *mutual* interest in antique thimbles. Over the past year, we have been exchanging *duplicate* thimbles since we met."

Here was another slam-dunk dichotomy of my mother. Lila doesn't know how to sew a button on a shirt, yet she collects rare and valuable thimbles.

"And the other *mutual* interest Ida and I have is a *headstrong*, independent daughter."

Before I could offer a retort, Gurn barreled into the kitchen. I turned to face a man who looked like he'd been wrestling an alligator and lost.

"What's the matter?"

He didn't answer me. In fact, he didn't even look at me but addressed my mother.

"I just got off the phone with Aunt Ida. She says you're coming with us, Lila?"

His look was one of pure amazement. He's had that look a lot since we married.

"After my *two-week* Core Survival Skills Training in Washington State *and* my Wilderness First-Aid Certification," Lila said proudly, "how can I *not* be an asset?"

"But the forests of Washington State are a completely different terrain than the Guatemalan jungle." He had begun to stutter. A by-product of a conversation with L. H. Alvarez.

"Pish tosh," Lila replied after taking a sip of her coffee. "*Survival* is the same the world over. Locate your *water* supply and *edible* plant life; *learn* to build a fire; *find* your compass points; watch out for *surrounding* wild animals, and be *aware*

25

of poisonous insects, snakes, and plants. I received *top* scores in all subjects."

His vocal cords may have come back to him, but his voice wavered when he spoke. "Congratulations, Lila, but—"

"And the timing has been *most* fortuitous, Gurn dear," she said, rolling on like the mighty Mississippi. "I have been *thinking* about temporarily handing *over* the helm of Discretionary Inquiries to Peter now that he has been *promoted* to the office of vice president. This is the opportunity to do so for two or three days. Plus, with my *recently* acquired survival skills and my *allegiance* to the family, I cannot, in *clear* conscience, *not* offer my services in this *time* of familial trouble."

And so there.

Chapter Five

Gurn and I sat side by side in the open cockpit ready for takeoff. He began the methodical engine check required before departure, a smile lighting up his face. While he would never admit it, his affection for the small jet was akin to that of a pet, coming in just behind the cats. I'll bet he even thinks he hears it purr when he nears it.

Lila parked herself behind us in one of the four passenger seats of the main cabin, reading a *National Geographic* magazine. Gurn and I were at last free to talk. Until that moment, she'd been by our sides circumventing any conversation we might have had along "this-can't-be-happening" lines.

Accelerating jet engines are on the noisy side, so we wore headphones in order to hear and be heard. Knowing my mother wasn't in on what we were saying, finally, Gurn turned to me and vented his frustration.

"I can't believe Rich would allow Lila to come along like this."

"Excuse me, Mr. Chauvinistic Aviator, but my brother can no more control our mother than I can. But here's an idea. Why don't you call up your Aunt Ida right now and tell her Lila shouldn't come? She can relay that info on to Mom. Then you can throw her off the plane before we take off."

It took a second for what I said to sink in, then Gurn burst out laughing. I joined him.

"Sorry, hon," he said. "When you're right, you're right. It shows you how desperate I am. But for whatever reason, even JJ is fine with Lila coming along, especially as Aunt Ida has sanctioned it. Of course, through the years JJ's learned to pick her battles with her mother. They seem to have a relationship similar to the one you have with Lila."

"You mean where I roll over like a puppy, all fours in the air ninety percent of the time?"

"That's the one. But seriously, now that my panic is dying down, I realize there's about a hundred people on-site. We'll find some job for her within the compound, so she'll stay busy but safe."

"That might work," I agreed, knowing the "x" factor in this plan was the cooperation of L. H. Alvarez.

A third voice came into the headphones and began the bibble-babble of takeoff instructions. Gurn lifted his forefinger to me in the universal pause-the-conversation gesture. A short time later, we were cruising at thirteen thousand feet.

"Want some coffee?" I took a sip of Tío's coffee donation. Leave it to my uncle to be able to pack a hamper of food for our journey including a fresh thermos of java in a matter of minutes.

"Love some," Gurn said. "What kind is it? Tío's own blend?"

"Not this time. This is Mi Esperanza coffee, something a friend sent him. From Honduras."

I poured some steaming coffee from the thermos into a travel mug while trying not to glance out the windshield at the clouds below. I don't do small planes well, and here I was, married to a pilot who was devoted to his. One of life's little ironies. Like a mother who doesn't sew but collects thimbles.

I put the mug into Gurn's extended hand while saying, "I understand JJ and Martín are quite a pair. Hasn't your dad referred to them as Indiana JJ and Medicine Man?"

A faint smile crossed Gurn's lips. "Only when he's imbibed a little too much. Fortunately, that's only on New Year's Eve." He took a large gulp of coffee. "This is surprisingly good. Not as good as Tío's own blend, but—"

"But what is?" I finished for him. "Richard told me JJ is the director of planning for the El Mirador Basin Antiquities. Care to explain what that is?"

"She maps out existing ancient cities, projecting the most efficient excavation of them without compromising the integrity of the discovery."

"That sounds important. And like you memorized it right off the page."

"I did. Otherwise, I'd have no idea what she does." We both chuckled for a moment. He went on in a more serious vein. "Then, if it's warranted, she designs new buildings for the site, such as bathrooms and eating facilities, for staff, tourists, and visitors, often including new roads for cars and buses."

"But her main job is to map all the existing sites in the Mirador Basin?"

"And their interconnecting highways. Aside from that, JJ also leads groups into the jungle, groups like the graduate schools of ornithology, USGS geologists, the Department of the Interior, and so forth. Even Guatemalan senators. Six years ago, it was supposed to be a six-month job, but the powers that be found an ongoing grant. Using something called LIDAR, they keep uncovering more and more ancient cities."

"Okay, now I have to know. What is this LIDAR?"

"I have absolutely no idea, sweetheart. Why don't you look it up?"

"Good idea." I grabbed my phone and did a quick search. "Here's what is says: 'LIDAR stands for Light Detection and Ranging. It's a form of technology. Using it, archaeologists find evidence beneath the Guatemalan jungle canopy of the way Mesoamerican civilization altered its landscape. Images made using LIDAR technology reveal previously unknown ancient Maya settlements with houses, temples, forts, ditches, moats, and roads. So far, they've unveiled a million acres of settlement patterns to prove that the population was greater than previously expected, and the cultural and natural system is totally, one hundred percent interconnected.' Pretty impressive stuff."

"All I know," Gurn said, "is the site she's scoping out now is supposed to have a temple that rivals the Pyramid of Kukulkan."

"If memory serves me right, that's the temple in Chichen Itza, Mexico, right? The Yucatan."

"Right. I visited JJ there once when she was collecting comparative data. It's unbelievable. Well worth the visit. We should go sometime."

"Let's see if I can get through this site first," I said dryly.

"You'll be fine, especially now that you've got Lila, Queen of the Jungle to look out for you." Gurn laughed uproariously at his own joke.

"Yeah, ha ha. Let's talk about Martín. What does he do at the clinic? And where is the clinic in relationship to the dig site?"

"JJ says it's on the perimeter, so they both live in one of the on-site bungalows. His clinic gives free healthcare for anyone who needs it. Martín takes care of more minor issues a doctor isn't needed for. And he sometimes travels to a village if the patient can't get to him. According to JJ, neonatal and nutritional issues are killing thousands of people in that country every year."

"Sounds like he's one of the good guys."

"I've only met him once at their wedding five years ago, but he came across that way to me. The whole family likes him, even Aunt Ida. That's not easy to do. She can be tough, unyielding, and brittle. Sort of like someone else we know sitting in the plane with us, minus the designer shoes."

"You mean there's more than one Lila Hamilton-Alvarez roaming the earth?"

"To her credit, the survival course Lila took is one of the more intensive ones."

"Really?"

"And she managed to get through it. She probably knows a few useful things."

"You mean aside from how to dress the part?" I felt a surge of guilt run through me. "I shouldn't have said that. I will admit, there's not much Mom doesn't do well."

"And don't knock the strong woman, Lee. I come from a long line of them. I suppose it's only natural I should have married one."

"Why, thank you, sir."

"And when I married you, I knew I was marrying the entire Alvarez family. But I did it anyway," he added after a pause. He laughed uproariously again. Sometimes he gets on my nerves.

"As did I," I said after a brief pause. "Of course, in all fairness, your family doesn't live across the driveway from us like mine do."

"But in their own way, mine are just as formidable. You know, Aunt Ida was a marine in her youth. She'd be on this plane with us now if it weren't for Uncle Samuel's surgery.

31

But enough of the ties that bind. Sweetheart, why don't you sit back and relax? We've got a few hours before we have to land again to refuel."

I needed no other inducement. I finished my coffee, took off the headset, and looked behind me. Lila was already curled up and sound asleep on two side-by-side seats. Following her example, I sat back and drifted off, awaking only when we set down somewhere in Southern Mexico to refuel.

Chapter Six

The bump of landing stirred me, not to mention my appetite. I opened the small cooler, stuffed to capacity by Tío. Inside were his incredible tortas, each wrapped in a pristine white linen napkin. I pulled out three, figuring everybody else was feeling a little peckish, too.

Nobody makes a better torta than Tío, which is a kind of Mexican sandwich. He'd made two types. One similar to a small baguette. The other was a flat, oblong, soft roll. Both types were filled with turkey, Oaxaca cheese, refried beans, and avocado; the sandwich was smothered in Tío's special aioli. Of course, included were some of his homemade pickled jalapeños, which always adds an amazing flavor.

I unwrapped one and handed it off to Gurn. He munched happily as he stepped outside to oversee the liquid feeding of our silver-winged steed. I sat down next to Lila, who was writing something in her journal. I handed her a torta, and she politely thanked me.

Lila neatly unfolded the napkin and placed it on her lap. The torta had also been wrapped in waxed paper that peeled away more or less like a banana skin. Very civilized and convenient. Tío thinks of everything.

"Mateo told me he'd made the aioli sauce with a *light* mayonnaise this time," Lila said, calling Tío by his given name. She took a delicate nibble.

"The *light* mayonnaise saves a few calories here and there," Lila went on. "Something of which *you* might become *more* aware, Liana," she added pointedly.

"What do you mean, Mom?" I turned to her while peeling the wax paper from my own torta. "I lost weight right before the wedding, and I haven't gained any of it back."

Unlike Mom, I bit off a huge chunk and closed my eyes in ecstasy as I chewed. Then I had a thought. I stopped chewing. "Do I look heavy to you?"

"Certainly not. And don't *talk* with your mouth full. *Why* would you think that?"

I swallowed quickly. "Because you just said —"

"Liana, my dear, I simply *mean* one must be aware of these things. You're *not* going to be young and svelte *forever*."

"I don't know that thirty-four is that young, Mom. But, of course, I guess you would think that in comparison."

"Well, *thank* you!"

"No, no, no," I said hastily. "I just meant you've managed to stay young and svelte throughout the decades. No, no. Scratch that. Bad phrasing. I meant since like forever. Hmmm. Not much better. How about this? You —"

"Why don't you *cease* speaking, Liana, and *eat* your lunch?"

"Another bout of foot-in-mouth disease? Okay, just let me say this: you're gorgeous, Mom, and never seem to age. Honestly, I've always suspected there's a picture of you lurking in someone's attic. Like Dorian Gray."

"Once again, *thank* you. I *think*." My mother managed a smile. "But we are *often* as young as we *feel*. And I feel like a teenager."

"And look like one. Preteen almost," I added, slathering it on.

"You have become *carried* away, Liana. Eat your sandwich, but in a more *ladylike* fashion, please."

"Okay."

I bit off more of one of the best tortas I'd ever eaten, and I've eaten quite a few. Maybe I'd have another after this. After all, I was four pounds to the good. I chewed and swallowed.

"But you know, Mom," I said, continuing with the same dicey subject because I am often a glutton for punishment. "How you manage to look the way you do is beyond me. Maybe I've inherited some of your genes. Boy, I sure hope so." I took another bite of Tío's torta, contemplating that happy thought. Mom's voice interrupted my reverie.

"You're *dribbling*, dear."

"What?"

"Your *blouse*. You're *dribbling* aioli onto your *blouse*. Maybe you should wrap the paper a little more *tightly* around the sandwich."

I looked down. "Well, crap."

"*Language*, Liana. And use your *napkin*. Where *is* your napkin?"

I found the napkin crumpled up on the floor. I picked it up and swiped at my shirt, leaving behind a greasy blob. Lila watched me in silent disapproval. I began to wonder if I'd been adopted.

Refueling done, I made my excuses to Lila and joined Gurn in the cockpit while he readied for takeoff. Safer that way. I searched the small hamper for another torta. Rats. Only some fruit and a bag of homemade chips. I shared the chips with hubby.

An hour or so later, Gurn looked at the clock on the dashboard. He gestured for me to put my headphones back on. When I did, he said, "We're running late. It took us longer to refuel than I counted on, plus we've hit some headwinds." He shook his head.

"How late?"

"Nearly forty-five minutes. I've got this at full throttle, but still. I'd better alert Flores."

He reached up, flipped a switch, and moved a dial on his radio. Static came through the headphones. Finally, he located the traffic tower at our destination airport.

"This is Seahawk M2095Y calling Mundo Maya International Airport. Acknowledge."

I listened to more static until a voice came in speaking almost flawless English.

"This is Mundo Maya International Airport IATA Code: FRS. Please identify yourself again. Acknowledge."

"This is Seahawk M, as in Mike, 2095 Y, as in Yankee, en route from San Francisco, California, to Flores, Guatemala. Acknowledge."

"Transmission understood. Are you in trouble? Acknowledge."

"No, but we are experiencing a forty-five-minute delay. We're on a tight schedule. Can you alert the ground crew? Acknowledge."

"Stand by." More static. "Affirmative, Seahawk M2095Y. Delay acknowledged. You are still cleared for landing. Over and out."

Gurn turned off the radio and gave a quick glance in my direction. "Lee, grab the sat phone and hit redial. That should reach JJ. Tell her to delay the helicopter meeting us at the airport for another forty-five minutes."

The phone answered on the second ring.

"Huckster," JJ shouted into the phone, using Gurn's childhood nickname. "Where are you? Are you nearly here?"

"JJ, hi. It's Lee. Gurn's right beside me. We're still en route. Lila's here, too."

"Thank God. The more people we have searching for Martín the better."

"So, no updates on him," I said.

"No," JJ said, "but something else has happened."

"Just a moment," I said, taking the phone away from my ear. I spoke into the mic of my headset. "Darling, didn't you tell me once there was a way of patching calls through your radio system so we can all hear the conversation?"

He nodded and reached up into the side pocket of his chair and pulled out a small wire with a connector on each end. After he handed one end to me, I put it into a jack on the phone. Gurn put the other connector into a jack in the control panel and pressed a few buttons. "Audio is connected. JJ, can you hear me?"

"I can hear you," she said.

"Hold on," I said. "Let me get Mom in on this."

I pivoted around in the chair and saw that Lila, who had been watching our activity, looked at me questioningly. I gestured for her to pick up the headset within her armchair and put it on. She did so and the conversation went on.

"We are all with you now, JJ," I said.

"*Jacqueline*," Lila interjected, "This is Lila Hamilton-Alvarez. We have *yet* to meet, but your *mother* and I are *good* friends."

"Yes, ma'am, I know. Thank you for trying to help, Mrs. Alvarez," JJ said in a very polite, Southern way. Her accent, while barely perceptible before, was in full force now.

"Call me *Lila*, dear. How are you *holding* up, Jacqueline?"

"Not so well, ma'am." JJ's voice sounded tight and strained.

"Well," Lila said with authority, "we're on our *way*. We'll soon get to the *bottom* of this."

Gurn glanced at me but didn't comment. He went on to more practical matters. "JJ, we're calling to tell you to delay the helicopter pickup in Flores for another forty-five minutes. We should be on the ground at six fifteen."

"Okay," she said hesitantly. "Raul doesn't like to fly at night, but I think he can make the round trip back to Flores before nightfall." Her voice lowered, becoming more intimate. "I'm so glad you're all coming. I'm scared. I'm just plain scared."

I reentered the conversation. "You mentioned something else has happened, JJ. What was it?"

"An hour or so ago, one of the workers found Alejandro's knapsack about a half a mile from here in some underbrush."

"Who's Alejandro?" I asked.

"Alejandro is Martín's assistant. The other missing man," JJ said. "The knapsack had the word 'uayeb' written on it," she added in a whisper. "The staff and workers are pretty freaked. So am I."

"What's the word you just used?" I looked over at Gurn, who shrugged.

"Uayeb," JJ said, "is the name for five unlucky, unnamed days in the Mayan calendar. The Maya consider uayeb to be a deadly time which could bring bad luck, danger, and even death."

I said, "And this was written on the knapsack?"

"Yes," she replied, then drew in a ragged breath. "In blood."

Chapter Seven

We taxied to the hangar at precisely six fifteen p.m. Dusk was beginning to set. Twilight hit at seven fourteen. Nightfall, seven fifty-one. Every minute seemed to count, so I paid attention to the numbers. That's also what comes of having an eidetic memory, which can be one royal pain in the keister much of the time.

Once we stopped moving, I opened the door of the plane. The moist, hot air hit me like I was entering a steam room. The Bay Area gets hot, but never with this level of humidity. True, it was the hottest time of the year in Guatemala, but the sun was setting. What was it like in the middle of the day? Yikes!

The assigned crew came running over. Fast orders were given in Spanish, and any words Gurn didn't know or get, I translated, being fluent in Spanish. Lila jumped in with a word every now and then, too.

Thanks to JJ's clout, customs took a scant fifteen minutes to get through. Then we rushed to meet the impatient helicopter pilot on the tarmac. Blades already churning, he gestured for us to get aboard.

We threw in our knapsacks and climbed in. Barely seated, he took off straight up into the air and hung there for a split second. Then darting off to the right, we flew over rooftops and into a vast expanse of dark-green and black shadows.

Meanwhile, we scrambled to put on our headsets, not just to talk to one another, but to block out the din of the rotors.

Of course, Lila maintained her usual sophisticated demeanor, acting as if she did this sort of thing every day. Gurn who has been in many a helicopter – can even pilot one in a pinch – wore a big grin on his face the entire time. I, however, commended my soul to God and wondered if my will was up to date.

I'm not a helicopter person, especially in the growing dark. Actually, I don't like them much in the light, either. Between the heat and my fear of this metal praying mantis, I must have sweated off another four pounds.

Some thirty minutes later, we set down in a small clearing in the middle of shadows. We barely tumbled out of the chopper when the pilot took off again, apparently trying to beat nightfall back to Flores.

Before anything else, Gurn removed two battered hats from his knapsack, handing me one that looked like a wilted mushroom cap. I put it on. He plopped his favorite Aussie military slouch hat, well-worn and sweat-stained, on his head. Lila donned her pith helmet. Standing silent, we were as ready as we were ever going to be for the wilds of Guatemala.

There was a split second of silence after the sounds of the helicopter died off in the distance. The surrounding jungle made its presence known.

I will never forget the sensory overload. The sharp smell of damp soil, pungent and rich, was nearly overwhelming. We listened to the encircling night sounds of cicadas and far-off cries of animals — small, I hoped. I sensed movement, too. Restless trees and bushes swayed from indiscernible breezes or maybe animal life. Everything around us was alive in the fast-coming night. Here, nature — primal and electric — ruled. I could feel its power.

Just as I was about to give off a Tarzan yell, JJ was upon us, her entourage hurrying into the clearing. Of medium height, slender, and muscular, she was accompanied by seven young men and one middle-aged man, who carried a small monkey on his left shoulder. The men hung back while JJ, talking nonstop, ran forward embracing each of us quickly, one after the other.

"Thank God you've come," she repeated again and again. "You're here."

"Of course we're here," Gurn replied, hugging her once more, maybe to quell her fears.

They broke free, her face stretching up to his, his leaning down to hers. Even in this poor lighting, I could tell they had the same sandy-colored, sun-streaked hair, green-gray eyes, and lopsided grin. They could have been brother and sister. And in that instant, I knew that's how they felt about each other.

She began talking again. "I was so afraid something would happen, and you'd have to turn around and go back."

"What did you think would happen?" Gurn tried to ask, but JJ went on, her voice topping his.

"Oh, I'm sorry." She turned to the man with the monkey. "This is Paco. He is our guide and the camp translator, being fluent in English, Spanish, and Mayan. He is also my dear friend." She reached out to the monkey. "And this is Afortunado, an orphaned baby howler monkey. Paco is tending to it until it's old enough to fend for itself."

Paco stepped forward. "*Mucho gusto en conocerlo*, or should I say, good evening?" Short and stocky, his weather-worn, bronzed face looked intelligent and friendly. He continually stroked the small monkey that seemed very much at home riding the man's shoulder.

Before any of us could give a return greeting to him, JJ took over again. "We should start back. We can talk once we get there. I'm so glad you're finally here," she added again.

She made a quick about-face and turned her attention to the rest of the men lagging behind her, seemingly awaiting orders. Six of the men were about the same height as Paco. They, too, looked to be natives but much younger, no more than teenagers. They were dressed in colorful, short- and long-sleeved shirts and long, dark pants. Each wore a beat-up hat or baseball cap.

Two of the youths seemed to be identical twins. Maybe sixteen years old, they both wore the same outfit as the other. On their feet were expensive Diesel high-top sneakers, stylish and new.

The two boys held superbright flashlights, flicking them on and off with almost nervous energy. The four other teens had actual firelit torches that burned like enormous candles in the ever-increasing darkness.

A seventh man, somewhat older, stood slightly aloof. A good head taller than the others, his light-blond hair peeked out from under the brim of a Panama hat. With the flickering shadows from torches, I couldn't tell his exact age, but his body looked young and fit. He wore a khaki long-sleeve shirt and matching pants tucked into heavy tan-colored boots laced up to mid-calf. I was betting he, too, shopped at Abercrombie and Fitch. I gave a quick glance to Lila. Yup, a matching set.

Balanced on his right shoulder was a lethal-looking machete. Let me be clear, if you're going to balance something on your shoulder, I prefer it to be a monkey. It didn't help that he was clasping and unclasping the long handle with taut fingers. Here was a man who managed to look elegant and threatening at the same time.

42

Mr. Machete and the other men stood silent, watching JJ. She turned back to us.

"I'll give the rest of the introductions once we return to El Cizin." Saying no more, JJ used long strides to pass the men standing between us and the jungle.

Before hurrying to join her, Paco gave us a fleeting smile. I think he was aware of how fast things were going.

"It will be a twenty-five-minute walk. We will need to go *rapido*," he added the last in Spanish. "It is not good to be in the jungle after dark."

Ominous words if I've ever heard them. I felt myself breaking out into a sweat again, but this time, a cold one.

Chapter Eight

Before we even moved, one of the two twins with a flashlight went to the front of JJ. The other went behind us. The four with torches flanked our small party, falling into place as if it were choreographed. It was as good as any dance routine I've seen the Rockettes do, but without the high kicks.

Mr. Machete headed to the side of JJ, whacking-instrument in his hand. He had yet to say a word. Paco joined JJ. The baby monkey threw his head back and let out a pint-sized howl, clutching the man's face and neck. I've read adult howler monkeys can be heard up to three miles away when they let loose. Maybe even in New Jersey. I felt a tic start in my right eye.

"Vamonos," JJ shouted. Over her shoulder, she turned her attention to us. "Don't step off the path, and stay close together. Keep your arms by your sides. Whatever you do, don't touch anything. You never know. Got that?"

Gurn and Lila verbally acknowledged the orders. I, for one, couldn't do much more than nod. Then I closed my eyes, hoping when I opened them again, I'd be back in my own bed with the dual foot- and head-massage modes. But no matter how many times I blinked, I only saw the green-black jungle before me. And not liking it one bit.

Almost like a marching band, we entered the jungle via a wide limestone path cut between palm fronds, tree branches, and undergrowth. The vegetation was so dense on either side, they seemed like walls, but wet, living, and oppressive.

Every now and then, Mr. Machete hacked at vegetation. It apparently grew so fast, it had reclaimed its space in the short amount of time the party came and went on this centuries-old path. A few insects buzzed near my face. I instinctively swatted at them, glad I'd remembered to put on some bug spray. But I was sweating it off at a fast rate, too.

I couldn't help but wonder why four of the men carried old-fashioned torches instead of flashlights. It was almost as if JJ was reading my mind. She dropped back to where we were.

"You may be wondering about the torches," she said, taking in the three of us. "Dusk is when larger cats like to roam searching for food. They are afraid of fire, and the torches help to keep them at bay."

I sucked in some air and was noisy about it. Gurn touched my shoulder in a comforting manner. Lila moved closer to me. It was all I could do not to reach for my phone and call a cab.

JJ came to the right of me, sidling into Gurn's place when she saw how I'd reacted. Paco dropped back as well, staying directly in front her in a protective manner.

"Nothing's going to happen," JJ said to me. "It's just a precaution."

"I'm sure it is," I muttered, even though I wasn't.

"We'll be at El Cizin soon," she said. "There's a hot meal waiting for you. We can talk for a while. Then you can take a shower and go to bed. Tomorrow at dawn we begin the search for Martín."

The beam from one of the lights flashed on a nearby tree trunk. I thought I saw movement.

"What's that?"

"A boa constrictor," JJ said. "I don't know the genus name offhand. I can find out for you if you like."

45

"No, no, I'm good," I replied with a tight smile.

She returned my smile with one of her own, shy and sweet. "It might be better to keep your eyes down when you walk, everyone."

"Consider it done," I said, ogling my feet.

JJ went on, "It's unlikely, but you don't want to run into a fer-de-lance. They're dark and hard to see, especially at night."

"Fer-de-lance," I said, my heart thudding against my back teeth. "They're poisonous, right?"

"It's one of many indigenous poisonous snakes," Gurn said, entering the conversation from the other side of JJ. "But they keep pretty much to themselves. If you don't bother them, they don't bother you. As a rule," he added.

"Not necessarily true," JJ countered. "I've witnessed one or two attack and come back for more, leaving the victim dodging the snake like an oncoming soccer ball."

"Well, you can find some with a little more testosterone than others," Gurn agreed, good naturedly.

"I'll try not to run into the Arnold Schwarzenegger of snakes," I said.

"Do you know what they're called in Spanish?" JJ asked, turning to me.

"Politicians or snakes?" I laughed at my own little joke. It didn't fly. "Sorry."

Even though we were marching at a fast clip and breathing hard, JJ seemed to want to chat. I put a lid on my sense of humor and went on.

"I believe they're known as barba amarilla," I said. "Yellow chin."

"That's right," she said. "I'd forgotten you're fluent in Spanish, Lee. It's a pit viper. Subfamily, *Crotalinae.*

46

Distinguished by a small sensory pit between each eye and nostril."

That was more information than I ever wanted to know about a snake, but she was reaching out to me, and I took it as that. I smiled companionably, breathing hard though I was. JJ didn't say anything for a moment, then slowed her pacing, dropping back a step or two. So did I.

JJ spoke so softly only I could hear: "Thank you for coming, Lee. Your reputation precedes you. If anyone can find him, you can. That's what Huckster says, and he should know."

"I'll give it my best shot. We all will."

She nodded and looked straight ahead of her. Just when I thought our conversation was over, she said, "It's not a good time to find out I'm pregnant, you know."

"I can only imagine," I said.

"We've been trying for so long, I never thought it would happen. A baby." She took in a deep breath. Her exhale was sharp and uneven. "I don't know what I'll do if we don't find Martín."

"Don't go there. We'll find him," I said, surprising myself with the certainty in my voice. Then and there, that was exactly what I vowed to do. Fer-de-lances, step aside, and take Arnold with you.

Chapter Nine

About fifteen minutes later, we emerged into another clearing. Full-blown night descended with a thud, and the misty sprinkles falling from the sky only added to the overall yuckiness I was feeling.

This clearing was much larger than where the helicopter had set us down. I wondered why we hadn't just been flown here. But straining my eyes, I saw what I thought, at first, was empty space filled with small, man-made foundations and forms.

Electric lanterns and floodlights were sporadically scattered around what seemed to be the perimeter. Additional lighting was clustered here and there in front of large tents or small buildings. I'm not always good with dimensions, but the whole shebang looked to be the size of a good New York City block.

In the murkiness of the night, coupled with the light rain, an unlit something loomed at the other side of the boundary. It might have been two or three stories high, but that could have been the night playing tricks on me. In short, I couldn't tell much. And frankly, I was too beat to care.

Our pace slowed. The six young men split up and simultaneously took off in different directions, their delivery of the goods—us—apparently done. Paco seemed to have disappeared as well.

JJ and Mr. Machete led us to a stucco cafeteria with huge glassless windows. The shutters on each side looked as if they closed securely over the windows when needed.

"Once we finish restoring this site and open it for tourism, this cafeteria will continue on," JJ said. "As you probably know, El Mirador is one of the largest and earliest Mayan sites in the world. To sound like a brochure for just a moment, it's set within Guatemala's thick Petén jungles. El Mirador flourished in the preclassic period prior to the accession of Tikal. Lots of tourists want to visit, and Guatemala needs the money they bring in. We have several buildings and bungalows that will be given over to that purpose once the exploration and repairs are done. That should take another year."

"This must be an exciting and rewarding time for you," I said.

"It would be if my husband wasn't lost somewhere in the jungle," she replied.

Several young men and women were congregated at the entrance, even in the rain. As we neared, they gave us suspicious glances and scurried into the night.

"Now what was that all about?" Gurn asked.

"I have no idea," I said, "but they act like we're tax collectors. I wonder what gives?"

"Don't pay any attention to them," JJ said, pausing at the entrance. "Most are here for the season, either as volunteers or finishing off their dissertations. They have a built-in loyalty to whatever doctor or professor offered them their position."

Gurn, Lila, and I flashed each other a miscomprehending look.

I saw Lila switch to her CEO hat. "Why would they find our presence a challenge to their loyalty to anyone? We are here merely to help."

"Something's going on, JJ." Gurn stopped walking and looked her directly in the eye. "What is it?"

Chapter Ten

JJ's shoulders slumped. "All right, I may as well tell you. There was a big debate among the staff this morning as to whether or not I should have asked you to come. Half voted against it. Not that I cared. It was either that or call the police. I'm not the most popular person around right now."

"I think we need the whole story, JJ, but not here," I whispered. We were clogging up the entryway, and even though we'd stepped to the side, people still threw glances our way. Linking arms with her, I said in a much louder voice, "I'm really, really looking forward to that shower and being dry. But first some grub!"

A laugh of relief escaped all of us as we went into the cafeteria. Once inside, I saw this was probably the spot where many people got together for more than just meals. The overall design was festive and party-like rather than a cafeteria for workers in the middle of a wild jungle.

As if reading my thoughts, JJ remarked, "This is the informal gathering place for most of us, when we don't have to meet in the conference tent. We wanted to make it more than just a cafeteria. It can easily seat one hundred people, so we often hold our larger meetings here. And you'll usually find Consuela, who is in charge, in here, creating homemade tortillas or desserts. The smells simply pull you in."

"The kitchen is *always* the heart of the home," Lila said.

"Well, I just love the Mayan symbols and animals painted on the concrete floor," I said, glancing down.

"They're beautiful," Gurn remarked.

"A few of the workers did that," JJ responded with pride. "They are very talented."

The large room was about fifteen feet high with overhead fans to keep a welcomed breeze blowing. Also hanging from the ceiling was a series of electric lights, making everything bright and cheerful.

Tables of varying sizes were spaced evenly apart and able to seat two to eight people, depending. There were also long, communal tables with benches instead of chairs to accommodate a much larger group.

But each table, no matter what the size, held a decorative and colorful Guatemalan piece. The smaller tables featured a wooden whistle figure or a crude doll dressed in traditional costume. The larger tables had a handwoven huipil, an embroidered blouse usually worn by Indigenous women, spread out in the center of the table. It functioned as the place mat for a vase of vibrant tropical flowers.

We were drawn to the open kitchen, where several women busied themselves either preparing food or cleaning up. Before them, a long counter held trays of cold food, salads, fruits, and so forth, covered by netting. Off to one side, was a smaller counter offering hot dishes, steam rising into an already steamy night. Bottles of water were stacked on each end, apparently there for the taking.

I took a whiff of something that smelled like beef stew and felt huge hunger pains. Tío's tortas can only go so far.

Paco showed up out of nowhere. JJ turned to him. "Paco, can you see our guests' knapsacks are put in their tent?"

"Si, JJ," he said, softening the J sound as he uttered her name. We handed him our knapsacks with thanks. I was glad to be rid of mine and wondered how smart it was to bring my battery-operated fan and so much shampoo.

JJ turned to us. "Come with me, please. I want to introduce you to the remainder of the team that is still up."

"Or talking to you," I said.

"True enough." JJ gave a self-deprecating laugh. "You'll find in the jungle, most of us rise with the sun and go to sleep when it sets. The workers left an hour ago to go back to their tents, except for the ones who came with us. They start their workday at seven thirty a.m. and are done at four thirty p.m."

We followed JJ down the center aisle. She paused for a moment as if to speak to a lone man sitting at a table and paging through a large book. Oblivious to us, his ponytailed, black hair bobbed up and down as he ran his fingers through columns of numbers. He was an odd-looking man, coming across as more of a 1960's hippy than a chaser of numbers. Thinking better of speaking to him, JJ turned and gestured for us to follow her once more.

"That man was Curtis Winston," she said as we moved along. "You can meet him later. He seems to be working now so I don't want to disturb him. Curtis is the site's comptroller and deals with all our financial matters."

I turned to Gurn. "What's a comptroller? Is that different from what you are, a CPA?"

"In a corporate setting," he explained, "the comptroller is the head of the accounting department. Other accountants answer to him. You could say I am my business's comptroller."

JJ went on, "I've been told to tell you if you have any reimbursements due, such as fuel for your plane, you should bring him the receipts. The foundation has offered to cover any expenses you incur. Although I feel I should be the one to repay you."

"While we appreciate the gesture on both counts, it's not necessary," Gurn said.

"Certainly *not*," Lila piped up. "This is a *family* matter."

Left with not much more to add, I gave a resounding, "Hear! Hear!"

"Thank you," JJ said softly.

She led us to a corner table large enough to seat eight to ten people. Four men and three women were either nursing cups of coffee or finishing up what looked like pieces of custard pie.

"Ladies and gentlemen," JJ announced in a formal manner, "I would like to introduce you to Gurn Hanson, my cousin; Lee Hanson, his wife; and Lila Hamilton-Alvarez, Lee's mother. They are here to help in the search for Martín."

Apparently, JJ didn't know I hadn't taken Gurn's last name but still used my maiden name. I said nothing, and JJ continued with the formality of the moment. She turned to a woman whose very bearing suggested she ran the joint.

"May I present Dr. Joan Lancaster, from Cambridge University, who is our project manager. She's in charge of… well… everything from accounting to mixing the limestone."

"How do you do?" Dr. Lancaster smiled, albeit a little stiffly. She was like a queen acknowledging her subjects. In fact, her accent sounded like Elizabeth the Second's. She rose to her regal feet and gave us, what came across to me, a rehearsed speech.

"Thank you for coming even though I feel it was unnecessary. But as I understand, you are here merely to support a family member in a difficult situation. In any event, tomorrow morning we will send out another full-scale search party. We are being joined by many of the locals as well. But I am sure there is a very logical reason for Martín and Alejandro's delay in returning."

"And what would that be?" My eyes narrowed, and I tried to keep any sharpness out of my voice.

"A possibility of many things. A village woman having a problem with delivery," she said, a fake smile returning to her lips. "But one must remember, there is an even stronger possibility if we call in the police, they may close down the site. But, of course," she said, looking at JJ, "if we are unsuccessful tomorrow in our search, we will do so. But for now, we appreciate the visit and bid you welcome."

The last part came across to me as a bald-faced lie. She didn't appreciate the visit, and she'd like nothing better than to bid us to take a hike. I studied the project manager, trying to put aside my initial negative reaction.

A petite woman, she could have been anywhere from her early forties to late fifties. It was hard to tell with a face etched with deep lines, either from sun or age, maybe both. Her short salt-and-pepper hair was arranged around a face that had a touch of aristocracy yet hardness about it. When she smiled, her teeth, contrasting a brilliant white against her tan, did nothing to soften her features. She extended a regal hand to each of us in turn.

"But allow me to greet you individually. Mr. Hanson, a pleasure," she said, then quickly moved on to me.

As she grasped my hand and repeated the name given her by JJ, she then corrected herself. "Actually, it's Ms. Alvarez, isn't it? When I heard of your family-owned detective agency, I glanced at your business web page, Discretionary Inquiries. You didn't take your husband's name, married though you may be."

"I didn't take hers, either," Gurn said, winking in my direction.

"Please, just call me Lee," I said.

"Oh, I'm so sorry, Lee," JJ murmured, her face becoming flushed. "I didn't mean—"

"It's not a big deal, JJ," I said, brushing it off.

Ignoring JJ's and my exchange, a small laugh burst forth from the doctor. "And good for you, Lee Alvarez," she said. "This tradition of the man declaring ownership of a woman through wedding vows is antiquated and barbaric. I never took my husband's name, but, of course, we divorced several years later."

She shot a look in JJ's direction, her sharp, dark eyes holding more than superficial mirth. The subject gone over more than enough, Dr. Lancaster turned to Mom.

"Mrs. Alvarez," she said, grasping Mom's hand, "and I know I am safe in saying that. You are the CEO of Discretionary Inquiries, I do believe."

"I am, indeed," Lila replied, shaking the other woman's hand.

"Most impressive. I thought I recognized your name when I read your bio. You and I have a mutual friend, Dr. Karen De León. She speaks of you often. We interned together at Tenochtitlan many years ago."

"Yes, of course. Karen and I go *back* to our Stanford days. She is now the *curator* at the Metropolitan Meso-American Museum in New York City."

"And aren't we proud," the doctor said. "From public housing in East Palo Alto to a penthouse in Manhattan."

Lila hesitated, smiled, and said nothing. I could tell she, too, found it interesting how Dr. Lancaster had mastered the art of giving backhanded compliments.

Anxious to get on with things, I said, "You mentioned just now that if you reported Martín as missing, the authorities might close down the site. Why is that?"

Dr. Lancaster looked uncomfortable. "We've had some incidents. A few things. Nothing major, but you know how local authorities can be."

56

I could tell she was striving to make light of this. I persisted. "What things?"

Either she didn't hear me or pretended not to. She abruptly turned to a seated woman, her junior by at least ten years. "Please excuse my manners. May I introduce to you Professor Felicity Adler. She is my assistant."

Even sitting down, you could tell this tall, hunched-over woman, possibly five eleven or six feet tall, was ill at ease with her body. Dry, brown hair framed a face with nondescript features. Nodding in our general direction, she murmured, "Hello."

Another woman, small, Hispanic, and possibly in her early thirties, rose from her chair. Tray in hand, she looked at us with a genuine smile. Even in this heat, a pink cardigan sweater was thrown over her compact shoulders. Dr. Lancaster gestured to her.

"And Carla Pérez, who is just leaving," said Dr. Lancaster, taking a seat. "She is the group's admin. Carla takes care of the things we muddleheaded academics, such as myself, can't seem to do."

An obligatory laugh rose up from everyone at the table. The queen made a joke, and the court must laugh.

"It is a pleasure to meet you," Carla said, her English betrayed only by a slight Spanish accent. "Welcome to El Cizin." With a quick nod of her head, she was gone.

Mr. Machete strode to JJ's side and whispered something in her ear. "Yes, yes, of course," she said to him, then turned to us. "You may remember Dr. Bjørn Pedersen. He insisted on accompanying me to bring you here. He joined the camp a few weeks ago replacing our previous expert in stratigraphy, who was suddenly taken ill. As you know, archaeology is about telling stories. In order to do that, we have to understand the sequence in which things happened. That is Dr. Pedersen's job."

He removed his hat, and I took him to be a man in his mid-thirties. His Scandinavian features were also deeply tanned, but unlike Dr. Lancaster, he wore the sun well. He gave us a curt nod and walked away.

A little embarrassed by his brusque behavior, JJ rattled on: "Dr. Pedersen has just advised me that we need to get you three fed, so the kitchen staff can clean up and go home. Dinner is usually served between five thirty and seven thirty. Breakfast is from five thirty to seven. We always take a bag lunch with us wherever we may be going for the day. So let me finish with the rest of the introductions as quickly as possible so you can visit the buffet stations."

She turned to the men and women seated at the table, silent so far except for their enforced laughter. They flashed tentative smiles, however, whenever I glanced in their direction. While the women remained seated, the men stood at her words. Even in the jungle, chivalry was not quite dead.

JJ turned to the woman sitting nearest us. "This is Dr. Josefina Sanchez from Mexico City. She oversees property assessment and field survey."

"*Encantado de conocerte*," a graying, slender woman in her mid to late forties said in Spanish. A hawklike nose dominated an otherwise small-featured face. She gave a graceful bow of her head.

"Nice to meet you, too," I said.

JJ went on briskly. "Dr. Phillip Whitewater from England. He leads the team in historical significance."

"Cambridge University, dear ones, just to clarify," he said, then sat down. He adjusted round, full-rimmed glasses on a bronzed face, while watching me specifically.

The glasses didn't hide the fact that here was a man who liked to come across as what's known in *GQ* as a man's man. He was taller than average, muscular, and had a certain roguish attitude about him. His face carried a scar or two, which made him look even more like writer Ernest Hemingway.

I concede Hemingway was a brilliant writer and loved cats, but he was also a drinker and liked to knock his women around. Personally, I think he had a lot to answer for. I tried not to let that prejudice get in the way of responding to this archaeological maven.

I smiled at him, and he winked at me. Then he gave me a lascivious smile. Okay, dead in the water was Dr. Phillip Whitewater.

Meanwhile, JJ moved on with her introductions. With a wave of her hand, she indicated a standing, pink-faced man with yellow hair and bleached-out eyebrows and lashes. Some people need to stay out of the sun.

"This is Dr. Benjamin Storrs, on leave from the Archaeology Department at New York University," JJ said. "He is the project administrator."

"A dirty job," Storrs said with a smile, "but someone's gotta do it."

I got the feeling this was a running gag of his. Before I could rev up a ha-ha, he went on.

"Thanks for coming to help find Martín. We're getting up another search party first thing tomorrow morning."

"You sound like you come from New York City, Professor Storrs," I said.

"Born and raised in Hell's Kitchen," he replied, banging his hand on the table for emphasis. Lancaster gave him a dirty look, which he ignored.

Storrs took his seat but continued to study me intently as if I were under a microscope. Then he wrote something in a small notebook sitting beside his plate of food. Weird.

"Thank you, Bennie," JJ said, bringing me out of my thoughts.

She turned to the last person standing, a young, sturdy man who seemed to be covered in thick, dark hair. Not just on his head and face, but tufts of chest hair peeked out from his short-sleeve shirt. More ran down the length of his arms to his fingertips. Here was a man who might want to have his testosterone levels checked.

"And our leader in site conservation is Professor Emilien Bernard from France," JJ said.

"Notice," Professor Bernard said, his French accent giving the room a continental air, "that as a mere professor, I am given last billing."

A little thrown by his pettiness, JJ said, "I meant nothing at all, Emilien. It's just that you were at the end of the table. I would never—"

"Of course not," he said smoothly. "I was only joking." But it was clear by the expression on his face he wasn't.

Chapter Eleven

After Mom, Gurn, and I gave our own fast hellos, we headed for the buffet table. The three of us huddled together making our selections.

"This is a tense lot," I said. "And did you see how Dr. Lancaster avoided answering me about what's been happening here?"

"It was fairly obvious," Gurn said, reaching for a plate.

"I'll sit next to her and see what I can glean," Lila whispered.

"And I plan to quiz JJ later," I said. "I won't go to sleep tonight until I learn more about what's going on at this camp."

"*Buenos tardes*," said a woman's voice, interrupting our clandestine exchanges.

We looked up almost as one to see the smiling face of a tall, buxom woman standing on the other side of the buffet table. Probably in her early fifties, she was dressed in a white uniform, her darkish hair swept up in a hairnet. An unlined face was devoid of any makeup and shiny from the heat of the kitchen.

"Buenos tardes," Gurn and I replied in unison.

"Good evening," Lila murmured with a smile.

"I am Consuela, and I see to the preparation of all the food you have here. Welcome." She gave each of us a warm smile. While her halting English came easily to her, her Spanish accent made you concentrate on each word spoken.

"Well," I jumped in, switching to Spanish, "it all looks delicious and smells heavenly."

"Gracias." Consuela also switched to Spanish. "It is a labor of love."

"Is that beef stew?" I pointed to a warming tray filled to the top with chunks of meat, potatoes, and veggies floating in a thick gravy.

"Goat," she said with a smile. "The goat stew is popular here. I try to serve it once a week."

I thought of the nanny goat, Iddle-Widdle, that lived on a farm in Marin. We visited her frequently when I was a child. She had darling floppy ears and soft brown eyes that just melted you. I wasn't going near that stew. Let's face it, I'm not as cosmopolitan as I'd like to think.

As we chatted, Consuela straightened up errant slices of bread with plastic-gloved hands, then moved on, wiping up drips of sauces with a wet cloth. It was obvious she had pride of ownership over the dishes before us.

"Do not hesitate to come back for refills. If you have a special request or food allergies, please let me know." After refilling a bowl with tomatillo sauce, she left with a friendly wave of her hand.

I heaped green salad with pomegranate seeds and slices of fresh papaya onto a plate. It looked elegant enough to have been created by Tío. I already missed him and the cats.

I also opted for a slice of rare roast beef — at least, it looked like roast beef — along with the salad. I smothered the salad in raspberry dressing and grabbed a few dinner rolls and butter. Lila did the same thing minus the dressing, rolls, and butter.

Gurn took several pieces of fried chicken, a dish he will choose over practically anything else offered. He finished his plate off with mashed potatoes and string beans. Comfort food. It was almost like being at a buffet table at the Hyatt Regency.

When we rejoined the others at the table, we were greeted with polite silence. Lila sat next to Dr. Lancaster and began a quiet conversation, the gist of which I knew she'd tell us later. Lancaster's assistant, Felicity Adler, sat lost in thought, as did JJ, both sitting at opposite ends of the table.

The academics departed within a few minutes, claiming fatigue or duties elsewhere. We three ate quickly and scooted off with JJ to our assigned sleeping tent.

"I hope this will do," JJ said.

We entered a square, roomy tent. It had more of a permanence about it than anything I managed to throw up in the backyard as a kid. But even with the shades on the screened windows rolled up to the max, it still offered very little flowing air. I was glad I brought my battery-operated fan.

Three single cots under mosquito netting were placed about three feet apart from each other on a plywood floor. The netting was a relief to me. While we were taking antimalarial medication to reduce our chances of getting the disease, it only reduced the risk of infection by about 90 percent. Taking steps to avoid bites was important.

Our knapsacks had been placed on the floor at the foot of the cots. Three hanging electric lights were overhead, similar to the ones in the cafeteria.

A rustic bench sat beside each cot. On top of the benches lay white muslin drawstring bags, each about the size of a knapsack. Next to one of the bags was a small notepad. I picked up a bag from the nearest bench and noticed it was lying on top of two others.

I turned to JJ. "What are these for?"

63

"Those are for your dirty laundry. We're encouraged to fill the bags with the clothes we've worn that day, and to do so each day. This keeps the laundry situation more manageable for the staff. We have four washer-dryers going all day. They're next to the recycling room. You'll notice the bags have numbers on them, coordinating with the numbers on each bench. Write the numbers down on the laundry slip, along with a description of what's inside, any washing instructions, and put the slip inside the bag. The clothes will be washed, dried, folded, and then returned to you the following day."

"Well, that's handy-dandy," I said. "We could use that system at home."

JJ laughed. It was good to hear. "I know what you mean. In the corner over there" — she paused, turned, and pointed to a corner of the tent — "is a black plastic bag inside a metal bin. That's for trash. No garbage. We don't encourage eating inside our sleeping tents. Less chance of animals and insects paying a visit."

"We wouldn't want *that*," Lila commented.

JJ went on, "The trash bin is airtight. We're asked to be sure the lid is tightly closed on it at all times."

"Understood," Gurn said.

She gave him a smile. "The showers and lavatories are outside and to the right, about two doors down. Just follow the sounds of the generators."

"I *wondered* what that hum was, "Lila said.

"Yes, we have our own generators. They are right next to the bathroom facilities. The doors are marked 'damas' and 'caballeros' with three stalls and showers in each. Wash cloths, soap, and towels are already in the shower rooms."

JJ let out a huge sigh, her body riddled with fatigue and stress. Lecture over, she lapsed into a more personal conversation.

"I can't believe I'm twelve-weeks pregnant. It's something I've dreamed of and yet—" She broke off.

My mother went to JJ's side. "You need to get some *rest*, Jacqueline, dear. We'll be *fine*."

"But before you go," I said, "what specifically has been going on around here that might give the authorities reason to shut the site down?"

With a sense of heaviness that belied her slender frame, JJ sat down on the nearest bench. She picked up one of the laundry bags and began playing with it. While opening and closing the drawstrings, she said, "Many things have happened, some small, some large. I can't speak for everyone, but I've been feeling so... I don't know... violated."

"In what way?" I prodded.

"Maybe not violated. Maybe helpless. You see, besides the Antiquities Room, nothing is locked up around here."

"Is the Antiquities Room," Gurn asked, "where you keep artifacts and other important finds?"

"Yes. Also, where objects are cleaned, categorized, and repaired."

I went back to the subject of the locks. "What do you mean, nothing is locked around here?" This news surprised me.

"The bungalows and tents can only be locked from the inside," JJ said, "more or less for a modicum of privacy. But there's no way to lock them from the outside."

"Everyone is on the honor system, I take it," I said.

"Yes, having no locks is supposed to reinforce the family-like attitude being promoted. And we've had no problems before on any of the other sites." JJ's words came hasty and apologetic. "But suddenly on this one, we've had nothing but. The natives blame it on, well, we can get into that later. Anyway, for the past few months, we've been having incidents."

65

"Like what?" Again, I prodded.

"It started with the theft of personal items. That was the first to happen. I had a locket stolen, one that Martín gave me for my birthday. It was his grandmother's, passed on to his mother, and then to me. It can never be replaced."

"How do you know these items haven't been lost or misplaced?" Gurn asked.

"Because whoever it is," JJ replied, "makes a mess when they take things. There's no way you don't know someone's been in your tent. Everything's strewn around. Then relics started missing. Some expensive, some not. With the thefts of the rare finds, we had to contact the police as well as the DC office. It's alarming. For one thing, how are they getting into the Antiquities Room? The building is locked, as I mentioned, and yet they manage to do it."

Gurn asked, "Who has keys?"

JJ reflected for a moment. It was as if no one had thought of that or asked the question before. "All of the heads of departments, Dr. Lancaster, and me. Sometimes I take visiting dignitaries in to see our work in progress."

"How many people is that in total?" I looked at Gurn and Lila after I asked the question.

"Maybe ten of us." She went into defense mode, her voice louder and sharper. "But these are people who have devoted their lives and their careers to the Maya legacy. None of them would steal from or endanger what we're doing here. I'd stake my life on it."

She was silent for a moment, possibly reflecting on the wisdom of that statement. "At least, I don't think they would," she whispered, more to herself than to us.

"Is that all that has happened," I asked, "or is there more?"

"I can't believe I'm saying this, but there's also been vandalism. Wanton destruction of equipment. Things have

66

been smashed or stolen. Some of it major. Necessary equipment. Waiting for replacements has set our work back." Frustration rang out in her voice. "But who? And why? That's what we keep wondering. There are one hundred people working this site, milling around all the time. How do you even begin to find out who's doing this?"

JJ threw the laundry bag down on the bench beside her. We watched her clasp and unclasp her hands, instead, before speaking again. "Recently it turned violent."

"Violent!" Lila let out a gasp.

"Yes, last week a visiting scholar was attacked. He's since gone back to the States."

"What *happened*?" Lila asked before either Gurn or I could utter a word.

"He was on his way to the lavatory one night when someone hit him over the head and stole his wallet and watch. Dr. Abeba checked him out, and even though he seemed fine, the doctor insisted on filing a police report."

"Now who is Dr. Abeba? We've got a long list of characters," Gurn said.

"Yes, I'm going to need a dance card soon," I said.

JJ smiled, letting go of some of her tension. "Dr. Kia Abeba is visiting from Ethiopia for the next eighteen months. She's doing a study on the similarities between the two ancient cultures, Abyssinia and Mayan, not that there are many. But she has some sort of grant, which means we can pay her less."

"She's an MD as well?" I asked.

"Yes. As you know, Martín is only a paramedic, not that he doesn't know a lot about the human body. But there are things he can't do. When she leaves, we will have to hire another doctor."

"Sounds like the dig is on a tight budget," I said.

"We're already months behind schedule," JJ said.

The fatigue of the day was evident in her voice. No longer animated, she spoke in a soft monotone.

"We're running out of time and money. And the donors, as well as the head office, are becoming impatient."

"That's enough for now," Gurn put in. "Get some rest, JJ. Tomorrow will be a big day."

"Yes," I said. "But first let me ask, can you get your hands on Alejandro's knapsack?"

"The one that has the word 'uayeb' written on it in blood?"

"Yes."

"I guess so, but why?"

I became vague. "I'd just like to see it, that's all."

"I'll drop it by your tent sometime in the morning, how's that?"

"Perfect. Thank you. Also, I'd like to retrace the path Martín took the day he disappeared. Is that going to be a problem?"

"We've been over it a dozen times. It's no use," JJ said, almost in tears. She pulled herself together. "I'm sorry. Forgive me. I'm just tired."

JJ rose from the bench, forcing a smile. I crossed to her and reached out, giving her a big hug. She returned it and held on tight.

"But we've got fresh eyes and sheer determination," I said, breaking free. "We'll find something. If nothing else, I want to see where he disappeared. Whatever else, don't give up hope."

"Of course not," she said. She smiled at each of us. "As Scarlet says, 'Tomorrow is another day.'" She gave a fairly good imitation of Vivian Leigh in *Gone With the Wind*. I was impressed.

She headed for the exit but turned back at the door. Her voice reverted to the desperation I knew she was feeling.

"We will find Martín, won't we? I don't know what I'll do if—"

"Yes," all three of us said in unison.

"We'll find him," I added. "It's a promise."

We watched her close the thin door behind her, there more for privacy than protection.

"It's interesting that JJ went to Flores to have a doctor confirm she was pregnant," I said to no one in particular. "Especially, as she's around twelve weeks. Any medical doctor should be able to tell when a woman's that far along. Why not have Dr. Abeba check her out?"

"I hadn't thought of that," Gurn said.

Lila turned to me. "Maybe we *shouldn't* have promised her we'd *find* Martín, Liana. We have *no* facts. We *know* nothing."

"I disagree," Gurn put in. "I think it's better for her to have as good a night's sleep as possible. She looks at the end of her rope."

I nodded, a lump coming to my throat. "Besides, I intend to keep that promise. We won't leave here until we know something, one way or the other."

Chapter Twelve

The thought of lying down and going to sleep was fabulous. But I needed a shower. I knew I couldn't go to sleep without washing some of the jungle doo-doo off me before we went to bed.

The showers, bathrooms were no more than a two- or three-minute walk away. I grabbed my all-purpose muumuu, one of the dirty laundry bags, and headed out.

A long, single-story building had a wall running down the middle. On either side of the wall was an open door leading to either the damas' or caballeros' bathrooms and showers, depending. The men's was on the left and the women's on the right. They were open-frame entrances. No doors to shut.

Even though there was a slight step up into the building, it still meant anything two, four, or eight-legged could walk inside and make themselves at home. This did not thrill me.

I stepped up and stood just inside the women's side. Before me was a blank wall. Turning right, I entered the facilities. Then off to the left was a short hallway leading to the showers. Silence. No running water.

Ahead of me and against the farthest wall were three stalls. These were what I like to think of as open-air stalls, covered partially by swinging doors. At the bottom of each door was a space of at least two feet between the floor and the door. If anyone was in there, you would see their feet and lower legs. I looked and didn't see anyone. At the top of the door was a good four feet of open space to the ceiling. Basically, privacy was an in-your-head sort of thing.

Across from the stalls were three white porcelain sinks. Each had a large, rectangular mirror directly above it. I walked to the center mirror and looked at my reflection. Big mistake.

The lighting in the room was ghastly. Overhead were yellow fluorescent lights. Combined with the light-blue paint of the walls, they created a greenish hue on anything in the room. Like my face.

Then I saw my hair. It had exploded in the 100 percent humidity. The results were a dark-brown frizz ball surrounding a green face. Lovely.

I thought it best not to panic. I wasn't there on a fashion shoot, anyway. To keep control of my hair, I'd braid it, that was all. Then hope for the best. Last-ditch effort might be having a crew cut.

I was in the process of determining whether it should be one thick braid hanging down my back, ala Lara Croft, or two braids giving me a *Little House on the Prairie* look, when I saw movement behind me. I pivoted a half turn from the mirror and faced the center stall. A butterfly trembled directly over the center stall. Black and white and gorgeous, it seemed to flutter in one place for a moment, stop, then flutter again. I concluded the tip of one wing had to be caught on an invisible thread of a spider's web.

It probably had flown in during the day and became trapped. Butterflies tend to fly during the day and sleep at night. I learned that, courtesy of the Butterfly Habitat in Vallejo, California, on a high school field trip way back when. I'd also learned they were classified as Lepidoptera, which I think is just a lovely word.

But I digress. I dashed over, opened the door, threw my muumuu on the tank, and stepped on the lid of the commode. It was just as I thought. One caught butterfly.

Fortunately, I'd also been taught how to hold a butterfly, so you won't damage its wings. I reached up with one hand, gently closed its wings, and using a light but firm touch, held all four wings together in one place. Then with the other hand, I reached up, took the spider's strand between my thumb and forefinger, and pinched the thread with my two nails as close to the caught wing as possible.

The thread of its imprisonment broken, I opened my hand to release the butterfly. But this gorgeous creature stayed in my palm, wings held together, absolutely still. I thought I'd hurt it no matter how careful I'd been. Or maybe it was past exhaustion into death.

Suddenly its wings sprung open. It took off, flying first in a circle and then, *whoosh*, out the open door.

I stood on the lid of the john basking in the glow of a good deed well done. It was short lived. Just outside the door I heard two women approach. I could tell they were women because they were in the midst of a loud, heated argument.

Angry feet clomped in on the cement floor, echoing throughout the room. I squatted down into a little ball on top of the john's lid, trying not to breathe.

"You had no right to send that op-ed to the magazine criticizing my work. It was vicious and spiteful," said one. She had a Spanish accent, but her English was good.

"It wasn't vicious, Josefina. It was my professional opinion of your work. Your article on the Maya development of farming was sloppy. Not up to the standards I have set for this archaeological endeavor."

While I couldn't see the two women, I recognized Dr. Lancaster's voice right away. Her tone was haughty, nasty, and dismissive, all at the same time. Some people have the knack.

I searched into the tired databanks of my brain for the other person's voice. Then it came to me. Dr. Josefina Sanchez, in charge of property assessment and field survey, whatever that was. Maybe the job included knowledge of farming.

"And be careful what you say in here," warned Lancaster. "There doesn't appear to be anyone, but I don't think you want it spread around that your latest paper was a failure."

"It wasn't a failure! I know more about ancient Mayan farming than you ever will, Joan." Josefina's voice was terse and thin.

Still cool under fire, Lancaster replied, "I doubt that very much. Now, if you will excuse me, I am going to take a shower." I heard the sound of her feet clomping down the hall.

Josefina shouted after her, her voice breaking with emotion. "You are jealous, that's what you are. You are jealous because you think he likes me. Well, I have news for you. He likes every woman. He is, as you English people say, a skirt chaser."

The farther away Lancaster got, the louder Josefina's voice became. One second later, the sounds of running water reverberated down the hallway toward us. With a small sob, Josefina exited, not so angry and not so loud of foot.

I waited a second or two, listening to the shower. I stepped down, opened the door, and peered out. Decision time.

Did I take a shower and have a possible run-in with Her Majesty, the Queen, whom I was disliking more with each passing minute? Or did I stay dirty until tomorrow morning?

It was a decision I didn't have to make. I heard the rustle of someone else coming in, not so loud and not so angry. It was Lila. She looked at me in surprise.

"Why, Liana, I *thought* you would be taking a shower."

"Uh… no, not yet. There was a butterfly… never mind."

"Well, I decided to *join* you. I felt a quick shower will help me *sleep* better. Gurn thought so as well. He's in the men's room. Do I hear the *showers* running?"

I grabbed my muumuu and went to my mother, who was standing just inside the entrance. Linking arms with her, I said, "Yes, but only one is in use. There's two more."

"I believe the soap and towels are *also* in that area?" It may have started out as a statement, but Lila's tone rose at the end, making it more of a question.

"We are about to find out, Mom. It is my goal to find out many things," I said as we marched toward the showers.

There was, indeed, a healthy supply of fresh facecloths, towels, and soap in a corner of the showering area. The water was hot and steamy. It felt delicious.

Moments later, I heard Dr. Lancaster's shower stop. Then more clomping down the short hall as she exited.

As I lathered up, I couldn't help but wonder who Dr. Lancaster's "he" was. And just how much of a mortal enemy she'd made of Dr. Josephina Sanchez.

Chapter Thirteen

Four the next morning came early. But I'd set my vibrating clock under the pillow to wake me. I needed to do some exercise, a ballet barre, even if there was no barre. The more I don't want to do one, the more I need to. Murphy's Law.

The air felt oppressive, heavy with falling rain. It was one of those days you'd like to stay in bed listening to the rain beat down on your roof. Or in this case, your tent. But this was pushing forty-eight hours into Martín's disappearance, and we needed to get moving.

I dug around inside my knapsack for my leotard and ballet slippers. I tried to dress as quietly as possible to let Gurn and my mother sleep on.

Snatching up my phone containing dance music and earphones, I crept over to one corner of the tent that afforded almost a five-foot space. Not enough to do a grand jeté, but one must learn to adjust. For forty-five minutes, I practiced, stretched, balanced, focused, sweated, and centered myself. It was heaven.

Five a.m. came, and the other alarm went off. Both Gurn and Lila roused. While they scratched and yawned, I followed Gurn's advice and shook out my boots for unwanted creepy-crawlies. I grabbed a change of clothes, threw my rain poncho over my shoulders, and made a dash for a quick shower. But not before I taunted the two of them to get with the program. They followed soon enough. All three of us were showered, dressed, and ready to go by five forty-five.

Grabbing what we needed for the day, we plodded through the mist and downpour toward the cafeteria. It was just becoming light. I glanced toward the shadowy gloom at the other end of this ancient Mayan city, but it was still just that for me, a gloomy shadow.

On the way to breakfast, I turned to Lila. "You know, when I told you both last night about the argument between Drs. Lancaster and Sanchez, we never got around to whether or not you found out anything of import on your end, Mom."

Lila sniffed. "Dr. Lancaster was *most* uncommunicative, almost to the point of being *rude*."

"She strikes me as a woman who really knows how to rub people the wrong way," I remarked. "Having a boss like that can be a double whammy when things aren't going well on the job."

"What about her assistant, Professor Adler, Lila?" Gurn turned to look at my mother as he walked along. "Did she have anything to say for herself?"

"Not a thing," Lila said. "But I did notice she seemed *quite* ill at ease, starting at every noise. She seemed unhappy at being at this camp. But she *appears* to be quite under the thrall of Dr. Lancaster."

"Other than being Dr. Lancaster's assistant," I asked of my mother, "does she have an area of expertise?"

"She's supposed to be one of the *leading* experts on the Maya script, *also* known as *glyphs*, the writing system of the Mayan civilization."

"Similar to the Egyptians?" Gurn threw her a questioning glance.

Lila nodded. "They *bear* similarities. Both cultures thrived around the *same* time on opposite sides of the world. If the Mayan civilization had existed in a desert instead of a jungle, it is possible they might have been discovered much *earlier*

76

and be as equally *revered* as the Egyptians. It's *certainly* food for thought."

"Speaking of food," I said, "we've arrived."

The cafeteria was alive with action, though it was barely past five forty-five. Fifty or sixty people were either standing in the fast-moving buffet line or seated at tables eating. Lively chitchat, mostly in Spanish, filled the air.

We made our way toward the heavenly smells of what turned out to be a bountiful Guatemalan breakfast. It was hard to believe Consuela and her assistants did this every day.

The buffet and steam tables were laden with black beans, fried plantains, cheeses, scrambled and fried eggs, fresh fruits, pancakes, white sausage, chorizo, wiener sausage, carne asada, which is charcoal-grilled beefsteak, and hot oatmeal. Side dishes of cream, bread, tortillas, bowls of red and green sauces, everything fresh made. Hot chocolate, orange juice, and, of course, coffee was there for the taking.

Just as we finished loading up our trays, JJ appeared and walked with us to an empty table. Her face was drawn. There were dark circles under her eyes, but she managed a smile and hugged each one of us.

She looked at me. "I dropped by your tent to bring you Alejandro's knapsack. You weren't there, but I left it under your cot, Lee. Out of sight. Although I don't know what you're going to find in it."

I smiled in a noncommittal manner. "You never know. And thanks."

"How did you sleep?" JJ's question took in the three of us.

"*Wonderfully,*" Lila said. "We found the cots quite comfortable. We slept *exceptionally* well."

Speak for yourself, Mom, I thought. *I was wide awake most of the night waiting for a puma to break down the door demanding to know what I was doing in his jungle.*

"You don't look like you got much sleep, JJ," Gurn said, reaching out and touching her hand briefly with his. "How are you holding up, cuz?"

"All right, all right," she said, trying to brush it off.

"Let me get you some *breakfast,* Jacqueline," Lila said, rising.

"No, no. I don't want anything," JJ murmured.

"*Nonsense.*" Lila Hamilton-Alvarez took on the challenge. "You're eating for *two* now. You need to have, at the very *least,* fresh fruits and vegetables."

"How about a mango yogurt shake?" I suggested. "It looked delicious."

"*Perfect* choice," Lila said, not waiting for JJ's response. Sweeping away, she said, "I'll be *right* back with it."

I sipped coffee, excellent, by the way, and kept a watchful eye on JJ, as did Gurn. Both of us knew things couldn't go on like this for too much longer. The mystery of Martín's disappearance was jeopardizing JJ's health and the health of her baby. We needed to find out what happened to the man ASAP.

After Lila returned to the table with JJ's yogurt drink, I asked, "JJ, where did the six men who escorted us from the landing strip go when they left last night?"

She thought for a moment. "Most returned to the workers' campsite. But we don't do a bed check. Sometimes they go to their village to see family or friends, especially if it's close by." JJ stopped toying with her drink and took a few healthy swigs of it.

"Is there a village close by?"

"Oh, yes. There are many small villages, comprised of mostly extended families or friends, scattered throughout El Mirador. Some of our workers come from one quite close, not quite a mile away." She turned to my mother. "This is good, Mrs. Alvarez. Thank you for getting it for me."

"You *must* call me Lila. And you need some *toast* as well," Lila said, standing up again.

"No, no."

JJ's protest fell on deaf ears. Lila hurried back to the buffet table, picked up a small plate holding two pieces of toasted grain bread and butter.

JJ turned to me. "Your mother is wonderful," she said. "She reminds me of how much I miss mine."

"Yeah, yeah. Moms are great," I said, not allowing us to be taken offtrack. "JJ, back to this village. Is it between here and the site where Martín went? What's the new discovery called, by the way?"

"We don't have an official name for it yet," JJ said, "But it seems to feature the god, Kinich Ahau. Kinich Ahau is the Lacandón name for the Sun God. So that probably will wind up being the name. But, yes, the village is between here and the new site."

Gurn leaned forward, recognizing the gleam in my eye. "Lee, you're thinking one or more of the six youths who were with us last night could be involved?"

"It's a possibility. I'd like to interview them, for sure."

Lila returned with the small plate of toast, butter, and what looked like raspberry jam. I picked up a fork and took a bite of chorizo from my plate — heaven — and waited until Lila sat down again.

"I think we should start," I said, after swallowing, "with a conversation with the white-sneaker twins."

"The twins? Geraldo and Jorje?" JJ asked in surprise. "Why?"

"Do you know them? They seemed a little nervous to me," I said, by way of explanation for my choosing those two.

"No more than I know the others who work here," JJ admitted.

"Eat at least *one* of those pieces of toast before you *leave* this table, young lady," Lila said to JJ before turning back to me, "I noticed that, *too*, Liana, but I *assumed* it was because it was getting dark, and they were anxious to get back."

"Let's not assume anything." *Never ASSUME*, I'd almost said, *because when you ASSUME, you make an ASS of U and ME.* I didn't say it, though, because puns like that don't fly with Lila Hamilton-Alvarez.

"Let me see if they've arrived for work yet," JJ said, ignoring her toast and standing. "Or if they're even coming back."

"What does that mean, even coming back?" Gurn also stood and looked directly into his cousin's face. "Have you had problems with workers not showing up?"

She looked away, not quite nervous or embarrassed but decidedly uncomfortable. She kept her voice low. "We've had some issues with keeping local workers."

"Why is that?" Mom, still seated, demanded. She stared up at JJ.

I could see JJ come to a decision. She glanced around before taking her seat again. She leaned in toward us, and gestured for Gurn to sit down as well. The four of us pulled our chairs in and huddled together at the end of the table in a conspiratorial fashion.

"As you've sat *down* again," Lila said before JJ could go on, "Please eat your *toast*, Jacqueline."

With a sigh, JJ picked a slice up and took a large bite. As she chewed, she said, "It's this site. This is the first temple we've found dedicated exclusively to the Mayan god, El Cizin. He's one of the major death gods and apparently much more important to the culture than we initially thought."

JJ paused and slathered jam on her toast before ripping off another bite with her teeth. "El Cizin," JJ said, chomping away, "is mentioned many times in the oral tradition of the Lacandón people. The evidence we're uncovering here says they believe he was the one to contend with, even centuries ago."

"How *interesting*," Lila commented. I could sense she was restraining herself from telling JJ not to talk with her mouth full. "You speak of this El Cizin *almost* as if he's real."

"Do I?" JJ seemed flustered. "I'm sorry. I guess, after a while, the way the populace feels rubs off on you. And the locals certainly feel he does exist. Many who live here are descendants of the Lacandóns, which makes these myths and legends very much a part of their lives."

"The Lacandóns," I asked, "still live in the Sierra del Lacandón, a national park nearby, don't they?"

"We're in the park now, sweetheart," Gurn said, softening the comment with a smile.

"That's right," JJ affirmed, also smiling.

"We are? Okay, putting my lack of geographical skills aside," I said, returning their smiles, "how does El Cizin tie in with your not keeping workers?"

JJ thought for a moment. "There is only one death god found in the Lacandón language, Kisin. K-I-S-I-N. In Mayan it means 'Stinking One.' He is the Mayan earthquake god and god of death, ruler of the subterranean land of the dead. In the English language, we spell it with a C, but it's the same god."

I thought for a moment, then asked, "So this El Cizin is believed to be the ruler over the world of the dead, the principal death god?"

"Yes," JJ said.

"Is he like the Aztec deity Mictlantecuhtli?" Gurn asked. "I remember you telling me about him when I joined you in Mexico a few years back."

"Somewhat," she said, "but in El Cizin's case, he's even more evil and vindictive. He takes an active part in pulling offenders into the world of the dead, or what we think of as hell. Most Lacandóns are terrified of him."

"He sounds like a pretty scary god," I said.

"Most definitely," she said. "And the legends are clear Mayan gods don't like to have their temples or pyramids disturbed any more than the Egyptians did. El Cizin is considered the most vengeful god of them all. That's why the natives are very squirrelly about working here. We have to pay them double. And still, many don't return whenever we uncover a new chamber or unearth artifacts that involve El Cizin. And... oh... I don't know..." Her voice dropped off. She reached for the last piece of toast and took a small nibble from it.

"Go on," Lila encouraged, leaning in. "This is *most* illuminating."

JJ set the toast back on the plate. Heartened by my mother's interest, she said, "The locals feel he is becoming angrier with each passing day. They don't like us digging around in his temple."

"Which temple is that?" I was all agog now myself.

JJ looked at me as if I had a screw loose. "The one here. Just outside. Didn't you see it on your way to the cafeteria?"

"It was raining pretty hard when we came in. It just looked like a gray blob at the end of the block."

"Well, the rain just stopped," JJ said, "and the sun is out. We're in rainy season, so grab your moment in the sun while you can!"

I was glad her sense of humor hadn't completely abandoned her. She sobered and went on. "Anyway, early into the dig, we found a mural on one of the walls of El Cizin eating offenders. Even their children."

"Wow," I said. "That's grisly."

"It is," JJ agreed. "That mural sent over half the men home then and there. They never returned, no matter how much money we offered them. And they need the money and the fringe benefits."

"Really," I said. "What are the benefits besides a salary?"

"For one thing, an education, if they want. We have a teacher who helps them learn to read and write. And then, of course, they have medical and dental assistance as long as they're in our employ. Not just for them, but in emergencies, their families. The workers have daily access to our on-site doctor, and we have a dentist that visits four times a year. You do know that Martín runs a free clinic right outside the perimeter? It's for everyone, whether they work here or not."

"Yes," Lila said, "I *understand* he takes care of the workers' families' general health."

"He's not a doctor, but sometimes he's all that stands between serious illness and health," JJ said. "He delivered six babies just this year."

"I take it," Gurn said, "most of these people are barely eking out an existence."

"Unfortunately," JJ said.

"And still some left the job, despite the money and the perks," I muttered. I turned to JJ. "Because they were afraid El Cizin might reach out and punish them?"

"Not just them," JJ said. "He would punish the entire village. Bad crops, illness, pandemic-like deaths."

"Do you ever visit these villages?" Gurn asked. "See what's going on?"

"Of course not."

JJ's answer was abrupt, almost harsh. Then she caught herself.

"I mean, it would be considered an intrusion into their private lives. Sometimes Martín goes into one of the villages, especially if the person is too sick to go to the clinic. But only if he's asked. The natives don't like it. We've learned to wait until they come to us."

"And the legends of El Cizin's evil ways have made this delicate truce-like living even worse," I said.

JJ looked at me. "You understand. Thank you. You'll notice most of the men working here are barely more than teenagers. They're the only ones willing to take the chance. The village women aren't allowed to come here at all."

"What about Consuela and her crew?" I asked.

"Consuela's from Honduras and has been with us for years," JJ said. "She doesn't—"

JJ was interrupted by a high-pitched, bone-chilling scream that came from somewhere outside. It was immediately followed by another scream, longer and shriller. Most people froze in place, only their heads turning in the direction of the sounds. But Gurn and I leapt up and took off, running toward the continuing and constant shrieks.

Chapter Fourteen

We darted from the cafeteria and into the brightness of the day. Turning in the direction of the screeches, I saw something so shocking I almost lost my footing. I stood paralyzed for a moment, staring at what lay before me.

The gray blob of less than an hour before had transformed into a magnificent Mayan temple, a pyramid nine or ten stories high. Still wet from the rain, its sand-colored stones glistened like gold in the newly emerged sun. The sight was awesome in every sense of the word.

I pulled myself together and rushed by several stunned people to join Gurn at the base of the stone steps. He'd stopped, looking up at Professor Felicity Adler. Dr. Lancaster's assistant was standing on a step halfway up the temple. Her face scrunched up in horror, she stared down at a body lying motionless on the step, her screeches turning into yowls.

One of the four men we'd met the previous night at the dinner table, Professor Emilien Bernard, was already running up the steep steps. We followed in hot pursuit.

Professor Adler's yowls evolved into whimpers by the time Professor Bernard arrived. Looking at him, she backed up and tripped, falling onto the next-highest step.

Professor Bernard took a moment, focused on the dead man, then backed away himself. Maybe the sight of immediate death overwhelmed a man who only dealt with it when it was centuries old, when bones and dust represented the one-time living and breathing.

Long-legged Gurn arrived before me. He dropped to his knees and put a hand to the inert figure's neck for a pulse.

A second or two later, and breathing hard, I reached the step and stood beside my husband. I looked down and could hardly believe my eyes.

There lay a Mayan warrior. Probably in his mid-twenties, the man had been laid out in all his combatant finery. A young and handsome face, his golden skin stood out against the red, yellow, and blue of the head-to-toe warrior regalia. Adorning his head was an elaborate feathered headpiece, now flattened by the rains. Exotic plumes lay forlorn and sad looking.

I managed to gasp, "Any pulse?"

Gurn shook his head sadly, gazing at the young man.

"Stand aside," a woman ordered, arriving seconds after I did. "I'm a doctor."

I stepped back, nearly colliding with the stone stair above. Gurn rose and stepped to the side. We both exchanged glances, then studied the woman bending down.

It didn't take much to figure out this was Dr. Abeba. Aside from her pronouncement of being a doctor, she was a slender, middle-aged Black woman with refined features that often go with the Ethiopian people.

But Gurn, always ready to double-check on things, said, "You are Dr. Abeba?"

"Yes," the doctor replied without looking up. "Be quiet now," she ordered. "I need to concentrate."

So quiet we were and watched practiced hands examine the body. I took this opportunity to look over the dead man more carefully.

Arms by his side, he was posed on a tan cape of rough, woven cotton fabric. Its red-leather fringes had been meticulously combed in place. He wore a loincloth also made from cotton. The wide leather belt was set with jade stones in a complicated pattern of size and colors. I couldn't help but admire the workmanship of the warrior's costume from the headpiece down to the leather sandals on his feet.

Covering his chest was a round shield of intricately carved leather, impressed with an image of a Mayan god. Which god, I didn't know.

I heard Professor Bernard's heavy breathing nearby. I turned and saw shock frozen upon his face. And something else. Recognition.

"Who is it?" I asked.

"Alejandro Rios, Martín's assistant," the French professor said. His voice held disbelief. "Oh *mon Dieu*! But how... what..."

"He's dead, dead!"

The shrillness of Professor Adler's voice bounced off the side of the temple as if she were using a megaphone. I'd forgotten about her and looked in her direction. She sat on a higher step at the other side the temple. Leaning into the riser above, it was as if she felt the stones themselves offered some sort of protection.

"I hate this place! It's cursed! Cursed!" She howled like a wild dog. "We shouldn't be here! I knew it, I knew it!" She sobbed anew. "I knew something like this would happen."

Ignoring the hysterical woman, Dr. Abeba lifted the colorful shield from the dead man's naked chest. I stepped closer.

"If there was any blood, it's been diluted, if not obliterated, by the heavy rain," I remarked, looking at Gurn. "But I can't see any wound, though, any cause of death."

Gurn also came closer. "Might have been stabbed in the back," he offered, looking directly at me.

87

"It's possible," Dr. Abeba said, coming into the conversation. Her Amharic accent was very slight.

"But I don't want to roll him over. I'm sure the police wouldn't like it. They probably won't like the fact I touched the shield. I should put it back." She returned the shield to the top of the man's chest. "Alejandro was so young," she said, suddenly giving way to emotion.

"The police," I said to Gurn. "They'll have to be called, right? There's no way to keep them out of this now."

"No, there isn't," Gurn said.

"Goodbye anonymity," I murmured. I looked down at the still-kneeling doctor. "Doctor, do you think this was some sort of religious sacrifice?"

Pulling herself together, she stood. "Possibly. We'll know after the autopsy. But whatever it was, it certainly won't make right this young man's death."

Chapter Fifteen

I tuned in on the cries of grief, wonderment, and fear from the ground. A few dozen people, a combination of natives and staff, were standing together at the bottom of the pyramid gaping up at us. Abruptly, as if by some unspoken command, the group split up, with most of the young natives running in different directions at the same time.

I dropped to the next lower step, moved past the doctor, and signaled for Gurn to join me. When he did, I wrapped an arm around his waist and pointed with the other.

"Darling, look," I whispered. "The white-sneaker twins are running away as if their lives depended on it."

His eyes followed the direction of my pointing finger. "What the—"

"Can you tail those two?"

"Consider it done," Gurn whispered back. "I've got everything I need on me, including my sat phone." His hand went to his side, and he tapped one of the many pockets of his olive-green tactical pants left over from his special ops days. "I'll keep you posted."

Without waiting for my response, he leapt down the side of the temple like a mountain goat. Mr. Sure-footed hit the bottom, pushed through any remaining gawkers, and tore after the two boys. He entered the jungle only moments after they did.

Leaving others to deal with the dead body, I made another split-second decision. While I didn't jump down with the same sure-footed goatness of Gurn, I got down a lot faster than I'd climbed up. Sidestepping the remaining people still staring up at the scene, I raced back to the cafeteria.

I found Lila at the entrance with a hand over her eyes, shielding them from the sun in order to see what was going on. Grabbing her by the arm, I pulled her to the side and didn't even allow her to speak.

"Mom, just hear me out. We've got to find JJ and head out now, before the police get here. Once they do, we'll have to stay put."

With not a moment's reluctance, Lila said, "Of course. *You* alert Jacqueline." She pointed to where JJ seemed to be in a heated discussion with Dr. Lancaster. Lila turned back to me. "I'll get our *things* from the tent and be *right* back."

I sprinted the length of the tent to JJ and Dr. Lancaster. "Pardon the interruption, ladies." Both women turned to me.

"I can tell from the look on your faces," I said, "you know Martín's assistant has been found on the steps of the temple, dead." Both tried to speak but I stopped them before they could respond. "We're leaving on the search for Martín immediately. Gurn's gone already." I turned to JJ. "JJ, come with or stay; make up your mind, but it's now or never."

"I'm ready," she said, also without any hesitation. "Just let me get my knapsack and hat." She turned and fled the tent.

"But wait," Dr. Lancaster called after JJ. She turned to me. "We need to think this through."

"No, we don't," I said.

The project manager fairly puffed up with indignation. "I can't allow you to leave like this."

"We have to go before the police arrive," I said, ignoring her puffiness. "I'm sure if you haven't called them by now, someone else has. A man is dead."

"Yes, but we must be prudent —"

"Gurn has his sat phone." I went on as if she hadn't spoken. "I have mine. Lila is getting our knapsacks. Everything we need for the day should be in there. Ah, here's JJ," I said as Gurn's cousin raced back into the tent, cramming her hat on her head.

Out of breath, she said, "I found Paco. He'll guide us wherever you want to go, Lee."

Paco, complete with monkey, rushed to her side. "I will get extra waters. Then we go," he said. As he left for the supply of bottled water on the counter, Lila returned and handed off my knapsack to me as well as my hat.

"Now, just a minute," Dr. Lancaster sputtered again, standing in one place but turning to each of us, condemnation in her tone. "There's protocol to be followed. I can't allow this. You need to wait."

"No! I will not wait," JJ said, shutting the older woman down. "Not one more minute. I listened to you. I gave you the time. I didn't call the police. And I should have. The more people searching for Martín, the more chances we have of finding him. Now his assistant is dead. I'm not waiting around for anybody else to die. I'm going to find Martín, and I don't give a damn about you or your protocol."

She turned on her heel, ignoring her superior, and threw her knapsack on. Shocked, Dr. Lancaster stared wide eyed at JJ's back.

"Let's go," JJ said to us, showing the authority she probably wielded during more normal times. "Paco," she bellowed without looking up while clipping the ties of the knapsack together around her waist. "Vamanos *ahora*!"

"*Estoy aquí*," he said, running to her side. "I am here."

He put on his own knapsack, laden mostly, I suspected, with water. An excited baby monkey jumped to the top of the man's head as we exited the tent and headed out into the jungle.

Chapter Sixteen

"Now that we've accomplished a rather *dramatic* exit," Lila whispered in my ear, "*where* are we going?"

"We follow the path where Martín was last seen and we try to locate Gurn," I whispered back. "He's following some very likely candidates in all this."

It had only been a few minutes of us tromping through the jungle, following a narrow path of flat limestones. Wherever I looked, the jungle was a vivid green, in shades varying from a yellowish to almost black. Occasionally, there would be a flash of another color, either an exotic flower or a tropical bird in flight.

Once an orange and blue caterpillar about a foot long dropped from above onto the sleeve of my shirt. Lila reached forward and brushed it off before I hardly knew what happened. Or could scream.

The lineup was Paco with monkey, JJ, me, and my mother. Lila may have been pulling up the rear, but she was so close on my heels, she tripped me up a few times. But she also got rid of the caterpillar, so I wasn't pushing her away.

After a time, the air grew heavy again with moisture. The overhead green canopy darkened. There was the sound of rain. I looked up. I'd like to say a drop of water landed in my eye, but it was more like a half of a cup. Temporarily blinded, I stopped short.

"Whoa," I said, wiping my eyes with the sleeve of my jacket. "What was that?"

"It's raining overhead." JJ said. "And it sounds intense. Likely a storm. The trees are keeping it from hitting us directly, but water gathers on leaves. When they become weighted down, they drop their load unexpectedly," JJ answered.

Another "load" landed on my hat. As it dripped off the brim onto my shoulder, I said in my best martyr voice, "So the heavens have opened up. Well, why not? Par for the course."

"Liana," Lila chastised, "please *don't* soliloquize about a little *water*."

And here, the fickle finger of fate took over. Right after she made that statement, something that looked like a snake plant on steroids bent one of its longest leaves directly over my mother's pith helmet and let loose a torrent of collected rainwater. She was drenched. A firefighter's hose could not have done a better job. I tried to keep a straight face.

JJ looked up. "This is not good. A storm's raging up there. Soon leaves and even limbs of trees will start falling. Maybe a small animal here and there. Be on your guard."

I cannot express how thrilled I was to hear that, especially the falling-animal part. A foot-long caterpillar had already dropped in on me. That was enough for one day. But having been previously chastised, I kept my mouth shut. Meanwhile, Lila shook the water off her like a delicate French poodle.

Muffled sounds of rain surrounded us. The world dripped. It was surreal.

"I can no longer use the machete," Paco announced, turning to face us.

JJ picked up the conversation. "This will slow us down. But when vegetation becomes too slick, you can mutilate yourself by using a machete."

"If we can't move ahead, maybe we should turn around and go back to the camp," Lila said. She actually gurgled the last of this statement. Runoff from her pith helmet had dribbled into her mouth.

"No!"

"Absolutely not."

JJ and I spoke over one another, our determination evident.

"We forge ahead," I said. "Gurn is out there looking for Martín, and they need our help."

Just then the sat phone rang. I scrambled to get it out of my pocket, looked at the incoming call, and slapped it to my ear. "Darling! Are you all right?"

"Sweetheart," he said, then static took over. All I got was every third or fourth word. However, the words "Martín," "boys," and "find" were clear. Then the line went dead. I hit redial. Nothing.

Ignoring the three people staring at me, I hit the speed dial for my brother. More dead air. I turned to JJ.

"Okay. I'm not going to panic. But tell me, when you get strong storms, do they interfere with the satellite dish?"

"They can," she answered instantly. "But only on this end. If we have to, we'll move to another spot for better reception."

After a moment's dead air, my brother answered.

"This is Richard."

"Richard! Thank God. Listen, because I could lose you at any minute. We're having some kind of jungle monsoon here. Track Gurn's phone right now, ASAP. Can you do that?"

"Does he have the one assigned to him?"

"Yes."

"I'll get back to you." He disconnected. Once again, he didn't waste time asking any unnecessary questions, just went about solving the issue. It's the way our working relationship has been for years. And why he's a treasure.

I turned back to faces staring at me. I even had the undivided attention of the monkey.

"Okay, everybody. We need to stay put until I hear from Richard."

JJ asked, "What did Huckster say?"

"You *should* have put it on speakerphone, Liana, so we could *all* hear," Lila said.

"Next time, Mom." I turned to JJ. "I don't want to get your hopes up, but he may have found something."

JJ's sharp, noisy inhaling of a breath interrupted me. "Is it Martín? Did he find Martín?"

I reached out and touched her on the arm. "I'm not sure. Most of what he said got lost in static, but it sounded promising. Richard is tracing his phone and will call me when he has anything. We'll just have to wait. And hope he can get through."

Facing one another, we formed a small circle, albeit a wet one. The jungle continued the sounds and beats of the storm overhead, with the occasional wind gust, never quite reaching us. But the water did. Soon, we were standing in ankle-deep mud. A small squirrel half ran and half swam by, but other than that, the rest of the wildlife was as eerily silent as were we.

It felt like hours, but it wasn't more than ten minutes before the phone rang again. I answered on the first ring, hitting the speakerphone this time.

"Richard, you're on speakerphone with Lila, JJ, and Paco, our guide. Just so I know, these phones are waterproof, right?"

"Right," he replied. "I never send you out with equipment that isn't Lee-proof. I've learned that the hard way."

"Ha ha. So what do you have?"

"I've got him. Or at least, his phone. Not much more than a mile from where you are."

With those words, all four of us exchanged looks of relief. Richard went on.

"I tried to call him myself, but he didn't answer. I've locked your phone on to his. It's a standard GPS locator. Do you see the button on the phone right below the compass?"

My eyes darted across the phone in a quick search, but Lila pointed to it immediately. Our mother is someone who actually familiarizes herself with the equipment she uses. I should try that sometime.

"We have it," I said.

"Good," Richard said. "Click on that button, and you'll see his location in conjunction with yours."

Holding the phone in the center of our little circle, I hit the key. A small map came up in the LTD screen with two blinking dots that made a coordinating beeping sound.

"I've got blinking, beeping dots."

"The farther you are away from his phone, the farther apart the beeps. The closer you get, the more rapid. It will become a steady hum when you intersect."

I looked around me. "Finding him might be dicey right now."

Paco took the phone from my grasp and studied the map. "I have lived in this jungle all my life. I know it. We will find him."

I could have kissed Paco. Here was a man who knew the power of positive thinking.

Richard's voice filled the air once more. "It can also give you longitude and latitude, should you need it," he said. "I'll be tracking both phones, so if you go astray, I'll let you know." He paused. "Are you in any danger?"

97

"Not sure," I said. "Could be."

"How prepared are you?" That was the polite way of asking if we had any weapons on us.

"A revolver, mace, and a hunting knife," was Lila's instant reply. My eyebrows shot up to my hairline. I gaped.

She looked at me in surprise. "One must be *prepared*, Liana."

"I have the machete," Paco offered without skipping a beat. He returned my phone to me, and our eyes met. We exchanged a look of solemnity, quickly overridden by a thumbs-up from him. I returned it. There was much more to this Paco than met the eye.

"I have twine and also a hunting knife," JJ said. "With me at all times."

I didn't bother asking JJ the whys and wherefores of the twine, but answered Richard's question with, "I'm good."

By saying that, Richard knew I was armed and just about as dangerous as any woman would be looking to save the life of the man she loved.

Chapter Seventeen

"Afortunado," Paco said, rubbing the wet head of the monkey, "bring us the luck." The monkey, in turn, squealed and chattered.

"*Guarda silencio.*" Paco ordered his pet to be quiet. Much better trained than either one of our cats, Afortunado ceased making noises immediately.

Paco turned and, looking at what was nothing more than a barricade of vegetation, began to push his way toward the coordinates. Now that we'd left the interconnecting roadway created by the Mayans centuries ago, it was slow going.

Trying to walk through just one mile of this dense jungle promised to take us hours. Between wet palm fronds, bushes, limbs, and actual trees coming at me from every which way, I was glad every part of my body was covered, gloved hands included.

The only exception was my face, which was slathered in insect repellent. The bonus of the storm was buzzing insects no longer were trying to get their share of me. But I knew I was going to need a facial after this trip.

At one point, Paco put up his hand for us to stop moving. Instinctively, we stood perfectly still, breathing as softly as possible. The rustle of a large animal, maybe a puma, passed close by. I thought I heard a low, throaty growl, but that could have been my stomach. Breakfast had been hours before, and I hadn't had a chance to eat much. After the sounds of movement died away, we continued our journey at a snail's pace.

Just when I thought we would never see the light of day again, Paco brought us to another man-made path. It was narrower and more ill-kept than the Mayan limestones, but I felt like we'd hit an eight-lane highway.

Paco turned to us with a look of satisfaction on his face. He gestured for us to come close as he whispered, "A village is nearby. It has no name, but the head of it is Juan Pedro Nacan, a descendent of the Mayans. A man of power. Not always a man who does the right thing, but I have learned to mind my own business about the ways of village leaders."

"Live and let live," I said.

"Yes, especially with someone like Juan Pedro. It is mostly his family that lives there. He is the father of the two *jóvenes* that work with us at the site."

"The twins in the white sneakers," I said. "Of course. Then that village is where we need to go."

Paco nodded, reached into his pocket, and pulled out a large date. He gave the fruit to Afortunado with another quick pat on the head before moving along the path. Afortunado munched as we went along. Easy for him. He had a ride.

Despite the rain, the heat was unending. Plus pushing through all the brush at 100 percent humidity made even breathing laborious.

I was dripping, and not just from the rain. My eyes burned from salty perspiration I couldn't brush away fast enough. Even Lila, who never did much in that department other than "glow," was sodden.

We only paused now and then to drink bottled water in an effort not to become dehydrated. JJ and Paco, more used to the weather, plowed ahead, but they, too, were soaked.

What kept me going were the two blinking dots that grew steadily closer. I tried texting Gurn repeatedly but had no reply.

Within half an hour we came to a large clearing. Twelve to fifteen primitive-looking dwellings centered around an impressive-sized pit lined with stones and rocks. Despite the rain, the pit had smoldering smoke rising from beneath layers of singed palm and banana leaves. Whatever was in there smelled delicious. Maybe wild boar.

Starving, I reached inside one of the many pockets of my cargo pants and pulled out a trail-mix bar. Just as I finished unwrapping it, Afortunado reached over and snatched it from my hand. I tried to retrieve my meager lunch by slapping at his paw, but he slapped right back at me.

Lila to the rescue. She waggled her forefinger in the animal's face, which gave him pause. You are not waggled at by the likes of Lila Hamilton-Alvarez and take it lightly. Even primates know that. Paco watched with a grin as Afortunado became docile, looking almost ashamed. Wordless, Lila took the bar from his paw with a *tsk-tsk* and handed it back to me. Maybe I did need my mommy along, after all.

Chewing on my hard-won prize, I noted the structures of the village were built of roughly hewed wooden planks or corrugated tin. Many supported a rounded, thatched roof but a few had flat, rusting tin roofs. Each was put together in a way that suggested extreme weather conditions other than heat, heat, heat and rain, rain, rain was never going to be an issue.

The village appeared to be deserted except for two women, an elderly man, and several small children. The women sat on logs under the overhang of a home. Chatting and laughing, they were making tortillas. I could have gone for one of those then and there.

101

The old man sat in a green plastic chair under another overhang, the largest building in the village, either a meeting hall or general store. I did a double take. The tin roof of the building was topped with a huge, gleaming satellite dish.

The old gaffer was wearing earphones. Eyes closed, he was either sleeping or grooving. The twenty-first century meets the Mayans.

While the downpour lessened, young children were protected as they played under a large ceiba tree, Guatemala's national tree. It was hard to tell how many children there were, each flitted around so quickly. Ah, youth.

I took another bite of my trail-mix bar and looked at my phone again. The two blinking dots, while close to one another other, did not jive. Gurn was nearby but probably not in the village or in any of its buildings.

I showed the phone to JJ and Paco and shrugged questioningly. Using hand gestures, JJ indicated we should walk around the edge of the village to the other side. Agreeing, Paco nodded. Lila, following the mime, joined the conga line.

In total silence, we snuck around to the other side of the village. With each step, the dots grew closer and became more rapid.

Finished with my snack, I took the lead and beat through the brush with my arms. We came to another narrow path, not much more than trodden ground cover.

A few minutes later, the two dots almost intersected. It was all I could do not to call out, but the possibility of whatever or whoever was around us caused me not to.

Covered with mud, Gurn rounded a corner and came into view. He was half carrying a limping man, whose expression said he was in a great deal of pain. Gurn's face lit up when he saw me. My heart leapt. He was okay.

JJ let out a yelp. Here, obviously, was the missing Martín. She pushed past me, and raced to her man, enveloping him in her arms.

This threw Gurn off-balance. He lost his grip on the wounded man. Strength nearly gone, Martín dropped to his knees in the mud. JJ also dropped to her knees, cradling her husband in her arms. Martín looked up and gave her a weak smile.

Gurn glanced at the three of us standing a few feet from him. He put his finger to his lips in a shushing gesture. We froze in place.

Eyes darting around, Gurn took in his surroundings. He leaned down to JJ, keeping his voice barely audible.

"He's severely dehydrated. If you've got water on you, give him some. I've already given him mine."

With all the water falling from the sky, I couldn't believe the dehydration part, but I'd learned to take Gurn at his word. JJ nodded and pulled a water bottle from her pocket, bringing it to Martín's lips.

No longer able to stay where I was, I ran to Gurn. Paco and Lila were close on my heels.

We gave each other a fast embrace, mud and all. I looked into his face with a smile. He gave me one of his lopsided grins before turning to the others. Instinctively, we all stepped closer to one another.

"The men of the village are off somewhere," Gurn whispered. "Maybe farming, but they could turn up at any minute. And I don't know when the sneaker twins or the other man will come to."

"There's a story here, I suspect," I said in a soft voice.

"Definitely," Gurn replied. "But first, we need to make tracks."

103

"I'm sorry," Martín murmured in barely audible tones. "I wish I could walk."

"Shhhh," JJ whispered, stroking his face. "It can't be helped."

Gurn turned to Paco, still keeping his voice low. "Going to need your help, my friend. He's got a bad ankle. We might have to carry him." Paco nodded while Gurn pointed to a nearby palm tree.

"It would be faster to drag him on a gurney. If we had some rope, we could use a palm frond. But whatever we do, we need to get going."

"JJ has some twine," I said, looking at the woman cradling the injured man. "JJ, give me your knapsack. Let's see if we can make it work."

Holding on to Martín with one arm, JJ ripped the knapsack off her back, and tossed it onto the mud-covered ground in front of me. Within seconds I found the ball of twine.

Gurn took it with a look of approval. "This will do if we double it," he said to no one in particular. He surveyed the surrounding trees, then stopped at one. He turned to Paco. "See that coconut tree? A tree of a thousand uses, that's the saying."

"Si," Paco acknowledged. "It is."

"We're going to add one more," Gurn said. "A makeshift gurney."

"Do you need any help from *us*?" Lila asked, anxious to help.

"Yes," I said. "Can we do anything?"

"Not yet, but stand by." Gurn went to the coconut tree and pointed to a particularly large palm frond, more than eight feet from the ground. "Paco, see if you can reach that frond up there."

104

Paco swung the monkey to the ground and crossed to the coconut tree. Afortunado trailed behind but at a safe distance.

The shorter man, barely five foot five, studied the frond for a moment. He extended the machete over his head, turned to Gurn, and shook his head. Gurn took the machete from Paco's hand and did the same. He, too, shook his head.

"Idea," Gurn said, without missing a beat. "Paco, you need to climb aboard my shoulders. Think you can do that?"

Paco broke out into a broad smile. "*Mis hermanos* and I were part of acrobatic team in Antiqua when we were jóvenes."

"Ah, youth." Gurn returned Paco's smile. "I knew you were a man of many talents. I didn't have any brothers, but it works pretty much the same way."

Crossing his hands at the wrist, Gurn reached out to Paco, then squatted down. Paco dropped the machete, then took both Gurn's hands in his. Springing up, the older man threw both legs around and over Gurn's shoulders in an almost balletic movement. When Paco was secure, Gurn rose to his feet and faced the coconut tree.

Not to be left out of things, I ran over, picked up the machete, wiped off as much mud as I could from the handle, and handed it to Paco.

"Gracias," he murmured.

"Hack it off close to the trunk," Gurn ordered. "I'll try to stand as still as possible."

After several well-aimed slashes, the palm frond fell to the ground, noisy and heavy, splattering muddy water everywhere. From one of the slender, elongated leaves, a small lizard made a break for it.

Gurn squatted down again, and Paco hopped off. He picked up the frond by its thick stem and looked to Gurn for further instructions.

"Drag it over to our patient, Paco," Gurn said, picking up the twine and unraveling it. "Okay, let's hoist him onto the gurney. Then we'll truss him to it."

JJ rose and got out of the way. Paco went to the other side of Martín. Following Gurn's example, he grabbed the moaning man under the arm.

"On the count of three, Paco. One, two, three, lift."

I looked up at the endless trees blotting out the sky. The rain still fell but lighter than before, and the wind had lessened. Maybe we were getting a break in the weather.

I turned my attention back to the two men as they lifted Martín onto the makeshift gurney. Martín tried to help, but it was a feeble attempt.

Gurn removed a shirt from his own knapsack and wrapped the garment around some of the twine. He then wrapped the cushioned twine around Martín's chest. I was to learn later this was not just for comfort but to prevent rope burns. Using the rest of the twine, he secured the injured man to the palm frond with fast, knowing movements. All of this was done in less than five minutes.

Coming to her husband's side, JJ grasped one of his hands. She looked at Gurn and said, "What now?"

"Now we go as fast as we can."

Giving a quick look to his pet standing by his side, Paco reached down and took the monkey's extended paw. In one deft movement he swung the wet, muddy monkey onto Lila's shoulder. Stunned, Lila turned and looked at the animal now sitting on her shoulder. Afortunado playfully nipped at her nose.

"Ow," she said in a surprised, yet ladylike manner.

"Afortunado," Paco said severely. "You behave."

"Yes," Lila hissed. "You *behave* or I shall have a new muff made of *monkey* fur."

106

As if understanding her words, the monkey settled down and, wrapping his long tail around her neck, snuggled into her like a good boy. What a suck-up.

Gurn turned to JJ. "Make sure Martín doesn't fall over. It's going to be rough in some spots, so keep one hand on his chest at all times. You're going to have to pay attention." She nodded.

"I will be the advance," Lila said, taking the machete from Paco. "I checked my compass as we went along, and we traveled in a north, northwest direction. I will reverse it. The revolver's in my jacket pocket, if I have to use it."

Having said that, she went to the front of our small but not-so-merry band. The monkey looked back at us and chattered.

"Shhhh," Lila commanded. Afortunado shushed.

Finally, Gurn turned to me. "Hon, you pull up the rear, and make sure nobody takes us from behind by surprise."

I dropped back. Led by Lila, Gurn and Paco began to drag the wounded man on his makeshift gurney, JJ by his side.

Unlike my mother, I withdrew my Glock 19 and released the safety. I may have aimed the gun to the canopied sky, but I was ready to shoot anything, man or beast, who tried to prevent us from getting back to camp.

Chapter Eighteen

Two hours later we neared the outskirts of El Cizin. The road became limestone again, widened, easier to navigate. Even though we were exhausted, we picked up speed and entered the clearing next to the temple within minutes. Naturally, just then the rain stopped, and the sun shone brightly.

Standing at a back corner of the temple, deep in conversation, were Carla Pérez and Professor Adler. The first to see us, the administrative assistant gave a cry of surprise. Both women hurried over, bombarding us with questions.

Their raised voices drew the attention of several nearby workers, who dropped their tools and came running. Dr. Lancaster showed up out of nowhere and began barking orders. We were now a full-blown parade complete with crowd control.

Exclamations and questions came at us in both Spanish and English. Everyone tried to help but only got in the way. We five had become a finely tuned machine and managed to push through them, heading for the first-aid tent. As we neared, Dr. Abeba emerged, drawn out by the ruckus.

"Martín, he is alive?" were the first words out of her mouth.

"Yes," JJ said, "but he has a wounded ankle and is dehydrated. There are moments of delirium."

"Bring him inside and we will see." She stepped back to let our small cavalcade enter. "Put him on the examination table," the doctor ordered.

Gurn pulled out his hunting knife and cut the twine binding Martín to the gurney. A young man, hardly more than a teenager, appeared out of nowhere. With his help, Paco and Gurn lifted Martín onto the table.

"Thank you, gentlemen," Dr. Abeba said. "I will take it from here." She turned to JJ and gave her a brief smile. "You may stay if you like, but I think you might want to get rid of some of that mud. I will clean up my patient as well. Come back in twenty minutes. I'll know more then."

"Of course, Doctor," she said, wiping her hand across her forehead, spreading even more mud. JJ turned to Gurn, Mom, Paco, and me. "Thank you for saving my husband's life."

It was a simple statement but filled with great emotion. Before waiting for an answer, JJ darted around Dr. Lancaster, who'd been standing in the doorway taking everything in. She wore a look of disapproval on her face. About what, I couldn't tell. Mud?

Dr. Abeba turned to us. "You should leave as well. I have to concentrate. That would include you, Dr. Lancaster. Thank you," the doctor added in clipped tones.

"I need to ask him some questions," Lancaster announced.

"Not now." Dr. Abeba turned away, her voice unyielding.

Monkey and all, we turned around and stared at Dr. Lancaster blocking the exit. By an unspoken but unanimous decision, none of us had any intention of going around her. She had no choice but to lead us out of the tent. Once outside, Paco took the monkey from Lila's shoulder and thanked her profusely for taking care of his pet.

I turned to Dr. Lancaster, hovering just outside the door. "Where are the police? Have they come and gone? Did they take away Alejandro's body?"

"They have yet to arrive," she answered. "They'd been called away to help put out a fire started by a group of illegal loggers twenty miles from here. As soon as they have the fire contained, they will come. Illegal logging is a big problem in Guatemala. Deforestation causes all sorts of difficulty with the environment. Meanwhile, Dr. Abeba has custody of Alejandro's body." She paused. "I am more interested in Martín. Did he tell you what happened?"

"No," Gurn said. "We were a little busy rescuing him, and frankly, he's not had many lucid moments."

"But," I said, "we'll find out what we need to know soon enough. I guess we should all get some of this mud off."

"Exactly," Lila said. "A hot shower would do us all a world of good."

"And some food," I added.

"Of course, of course," Lancaster said. "Lunch is long over, but there is always fruit and beverages in the cafeteria. That should hold you until dinner." She paused again. "Well, I see there won't be any answers now. I will have to speak with Dr. Abeba later. If you will excuse me, I have some files I need to review." With her head held high, she strode away.

"Dr. Lancaster's an odd bird," Gurn said as we headed for our tent. This comment was unlike him. He's from the school of thought that if you don't have anything good to say about someone, don't say anything at all. And believe me, here was a lady we were all keeping mum about.

"She seems oblivious to other's misfortunes," I said.

"Indeed," Lila said. "In passing, I've heard a few people say she can be a bit of a w-i-t-c-h."

"They just don't know how to spell," I said.

"Liana," she chastised, "watch your language."

"I didn't use any bad language. Yet. Give me a chance."

Taking all this in, Gurn burst out laughing. Lila and I stopped walking and stared after him.

"Sorry," he said after seeing the expressions on our faces.

We entered our tent, Lila being the first to reach for a change of clothes. It's amazing how fast she is when she wants to be.

"Don't forget to check yourselves over for leeches," she sang out and left for the showers.

"I'll check you over, and you can check me," Gurn said with a waggle of his eyebrow. It was a weary waggle, but I appreciated the effort.

Not sure how soundproof the canvas walls were, I looked around, then leaned into Gurn and whispered, "Want to tell me what happened?"

"You mean, details of how I found Martín? Why are we whispering?"

"I thought you had to be careful what you said in a tent. Something about a camel's nose."

Gurn looked at me in surprise, stopped rooting around in his shaving kit, and let out another laugh. "First of all, sweetheart, there are no camels in Guatemala. They're not indigenous to the country, my love."

"Someone might have a pet, dear heart," I contradicted. "Or it could come from a circus."

"Secondly," he said, overriding my glib comeback, "the term comes from an old Arab proverb meaning once you let a camel get his nose inside the tent, his body will soon follow. It doesn't have anything to do with conversations being overheard."

I mused. "The camel's nose being a metaphor for a situation where the permitting of a small, seemingly innocent act will open the door for larger, undesirable ones. Although a camel's nose sounds kinda cute."

"They spit. I can attest to this."

"You don't like camels? But you're such an animal lover."

He sat down on the bench with a groan and stared up at me. "Just how did we get into a thing about camels, beloved?"

"Not sure, darling," I said, sitting beside him. "Tell me how you found Martín."

"I followed the two kids to a spot past their village. The storm hadn't started yet, so it was easy to do. They led me to a cluster of rocks near a hill, shaped like a horseshoe. A perfect place to hide a small prison made of bamboo."

"That's where Martín was being held? Inside a bamboo prison?"

"Yes, right inside a cave and sheltered by an overhang. He was lying inside and moaning. They watched him for a moment, then one of them pulled out a sat phone, made a phone call, and had a conversation."

"Wait a minute. They have a sat phone? Those things cost over a thousand dollars. I should know, Richard hawks me every time I damage or lose one."

"Those are the good ones," Gurn said. "You can get cheaper versions for around three hundred, but the monthly rates are what kill you."

"Now, this is interesting," I interjected.

"Monthly rates?"

"Well, those, too. But two kids living in a jungle with designer sneakers and a sat phone. And in their village is a large, modern, and expensive satellite dish. I'll bet you the monthly rate on that is a killer, too. But go on."

"I couldn't catch every word they said because they were talking half in Spanish and half in Mayan, but they seemed pretty spooked about Alejandro being found on the temple steps."

"So, what happened next?"

"I waited until they finished their call and knocked them both out. I was in the middle of cutting the ties on the bamboo door to get to Martín when another fellow showed up."

"Probably whoever they called."

"He tried to do something to me with a blow dart, but I took his blowpipe away from him. I'm sure he had a pretty nasty headache when he came to. Same for the boys."

"Where's this blowpipe now?"

"I broke it in half. I have one of the darts wrapped in gauze in my knapsack. After I freed Martín, he told me they hadn't given him any food or water since he'd been imprisoned, two days ago."

"So that explains the dehydration even though it's raining every time you turn around. Why did they kill Alejandro and not him?"

"From what Martín said, Alejandro just keeled over when they were running away."

"Blow dart?"

"Could be. We might not have noticed the puncture mark when we found him on the steps. You have to know what to look for."

"Meaning we should show Dr. Abeba the blow dart after we take our showers. And what kind of poison it contains. You know, it's too bad you didn't take their sat phone. We could have traced the numbers. Might have led to something."

"Of course I took it," he said with a smile. "I didn't want them to make another call for reinforcements when they woke up. Always thinking," he said, tapping the side of his forehead. He reached inside one of the ubiquitous pockets of

113

his pants and pulled out a sat phone, smaller than the ones we had, with far less gewgaws.

"Well, this has been your day, mister," I said, reaching for the phone. "You found Martín, and you might have found out who and what killed his assistant."

He winked at me. "All in a day's work, miss."

"I told you I'd be worthless on this trip. Although..." I broke off.

"You're not worthless. It would have been tough to get him back here by myself if whoever captured him caught up with us," he said. "It was a big relief when you turned up. But what's the although for?"

"Something's going on around here. I can tell."

"You mean apart from people dying and being kidnapped?"

"Apart from that. Those things should make the others anxious or, at worst, scared. This is something different. I can't quite put my finger on it... yet..." My voice dropped off.

"But a thousand-and-one minute details are adding up to something sinister in your subconscious mind? Like what?"

"I know we've only been here less than twenty-four hours, but there doesn't seem to be any sense of joy or camaraderie. Something you find when like minds have this kind of work opportunity. And take last night, at dinner. Academics are known for being a curious group. We should have been bombarded by questions, showing the standard inquisitiveness of the academic mind. They didn't ask us one thing."

"Maybe they were tired after a long day."

"Academics never have days that long."

"You know this from personal experience?"

"I do."

114

Something jogged his memory. "Of course. Mira, your best friend from college."

"Right. Mira was a geology major. I dated a few of her classmates. Their idea of a hot date was sitting around asking questions about me being a criminology major."

"Okay, maybe their lack of enthusiasm is a result of their illustrious leader. Dr. Lancaster comes across to me as a pretty uptight person."

"No, that doesn't quite explain it. There are a lot of mega-egos sitting on themselves like they're just waiting for something to happen. Or that someone will find out what's happening. I can almost smell their angst. And speaking of smells, we should hit the showers."

Gurn stood. "Before we do, I want to add one more possibility for the feel of this place."

"What?"

"Everyone could be afraid of the El Cizin temple and the legend. This god seems to pack a powerful punch."

I shook my head. "That might explain the natives but not the professionals. They take gods, legends, and stuff like that in their stride. It's all part of the business. But thank you for playing the devil's advocate."

"Anytime."

"Having talked this out, I want to find out more about the thefts and vandalisms. I think that's the key."

"Well, we might not get a chance to do that, sweetheart, darling mine. We came down here to find Martín and we did. Now we've done that, I don't know if we can just hang out."

"That's true."

"Besides, I thought you were just dying to get out of the jungle—"

"And back to civilization?" I interrupted. "That was before. Now I want to know what's going on." I stood. "But

115

first things first. Time to hit the showers. And what's all this stuff about looking for leeches?"

"If I find one on you," Gurn said, also standing and stifling a yawn, "I'll show it to you."

"Please don't and say you did."

Chapter Nineteen

A half hour later found us hurrying to the first-aid tent for an update on Martín. We passed the cafeteria, where Consuela and her assistants were preparing dinner. Several delicious flavors wafted toward me, including fried pork. I felt weak at the knees, made a quick detour, and grabbed two bananas.

I discovered tramping through the jungle can bring on an appetite. Not that I need much help in that department.

Inhaling our bananas, Gurn and I entered the first-aid tent. A cleaned-up Martín was no longer on the examining table but lay on a cot, hooked up to an IV. At the foot of the cot, JJ stood in conference with the doctor. Lila waited at a discreet distance but watched the action.

The young man who'd appeared out of nowhere earlier stood in a corner of the tent, unobtrusive but standing almost at attention. He might have been Dr. Abeba's assistant. We hadn't been introduced, but I flashed him a smile of acknowledgment, anyway. He returned one of his own, then blushed and looked away. When things calmed down—if ever—I would learn his name.

Dr. Abeba turned to us. "I've alerted the hospital. JJ and Martín leave shortly, so his head and ankle can be X-rayed. I believe he has a mild concussion, but I want to make sure. As for his ankle, that is more serious. I think there are multiple fractures. He doesn't appear to have any internal injuries, but he should be looked at more closely than I can do here."

"A helicopter will meet us at the landing field. Where you flew into yesterday," JJ added.

"Why can't it land here?" Lila asked.

"There are too many fragile structures scattered about," JJ said. "We'll have to carry him out by mule."

"Meanwhile," the doctor added, "He is on a saline-based electrolyte solution to help replenish his fluids."

"Before you take Martín away," I said, moving toward the injured man, "we need to talk to him, if possible."

"Of course," Dr. Abeba said. "But you will have to hurry. I've also given him something for the pain. He might be a little woozy."

"We'll chance it," I said.

Gurn and Lila joined me on the other side of the cot facing JJ. Gurn's cousin looked at us with a tired smile. Joyful as she was that she hadn't lost Martín, the stress of the past few days played on her face.

Seeing the dark circles under her eyes and paleness of her skin, I said, "Hang on, JJ."

At the sound of my voice, Martín opened his eyes. While he no longer looked to be in severe pain, I could see he would be visiting la-la land soon enough from whatever drug the good doctor had given him.

"Martín, it's Lee Alvarez. You may not know me —"

"I know who you are," Martín interrupted drowsily. While his Spanish accent was almost nonexistent, his strained, soft voice was difficult to understand. I leaned in as he tried to speak.

"You are my wife's cousin. And one of my saviors." He looked past me with a faint smile for Gurn. "And there is my hero, the man who rescued me."

"That's us," I said, "but we need to ask you a few questions before they take you away."

He looked confused. "Away? Where do they take me?"

JJ spoke before anyone else could. "We're going to the hospital, Martín, so they can X-ray your head and ankle and take care of you. You're going to be fine," she said, her voice breaking at the end.

"Tell us what happened," Gurn said, leaning in. "I was so busy getting you out, I had no time to ask. But we need to know."

Martín licked dry lips before speaking. "We were coming back... I can't remember... yesterday? The day before? I can't remember," he repeated.

"It doesn't matter. Go on," I prompted.

"Alejandro and me. He wanted to show me something in the jungle. A surprise. We walked for a while. He said it was not too far. Men came out of nowhere. They chased us. We ran but Alejandro collapsed. Then I... I... my foot got caught in the root of a tree. I fell and hit my head on a rock... or something. I... woke up in the cage."

His face clouded over. He tried to look around but couldn't seem to move. Martín fought to keep on talking.

"The way Alejandro fell, I could not believe it. To drop to the ground like that. And yet, he did."

"Martín, what was it Alejandro wanted to show you?" I asked another question before waiting for an answer to the first. "Did you know where he was taking you?"

His brow furrowed. "Taking me? I... I can't remember. Why were we there... "

"You were coming back from the other site," I prompted. "The one with some god's name."

"Kinich Ahau," JJ put in.

"Yes," Martín said, rousing himself. "Just a short detour he said. Wanted to surprise me. He is a herpetologist, you know."

I looked questioningly at JJ. She said, "The study of amphibians and reptiles. In Alejandro's case, rare frogs. Guatemala is filled with many rare species of animals."

I could see Martín succumbing to the drug given him. He closed his eyes and in a sleepy voice said, "Yes, he was always on the search for a frog sometimes found in the jungle, the poison dart frog."

A sudden clatter of falling metal and breaking glass caused us to turn and look in Dr. Abeba's direction. She looked down at the dropped tray of slides and test tubes. But it was the doctor's coloring that drew my attention. It had become ashen.

"Sorry, sorry," she muttered when she noticed us staring. She bent down to pick up the debris. The young man rushed to her side. In hushed tones, she told him what to do.

I returned my attention to Martín, fast slipping into unconsciousness. I reached out and touched him on the arm, hoping to bring him around. It was useless.

Dr. Abeba joined us after a moment. "He is sleeping now. It was a strong sedative I gave him. I know we can't do anything for him for at least a couple of hours, maybe more. I wanted to give him something to relieve the pain," she added.

"I'm so sorry," JJ said to me. "I know how frustrating this must be for you."

"Don't be silly." Disappointed but resigned, I said, "We'll find out what we need to know another way. Let's go."

"May I speak with you before you leave?" Dr. Abeba looked at Gurn, Mom, and me questioningly. "In the other room."

"Of course." Lila was the first to reply. She turned to JJ. "My dear, we *leave* you for a moment but *shall* return."

With a gesture of her head, Dr. Abeba indicated we should follow her into what appeared to be the lab section of the tent.

Aside from medical paraphernalia, a body lay on a cot covered by a white sheet. Alejandro, of course.

Dr. Abeba, ignoring the corpse, crossed to a worktable laden with vials and bottles. Picking up a glass tube, she turned to us.

"I want to show you something."

Almost as one, we moved forward and studied the tube. Floating inside a clear liquid was a small, indiscernible yellow blob.

"What *is* it?" Lila was the first to ask.

Keeping her voice down and looking in the direction of JJ and Martín, just on the other side of the partition, she said. "This is a Phyllobates terribilis."

"A yellow dart frog," Gurn said. "Highly poisonous. Which reminds me..." He broke off speaking and opened a small compartment of his knapsack. With great care, he pulled out the gauze-wrapped dart by its feathered back end. "I wonder if that guy's poison, or one of his relatives, coats this dart?"

Dr. Abeba set down the vial. With the same care as Gurn, she took the dart by the feathers and undid the gauze at the tip. Staring at it, she said to Gurn, "Should I ask where you got this?"

"I took it off somebody. The first one got stuck in a tree."

"I see," the doctor said, looking at Gurn with something akin to suspicion. She rewrapped the dart in the gauze and set it aside. "If what you say is true, had you even touched the tip of this dart with your naked hand, you might be dead many times over."

"Yes, I know. A single frog can contain enough poison to kill at least ten people." Trying to allay her unease, he added, "I have spent time in the Amazon jungle, Doctor."

"That would explain it. I had forgotten you were an expert on the jungle."

"Knowledgeable," Gurn corrected, with a smile. "No expert."

"In that case I should tell you, death usually occurs in less than ten minutes. And there is no known cure."

Dr. Abeba picked up the vial again. This time the liquid inside began to swirl, revealing two legs, body, and the head of a frog whose name I couldn't pronounce but didn't want to think about, anyway. Then something occurred to me.

"Where did you find the frog, Doctor? Underneath the body? Otherwise, one of us would have noticed it."

"When I gave the body a closer examination, I discovered it in the dead man's mouth."

Chapter Twenty

"Are you telling us," Lila demanded, her face draining of color, "you found that *thing* in his mouth? How *despicable*."

I stared at the yellow blob. "Is that what killed him?"

"I can't be certain," the doctor said. "It could have been put there after death."

"Why would someone place a *poisonous* frog in the *mouth* of a *dead* man?" Lila asked. "For what *earthly* reason?"

"Symbolic maybe," Gurn said.

"One thing about the ancient Mayans," I said. "They had a keen sense of drama. They knew how to use the fear factor of superstitions, myths, and legends to their own advantage. I'm sure that trait's been passed on from generation to generation."

"So, you're saying," Lila said, getting on board, "the killer or killers wanted to *frighten* anyone who found the body with the *deadly* frog?"

"Possibly," Gurn said.

"An ulterior motive is not uncommon," I added.

"I see you three are used to puzzling things out together," Dr. Abeba said with a slight smile. Her smile vanished. Her entire demeanor became sadder. "However, we will know more after the autopsy. We know nothing right now. Only that a young man is dead."

"Doctor," I said, "I don't remember seeing any signs of poison the way you usually do on a body,"

"You wouldn't," the doctor replied. "The first thing this particular poison does is paralyze the victim into a seemingly relaxed state. Then the venom prevents nerves from transmitting impulses, which leads to instant heart failure. This pretty little frog is considered the most poisonous animal in the world." She looked again at the vial containing the deadly frog before setting it down on the counter again.

"What are you talking about?" JJ said, standing in the doorway.

"Oh, Jacqueline, my *dear*," Lila said, rushing to her side. "We *disturbed* you. I am *so* sorry." She took one of JJ's hands in both of hers.

JJ gave her a brief smile, then turned to us. "What is this about a poisonous frog? Is that how Alejandro died?"

"We will know more," Dr. Abeba repeated, "after the autopsy. I should check on my patient," she said, ending the discussion. She moved past JJ, and into the first-aid room.

I looked at JJ. "How's Martín doing, JJ? And how are you feeling?"

"He's resting. At least, I know he will survive, unlike Alejandro. Dr. Abeba assures me once he gets his ankle taken care of and his fluid levels stabilized, he will be fine."

"I take it you're flying to the hospital with him," Lila said.

"Yes. He still doesn't know about the baby. I'd wanted to be sure before I told him." Her face broke out into a smile which left as soon as it came.

"Is the hospital *in* Flores?" Lila asked.

"No," JJ said. "We're flying to the regional hospital in San Benito, maybe a mile farther. It's larger, and they have facilities to do the" — here she paused — "the autopsy."

"*Don't* think about that," Lila said, continuing in her motherly vein. "*Liana* will resolve all of this, *probably* before

124

you return." She pushed back an errant hair from JJ's forehead.

"Pay no attention to that man behind the curtain," I said.

"That's a line from the *Wizard of Oz*. I love that movie," JJ said, again smiling.

"You just keep impressing me more and more. I'm so glad I married into your family." I chuckled for a moment, then sobered. "Anyway, pay no attention to Mom's latest press release on me. Truth be told, we're going to solve this together. And that includes you, JJ."

"And *together* we will do it," Lila said, not missing a beat. She went on, "Martín will be *fine* and soon; you both will have a *beautiful* baby. Try to *concentrate* on that."

"Let me interrupt this ode to motherhood with a thought," I said. "JJ, last night you mentioned destruction and vandalism done in the past few months. Did you document any of it?"

"Oh, yes," she said. "I took pictures and videos on my phone after each attack. I compiled them into a folder for further study."

"Could you send a copy of that folder to my phone? I'd like to see it," I said. "Do we need internet connection to do that?"

"I shouldn't think so. I think you and I have duplicate phones. All I have to do is tap a few buttons, lay your phone on top of mine, and transfer the files. It's one of the newer features."

"Ah! The wonders of modern technology," I said, handing her my phone.

Taking it, she removed hers from her pocket. "See? They're identical." After a couple of taps on both phones, she handed mine back to me. "There you go. Done."

"Thank you," I said.

She didn't reply but seemed lost in thought. After a nanosecond, JJ made a decision. Her voice became secretive.

"I want to tell you something I should have mentioned before. Let's take a walk."

Whispering something briefly to Dr. Abeba, JJ turned and left the first-aid tent. We followed. Dr. Lancaster appeared out of nowhere. Either this was something she excelled at, or maybe she'd been waiting for us to exit.

"JJ," Dr. Lancaster said, "how is your husband doing?" Her eyes searched JJ's. "Has he said anything? I can't get anything out of Dr. Abeba."

"No, he hasn't," JJ said. "But I hold myself responsible for how this turned out, Dr. Lancaster. I should have never put off bringing in the police. Maybe if we had sent for them right away, Alejandro wouldn't be dead, and Martín wouldn't be in the condition he is in now."

"You're not thinking rationally," Dr. Lancaster replied. Her patronizing tone reverberated in the air. Lovely way to talk to a near-widow.

"Excuse me?" JJ took the remark the same way I did. Her response was confrontational if not downright combative. "Exactly what do you mean by that?"

Unruffled, JJ's superior went on, her tone still filled with condescension. "My dear young woman, as you know, we did call the police several hours ago. They have yet to appear. In situations such as these," she went on in her clipped British accent, "it is best to try to handle things internally. I made the right choice, even with this unhappy outcome. There was no other way. You'll see, once you calm down, it was better to keep their disappearance unofficial."

"Was it?" JJ stood with her hands on her hips. "I don't think so, Dr. Lancaster. You and I will continue this discussion when I return from the hospital. Make no mistake,

126

it will not be a two-minute conversation standing outside the first-aid tent. I have a lot to say about what's been going on for the past six months. And it will be official."

The angrier JJ became, the more her Southern accent surfaced. If she'd added a "y'all" to her speech I, personally, would have headed for the hills.

Chapter Twenty-One

Five minutes later, JJ, Mom, Gurn, and I sat on the remains of a four-thousand-year-old eatery. Worn-down and broken stones, plus a faded fresco with paintings of a sheep, chicken, and goat were all that were left of this fast-food takeout stand. I couldn't help but wonder if they, too, served fries with your burger.

"I don't have much time," JJ said, looking at her watch and bringing me back to the present. "I have to see that Martín's ready when the mule arrives."

"Can we help?" Gurn asked.

"Thank you, no. You've already done more than I dared hope. You found my husband," JJ said with a tremor in her voice. She cleared her throat. "Dr. Abeba, Alfredo, Paco, and I can handle it."

"Is Alfredo the young man who was helping in the first-aid tent?"

"Yes, he's Paco's son." She saw the expression of surprise on our faces. "Oh no! Didn't I mention that? Oh, I'm so sorry. With everything going on, I guess it slipped my mind."

"That's *quite* all right, Jacqueline," Lila said, reaching out and patting her on the hand.

"Exactly," I said. "No harm, no foul."

"Still, I am sorry," she said. "Paco has been with the organization for several years. He's originally from El Mirador, and he's really happy to be back on his home turf. His wife passed away recently, and his son came to live with him. Alfredo wants to be a doctor. He graduates from our school this year, and we're all hoping he will get a scholarship to Universidad de San Carlos de Guatemala."

"I read it's the number *one* university in Guatemala," Lila said.

"Yes, and tough to get into. But Alfredo has the grades and he's brilliant. Martín saw his talent right away. He's the one who's been really pushing for the scholarship, trying to make it happen." She smiled at the thought, then looked up at me. "Look at me. I'm bragging on my husband."

I smiled back. "Speaking of Martín, how will you get him to the helicopter on horseback? Or should I say, mule back? He's out like a light."

"We have a type of a howdah. We put it on the mule's back for people who are injured and can't sit up. We're leaving for the chopper as soon as the mule is brought in from the village where they're kept. They should be here with it any minute." She turned to me. "But here's what I wanted to talk to you about. Lee, open up the folder I loaded on to your phone."

I obeyed. "Okay, got it."

"Look at the images of a room down in the bowels of the El Cizin temple. Newly discovered. Secret," she added. Her voice had taken a decided provocative turn.

"Well, I hope you meant that to be intriguing," I said. "Because it sure came off that way."

"I do. The specific image I want to talk about is one of the walls in the burial chamber of a king. We only discovered the chamber by accident a couple of weeks ago. Actually, Bennie Storrs is the one who made the find and brought the other three of us to see it."

"Who were the others?"

"Dr. Lancaster, Professor Adler, and me. The rest were out on an expedition to the Kinich Ahau site."

129

"Where they had the cave-in," Gurn said, once again, clarifying things. "And where Martín went the day he disappeared."

"Yes," JJ said. "The discovery came late in the day, and we were tired. We were checking out hallways, when out of nowhere, Bennie stumbled across a hidden staircase that led down to an untouched funeral chamber belonging to a king. He came back up and got us."

"That must have been *quite* exciting," Lila commented.

"It should have been," JJ said. "No one had any idea it was there, but we're still exploring this temple. We also suspect there's a tunnel somewhere leading to who knows where. There are mentions of one in a glyph, but we have yet to find it."

"A glyph," I said. "That's a symbolic figure or a character used by the Mayans to represent words. Mom mentioned those earlier."

"Yes," JJ said. "Professor Adler did a quick read of the glyph over the chamber entrance. She said it was the tomb of a seldom-mentioned king, B'alaj Chan K'inich. Early preclassic Maya, 1800-900 BC.

"That's pretty old," I remarked.

JJ went on. "Judging by the jade, gold, and silver included in his sarcophagus, he may have been more important than we previously thought."

Gurn asked, "Isn't it a big find?"

"Yes, it is," JJ said. "And Dr. Lancaster is sitting on it. Bennie is furious. So am I."

I was surprised at the vitriol in her statement but didn't say anything. JJ went on. "When we first found this unopened tomb, we couldn't believe our good fortune. Finding a tomb with all its preclassic funerary antiquities still intact is rare. None of us paid much attention to the murals on the walls even though they were beautifully preserved. As I said, we'd had a long day; it was late; the others weren't with us, so we tabled it, thinking we could come back the next day and do a proper job. That's what we thought."

"What happened?" Lila entered the conversation again.

"Something unexpected and… horrible," JJ said with an edge to her voice. "But I want you to see it rather than have me tell you. I managed to take several quick pictures of the walls of the tomb the evening we discovered it. One in particular was a little different than your ordinary fresco."

I was intrigued. What a world I'd been dragged into. "How so?"

"It's a mosaic rather than a painting. Not unknown for the Mayans but unusual in this area. Anyway, there are two specific images, numbers three-two-four-six and three-two-five-three. They'll be near the end. Can you find them?"

I scrolled through the folder, paying attention to the sequence of numbers. "Yes."

"Look at image number three-two-four-six."

There was total silence as I studied the number in question. Even in the small picture on my phone, the image was spectacular, colors still as vibrant today as they must have been centuries ago.

The background consisted of what looked like a cultivated part of the jungle. Sun-dappled trees were spaced evenly apart and devoid of undergrowth. Off to the left, a mountain with two peaks rose. On the right, a river snaked into oblivion.

Front and center was a large figure. The king. The highest member of royalty in all his magnificence. Dressed in a tunic of orange, yellow, and green, jade jewelry adorned his hands, neck, and ears. His headdress was a yellow peacock with green feathers fanning out and cascading down the upper portion of his body.

On either side, a half-dozen kneeling priests and warriors worshiped at the king's feet. Captives and slaves lay prostrate on the ground facedown in the dirt, not even daring to look up at this earthly deity. Impressive, to say the least, but standard fare for representing Mayan kings of the day.

As I looked closer, however, splattered throughout the trees in the background were small shapes in unlikely shades of pink, lavender, white, and the occasional maroon color. The fact this was done in mosaic tiles, no matter how small they were, made it a little harder to distinguish details, especially with the bad lighting.

I don't know much about Mayan artists other than they used specific colors to represent different people in their culture, mainly name, rank, and serial number. Slaves and nonentities were clothed in muddy browns. Black and red were worn by warriors. Blue-green was used for priests and sometimes as a symbol for death. Only royalty could be painted in pure green.

So where did these other colors, especially the pastels, come from? No matter how much I enlarged the image, I still couldn't make out what these odd little shapes were.

"How big is this mosaic, JJ?"

"Maybe twenty by thirty feet," she said, watching me. "Lee, now look at another image, three-two-five-three, taken the following morning."

I moved to the second image. "What is this? It looks like a black blob."

"That was image three-two-four-six after the destruction. It's been covered over completely with black paint."

"Holy chamole!"

My shock at the defacing of the centuries-old work of art caused Gurn and Lila to lean even more over my shoulder. I held my phone up for them to see. Gurn took it from my hand and shared it with my mother. JJ never took her eyes off me.

"The vandalism had to have happened," JJ said, "between the time we left that night and returned the next morning with the others. After the vandalism, Dr. Lancaster sealed the room off, claiming the walls were too unstable for the tomb to be gone into again until we brought in a team of experts to build supports. Meanwhile, she won't allow any of us access."

"But *shouldn't* someone remove the black paint as soon as *possible*?" Lila asked a reasonable question as far as I was concerned.

"Exactly. Much of the staff, including me, were willing to take the chance," JJ said. "The longer the paint sits, the more damage it does."

I asked, "When are these experts due?"

"Unclear," was JJ's reply. "It's already been two weeks."

"This doesn't make any sense," Gurn said.

"The work may be unsavable already," JJ replied. "Maybe all we have left of the mural is this image on our phones. It was after this incident two weeks ago the vandalisms and thefts increased. Something seems to happen almost every day."

"Hmmm," I said. "Does Dr. Lancaster know you took these pictures?"

"No, I took them when she wasn't looking. I'm not sure why I did that, but she's been behaving strangely for a while now. She's more uptight than usual and... I don't know... secretive. I didn't want to deal with confrontation at the time. Now I don't care."

"Where is this hidden tomb? Can you locate it again?"

"Of course."

"Is it on the map you made of the temple's interior?"

"Dr. Lancaster wouldn't allow me to include it in the mapping of the building yet."

"Why is that?" Gurn asked.

"I'd have needed the actual specifications of the tomb, before it could be included in any official mapping."

"That's how it's normally done?" I asked.

"Yes, you don't want anything that's inaccurate, Lee," JJ said. "It messes with the data. However, I made my own map of where it is within the temple. I included it in the folder."

"Where?" I scrolled through the folder.

"Look under a subfile named 'King's Tomb.' It's the very last entry."

"Got it. I'll look at it later. On to the missing relics. You don't happen to have images of them somewhere, do you? I'd like to see just what's been taken."

"Yes, I do. I pulled the catalogued pictures of the stolen finds and included them in another subfolder called 'Relics,' just in case."

"You've got all the makings of a first-rate detective, JJ."

"Thanks, but I'll stick to city planning. It's dangerous enough."

Despite the situation, the four of us laughed. Never did I appreciate my new cousin more.

"Let's get back to the mural before it was damaged," I said. "In the background, there are different colored splotches in the trees. What are they?"

She looked at her screen, even enlarged the photo. "I have no idea, Lee. The lighting wasn't so good, and as I said before, I wasn't paying that much attention to the murals. I was more focused on the sarcophagus." She thought for a moment, then shook her head. "Maybe birds or butterflies? But why a warrior king would have a mural done of himself with either one of those is beyond me. They were usually way too macho for that. It doesn't make any sense."

"You know," I said, "here's another thing that just occurred to me and doesn't make sense. Not to be too graphic, but a two-day-old dead body in this heat should have been more decomposed than Alejandro's was."

Everyone was silent for a minute or two, letting what I said sink in.

Gurn was the first to speak. "You know, you're right. The body looked pretty fresh."

I continued on in this vein. "We didn't know the probable time of death this morning, but if we go with the premise Alejandro collapsed and died the same day Martín was captured, that would make it two days ago."

"Then to *look* like it did this morning, his body *must* have been *kept* under some type of *refrigeration*," Lila finished for me.

JJ's stunned but comprehending look matched the rest of ours. "But there's nothing like that anywhere at camp. Dr. Abeba certainly doesn't have the facilities to have a morgue-like setting. Consuela is always complaining she doesn't have a refrigerator big enough to keep her meats and produce cold. In fact, I cannot imagine any type of refrigeration large enough to hold a human body in all of El Mirador. It would be extremely costly."

"That's what I thought," I said. "So, either he didn't die right away as Martín supposed, or somewhere out there exists a very cool place. Let's just add this to the ever-lengthening list of what doesn't make sense at El Cizin."

135

Chapter Twenty-Two

Right after we left JJ to deal with the trip to the hospital, I spied Dr. Storrs watching us from behind one of the larger statues in the park.

I turned to Gurn and Lila. "You know, Dr. Benjamin Storrs fascinates me. Putting aside I have no idea what a project administrator does, this is the second time I've caught him watching us since we've been here. He's also making copious notes in a little notebook."

As if hearing me, Storrs turned and dashed away, notebook in hand, in an almost furtive manner.

"You know," I said, "I'm going to do a little watching of my own and follow this guy. Gurn, Mom, care to join me?"

"Lead on," Gurn said.

"I think I'll see if I can be of some use to Jacqueline *rather* than go with *you*."

"Then let's meet at the conference tent. I've heard we're all being interviewed by the police this afternoon about Alejandro's death, now that they've arrived."

Gurn and I followed Storrs directly to his lodgings. Again, with a furtive glance in every direction, he entered his bungalow. I did some furtive glancing of my own, and seeing no one else around, I crept up on his narrow porch. Gurn waited behind a nearby bungalow, no doubt being the lookout.

I glimpsed in the window as he was just sitting down at a desk and opening his laptop. Becoming more brazen, I watched as he read from his notebook and input whatever was there into the computer. Then he started typing faster than even Stanley, D. I.'s general manager.

Thinking about Discretionary Inquiries gave me a pang of homesickness. I missed work. I missed Stanley. I missed Tío. I missed my life. But mostly, I missed the cats. *I wanna go home,* I wailed internally.

Pulling myself together, I was determined to find out what was going on. I stealthed off the porch and had a fast rendezvous with Gurn.

Plan in place, not two minutes later, I ran around to the back of Storrs' bungalow. Gurn knocked on his front door. I hoisted myself on top of a nearby log and listened right outside one of the open windows. I heard Storrs go to the door.

"Why, good afternoon, Mr. Hanson. What can I do for you?"

"I hate to bother you, Dr. Storrs."

"Not at all. You and your family are heroes, rescuing Martín the way you did."

"Thank you. We did our best."

"And isn't it a shame about Alejandro. I didn't know him well, but he seemed like a good kid."

"I'm sure he was, Professor Storrs."

"Please, call me Bennie. Everyone does."

"Bennie. And you can call me Gurn. Everyone does." He laughed. Bennie laughed. I fought back annoyance because they were standing in the doorway laughing while I was perched on a shaky log trying to keep my balance.

Do something, darling. I need to get into the bungalow before we have to report to the police to be interviewed.

"So, what can I do for you, Gurn?"

"I just need to know exactly what a project administrator does. For our files. It's crucial."

137

"It is?"

"Yes," Gurn said, then repeated, "Crucial. But it should only take five minutes. Maybe we could take a little walk. Unless you wanted to invite me in?"

That's chancy, darling. Well, maybe not. Whatever he's doing on his laptop, I don't think he wants anyone else to see.

"A walk, a short walk," Bennie fairly yelped. I heard the door close. Their voices grew fainter with each passing word, but I could still make things out. "Sorry, I only have a few minutes. For the record, I should be the project director not the project administrator."

"Oh? Tell me about it."

"I have the experience and credentials. But Dr. Lancaster likes to keep a certain amount of power to herself, and I agreed to do the dig because I've been into the legends of El Cizin for decades. This is a chance for me..." And then his voice faded away.

Knowing I only had a few minutes at best, I pushed the window wide open and hauled myself up. I was inside one-two-three. His was a messy place and had an overall smell of dirty clothes and unwashed dishes. Several flies buzzed over the sink. Lovely.

I hastened to the laptop, hoping he hadn't turned it off. This password stuff to get in and out of someone else's computer really hinders a PI, especially when they're in a hurry. But I was in luck. He'd left it on, and the document he'd been writing was on the screen.

Bennie was on page 115. A lengthy piece. I read the title in the header: *Extermination by Excavation.*

What the – ?

I sat down, more than curious, and began to read.

Chapter Seven

She never had a chance. He came at her with the hatchet and swung fast and hard. Blood spattered over the Mayan jade mask, blotting out the symbol of eternity.

"Aha," he said. "That does it for you, Dr. Jane Lundcaster. You are dead meat. Now I will take over the dig."

And so on and so forth. I only read about a page and a half when I heard footsteps again on the porch. But I'd read enough.

I leapt up and threw myself out the window, just as the door opened. I landed on something thorny but a small price to pay for knowing the reason for Dr. Benjamin Storrs' odd behavior. He was writing a novel. And from what little I read, not such a good one. No wonder he was skulking around.

I got up and went back to the window, daring to look in once more. They were in the same positions as before. Storrs was facing Gurn with his back to me. The top of his pale-blond hair glistened as the afternoon sun struck it.

"So that's it in a nutshell, Gurn. That's what I do on this dig. Now, if you will excuse me, I gotta get back to work."

"Of course, of course, Bennie. And thanks so much for clearing up your job description. Which sounds impressive, I must say."

Boy, Gurn was sure laying it on.

"If I ran this dig, you would see something really impressive," Storrs bragged. "I'm afraid Dr. Lancaster is too full of herself to do justice to this site. But forget about it." He pronounced the phrase as if it was one word: fuhgeddaboutit, then went on. "She's the boss. Unfortunately."

And that must be why, I thought, *you are killing her off in your novel.*

"Yes," Storrs continued self-importantly, "in this business it's all about making a name for yourself. One way or another. And in one field or another. Now I gotta get back to work."

The door closed, and Gurn's footsteps left the porch and crunched on the gravel heading away from the bungalow. I caught up with him while he waited on the other side of one of the tents.

"Psssst! Here, sweetheart."

I ran to him, giving him a quick hug. "Thank you, darling."

"Did you find out anything?"

"I did. Good old Bennie is a budding author. He's writing a mystery or suspense novel called *Extermination by Excavation*. I'm hoping it's a working title because it's not so good. But I read the last page he'd written, where he kills off the project manager, one Dr. Jane Lundcaster. That's not very good, either."

"So that's why he's always watching people and making notes about them. I suspect you're in it, too, being a live private dick."

"My claim to immortality."

"Seriously, though, I did learn he thinks he's the one who should be in charge of this dig. Or, at least, the project director. Apparently, the title of 'director' gives the person more latitude and decision-making rights. As merely the administrator, he has to run everything by Dr. Lancaster. Who, he says, cuts him down at every opportunity."

"She doesn't sound like a much-loved head honcho. Which could be dangerous. On the face of it, some of these people seem pretty competitive, if not downright cutthroat."

"Don't go by the fact Bennie kills her off in a book, sweetheart. There's a big difference between fiction and real life."

"But this archaeological dig is a very intense, insular world. Rational thinking seems to be at a premium, if not missing altogether. What they feel or think, they just might do."

"Your observation surprises me, sweetheart. But now that I think about it, your insight just might be spot-on."

I glanced at my watch. "Whoops, we should get over to the conference tent. It's time for our interview with the local police."

But Gurn didn't budge. He took one of my hands. "If you think something's up around here, then there is. Which means we should stick pretty close together from now on. We need to be careful." He paused. "Especially you, sweetheart."

Chapter Twenty-Three

"Señora Alvarez," Sergeant Juárez said. "You are telling me you did not know..."

The young, almost adolescent police officer stopped speaking. Glancing down, he read through his scant notes, shorter than most of my grocery lists. He looked up at me again, having found the name he wanted.

"Ah... yes! You are telling me you did not know the deceased, Alejandro Rios."

"No," I said, "I didn't."

Two hours had passed since JJ and party had left for the hospital. On the way to the helicopter, they'd crossed paths with the Policia Nacional Civil, whose stated mission was to "protect people and property and contribute toward public and national security."

But maybe not today, I thought. From the look of Sergeant Juárez, he was done in. Eyes red and irritated from smoke and fatigue, his khaki uniform was covered with soot, dirt, and smelled like an autumn bonfire. His shirt was ripped near the collar and a button was missing. A five-o'clock shadow did nothing to improve his appearance.

After apologizing profusely for the exhaustive state in which he and his fellow officers finally arrived, he then tried to make light of it. But they'd come directly from the massive fire, been up for over twenty-four hours, and had nothing to eat for twelve. They were a spent force, no pun intended.

An empty tray filled with food and coffee had been brought in by good-hearted Consuela once she'd learned the men hadn't eaten. A half-consumed tortilla sat on a small plate within the sergeant's reach.

Slurping on a cup of coffee, he and I sat at a long table in the conference tent normally used to discuss the coming day's work, projects, findings, or anything else they needed to confer about. Upon arrival, the police commandeered it for interrogation purposes.

Sergeant Juárez's underlings were checking out Alejandro's sleeping quarters and the temple steps. The sergeant was interviewing witnesses and suspects. I'd stood for nearly an hour in a long line that snaked past the cafeteria, waiting my turn. But lucky me, here I was.

"You did not know this Alejandro Rios before, either?"

"No, I never met him," I said. "The first time I saw him was when my husband and I found him dead on the temple steps this morning. We only arrived in Guatemala yesterday evening."

"*Bueno.* Very Good. You do not know any reason why anyone would want to see him dead?"

"I can't say that I do. I don't know anyone here, and as I say, my husband, mother, and I only arrived last night."

"That is too bad," he said with a keen sense of regret. "It is too bad you know nothing more. Because the doctor who examined him—" He broke off again and looked at his notes for a name.

"Dr. Abeba," I volunteered.

"Yes, Dr. Abeba. She believes you think Alejandro... ahhh..." He drew the word out, looking down again at the paper.

"Rios," I said sharply. "Alejandro Rios."

"Gracias. You think he may have been murdered?"

"It certainly looks suspicious."

143

"Possibly, it does. To you." He smiled, looking at me once more. "That is because you are professional investigators: you, your husband, and your mother."

Despite what Sergeant Juárez had been through for the past twenty-four hours — or maybe because of it — it was hard to believe he would be put in charge of anything more than a missing Tootsie Roll. He looked to me more like a college kid hung over from his older brother's frat party. He blinked, seemingly at a loss for anything to say or ask. I decided to rescue him.

"My husband is not a professional investigator, although he is a retired Navy SEAL. My mother, brother, and I do run a detective agency back home. But I have to say, a victim dressed up as a fourteenth-century Mayan warrior with a poisonous frog in his mouth was a big clue that it may not have been a natural death."

My sense of irony seemed to be lost on him. He merely nodded, his eyebrows knitted together in thought. "The three of you found the other missing man?"

"Martín Rodriguez. Yes, we did," I said with a smile I did not mean.

Silence loomed. I could see him thinking.

"That is what you do in the States? You find people? Your detective agency?"

"Well, not as a rule. But occasionally, it does happen. Discretionary Inquiries deals more with software, hardware, and intellectual property thefts."

"I took a class in intellectual property when I attended Columbia University. I obtained a Bachelor of Arts degree."

Although this remark came out of nowhere, he said it with a certain amount of pride. I looked at my watch while he took more time to think. Just when I thought I would start screaming, Juárez went on.

144

"Discretionary Inquiries? That name is familiar to me. But you do not do homicide investigations, you and your family?"

"As I said, not as a rule, no. But we have done a few."

"My mother was from Arizona. You went to college, señora?"

"Yes, Stanford."

"Ahhh," he drawled again.

Apparently, that meant something to him. Then he stared at me as if he'd run out of questions. I stared back at him having run out of answers.

Without looking down, he set his coffee cup half-on, half-off the saucer. Toppling over, the contents of the cup spilled out onto the table.

He swore under his breath in Spanish. While he looked around trying to figure out what to do, I grabbed some paper napkins from the tray and mopped up the liquid. I felt this scenario could be symbolic of our relationship.

"Gracias, señora," he said with a smile. "You are like my mother. But not so old," he added hastily.

"Thank you, but I'm feeling older by the minute. However, if we are through here—" I broke off and stood.

"Yes, yes, we are through," he said, rising courteously. If nothing else, he was well-mannered. "You and your family arrived after the man disappeared. There is no way you could have had anything to do with his disappearance or death. No way," he added in a reassuring manner. "The native superstitions took over. It has happened before. However, I must ask that you do not leave El Mirador yet. I must keep your passports until this death is more... what is it?" He seemed at a loss for the phrase.

"Sorted out?"

"Excellent. Si. Sorted out. It should only take a day or two. You understand. But I apologize for any inconvenience to you and your family. And, Señora Alvarez, you have a business card?"

"A business card? Uh… maybe. Let me look."

I rummaged through the pockets of my cargo pants and came up with a bent card, melted chocolate and lint adhering to the edges. I brushed off as much lint as I could. I would have licked off some of the chocolate, but I didn't know Sergeant Juárez that well.

"I'm afraid it's not a good one. I can get a better one from my knapsack in our tent, if you want."

"That will not be necessary. This is sufficient," he said, palming the card. "And you will take my card?" He removed a card case from the breast pocket of his shirt, took out a business card, minus the chocolate and lint, and handed it to me. "If you should have any thoughts. Muchas gracias."

He bowed and scraped a little bit more, all the while smiling graciously. Okay, I saw a future for this kid in the world of diplomacy. Maybe not in police work, but certainly diplomacy.

Chapter Twenty-Four

Gurn and Lila were standing outside the tent, obviously waiting for me to exit. Lila was texting on her sat phone, but Gurn opened his arms wide and I walked right in.

He whispered, "How did it go?" I leaned my head into the crook of his neck.

"I think Sergeant Juárez is at best inept, at worst an idiot," I whispered back. "And then he asked for D.I.'s business card. I wonder if he suspects us, despite what he says? It was a bit unsettling."

"He told me his father is the capitán of the Flores division."

"Oh, great." I let out a long and deep sigh.

"You must be tired, sweetheart," he whispered back.

"I am," I murmured. "How do you feel?"

"Like somebody beat me up." We broke free and he looked into my face. "I can't take three men down and drag gurneys through the mud the way I used to." He let out a laugh. I joined him. "I'll sleep tonight."

"Me, too."

We kissed lightly, then turned to look at my mother as she came to our side.

"Mom, who were you texting? Richard?"

"Peter. As *acting* CEO, I wanted to make *sure* he was *aware* of the situation that arose with Baltic Mergers right before we left. Now that I know we can't return for *a while*—" She stopped speaking.

Reverting once again to work mode, I said, "I think Pete's on top of it, Lila."

"I needed to *assure* myself that all will be taken *care* of."

I fought the urge to say something about ending a sentence with a preposition, but had no idea what the sentence should end in. Whoops. I mean, in what the sentence should end? Good golly, Miss Molly, sometimes English sucks.

Lila, not having a clue as to the spin my brain was taking, went on. "Liana, Gurn, it is *nearly* five thirty. It is *time* to dine."

Only my mother would use the word "dine" in the middle of a jungle. She went on.

"It is only good *manners* to arrive on time. Consuela informed me she was making a foie gras appetizer in *my* honor, as she knows I enjoy French food. But instead of using goose liver, she used duck. I felt it was *not* incumbent upon me to inform her that in that *particular* situation, it would make the dish a pâté *rather* than a foie gras. Also, I do *not* eat foie gras, as I consider the *process* to be cruelty to animals. But I did not say so, as she is so *very* sweet."

"So, you are friends with the cook, huh, Mom?"

"*Always* know those who *support* the industry, Liana. That's where the *true* power lies."

I stopped walking, frozen to the spot. "Holy chamole." I looked at my mother. "Mom, truer words were never spoke."

"Spoken, Liana. *Spoken*," she corrected.

"Whatever," I said, brushing it off. "Mom, why don't you and Gurn go to the cafeteria and save me a place? I'll be right there. I want to check something out first."

"I know that look in your eye," Gurn said. "You're going sleuthing. I can tell. I'm coming with you."

Lila bristled. That's the only word for it. "Gurn, dear boy, I had *hoped* when you two married, you would help *curb* this urge of Liana's to *rush* in where wise men fear to *tread*."

"But where's the fun in that, Mom? Besides," I said, "this might involve JJ and family."

"You can't fight that logic, Lila," Gurn said, grinning at his mother-in-law.

Before she could say anything more, I added, "Ten minutes, Mom. Then we'll be right there."

I strode away at a clipped pace. Gurn caught up and said, "What exactly are we doing, dear heart?"

"Remember JJ telling us none of the doors are locked except for the Antiquities Room? Well, there are a few people around here that can go anywhere they want without a backward glance. And I want to know more about them. You can be my lookout, darling."

"We will negotiate that as we go along, precious."

We walked away from the public tents, which included our guest tent, heading toward the housing for permanent and on-site personnel. Less than two minutes later, we arrived at where the archaeologists stayed.

Facing the temple and open courtyard were wood bungalows occupied by Dr. Lancaster and other department heads, including JJ and Martín. These dwellings would eventually be used for tourist functions when the restoration was complete.

Besides the bungalows, there were tents which housed assistants and volunteers. The tents could sleep from one to four, depending on their status. The lower in the pecking order you were, the more people shared the tent.

The tents sat in two rows. The front row faced the courtyard, the ones behind faced the jungle. Running in between them was a wide, graveled path.

149

"Well, lookee here," I said, coming into the tent area. "The map says there are nameplates for each person or persons occupying the tent. And there they are. How helpful is that?" Then I pointed a finger at one well-lit tent. "And equally helpful is any light on inside shows through the canvas. With the jungle's evening gloom descending, if a tent is lit up, it's probably occupied."

"Not necessarily," Gurn said. "People have been known to go away and leave the lights on. And people have also been known to take a nap with the lights off."

"Okay, Mr. Spock, stop being so logical. Even though I am guilty of doing both those things myself," I muttered as an aside.

Gurn laughed and asked, "Whose tent are we invading?"

"I don't like to think of it as invading, *mi cielo*. More along the lines of exploring."

"I love it when you call me your heaven. Whose tent are we exploring?"

"The administrative assistant, Carla Pérez. I understand she has one to herself. I think hers is in the back row. Come on."

Tiptoeing in between tents, we were rounding a corner when I stopped short. Gurn did, too. Coming toward us on the graveled path were the crunching sounds of feet.

Instinctively, Gurn and I backed up, hugging the canvas tent, trying to look as small as possible. We needn't have bothered.

Mr. Machete, aka Dr. Bjørn Pedersen, came into view. Puffing wildly on a cigar, he moved as if he had some place to be, and where we were wasn't it.

I reached inside my pocket and pulled out my phone to take a quick pic of him. Then I took another. He was completely oblivious.

Deep in thought, he whipped out his sat phone and dialed a number. Speaking Norwegian in hushed tones, he walked past the tents and entered the jungle.

"Now there's a man just begging to be followed," Gurn said, keeping his eye on the prize.

"You do that," I said, "and I'll find Carla's tent. Meet you at dinner in, say, twenty minutes? If either of us is going to be later, let's text."

"That should work. It will be dark in another fifteen or twenty, anyway." He blew me a kiss and hurried after his prey.

About to seek out the admin's tent, I heard yet another oncoming crunch of feet. I whipped out my sat phone, slapped it to my ear, and pretended to be ending a conversation. I heard the person coming up behind me but pretended I didn't. There was a lot of pretending going on.

"All righty, Fred," I said to nobody. "Thanks for bringing me up to date. Bye now."

I turned around to come nose to nose with a grinning Dr. Whitewater. He had absolutely no problem invading my personal space. I stepped back.

"Good evening, Dr. Whitewater." My tone was formal. I have a lot more of my mother in me than I care to think about.

"Call me Phil, baby." He showed me even more of his pearly whites. "And I will call you Lee, lovely lady, even though your husband may not like it." He leaned in with a lusty look.

I decided not to respond to his flagrant attempt at salaciousness. "Well, now that I've finished with my phone call, I think I'll join my mother and husband for dinner."

I tried to step around him, but he blocked my way. "I'm glad I caught you alone."

151

"Oh?" If Phil Baby wanted me to demonstrate some of my karate defense moves on him, bring it on.

He looked around and leaned in again. His breath smelled of stale cigars. "I had hoped you might tell me the real reason for your visit. It can't have been solely to locate the winsome JJ's husband."

"It can and was," I said.

I backed up a bit more. He pressed in a bit more.

"I should tell you the powers-that-be feel you are also looking into the missing relics, hoping to locate them. Maybe trying to make names for yourselves as specialists in stolen Mesoamerican art. Maybe do a series of specials on Netflix or something."

Okay, that hit me out of nowhere. It took me a moment to even wrap my mind around what a television production company had to do with any of this. I couldn't come up with something snappy right away, but when I did, it came straight from the heart.

"I'm not sure what the powers-that-be are smoking, but they might want to switch to chewing gum."

I guess I'd missed my allotted time for a comeback, though, because he went right on as if I hadn't spoken. "I myself am in the process of negotiating with Netflix for a new series, starring me. Of course, I have to come up with a certain amount of seed money, but that is something I am working on. But here is how I see it."

He swung one arm up in a wild gesture, almost as if he were writing on a marquee. I ducked.

"*Central and South America's Deepest Digs with Dr. Philip Whitewater*," he announced. He lowered his hand and looked at me again, eyes burrowing into mine. "So, I know how this goes, this seek and find. One must take one's opportunities as they arise."

152

"And with your charm and intelligence, not to mention being a dead ringer for Ernest Hemingway, how can your opportunities not arise?"

I'd meant it tongue-in-cheek, but he preened, anyway.

"So true. And I don't need anything upsetting the applecart, so to speak."

Abruptly, his persona changed from being a slightly over-the-hill rake to that of a dangerous opponent. *En garde,* I heard my French fencing master say in my head. This time I leaned in.

"Meaning what?"

"Meaning, lovely lady, if you are looking to exploit the situation, it would be better if we joined forces. Besides, you and I could have a lot of fun together." He paused before going on. "You don't want to cross me. This may be Dr. Lancaster's dig, but she's not the only one in control."

The not-so-subtle change in him was deliberate. Here was no randy buffoon. Well, maybe randy. But here was a man who liked to manipulate, lull people into a false sense of security, and catch them off guard. I gave him an unwavering stare.

"If you'll excuse me, I'm late for dinner. Have a nice evening."

"You, too, lovely lady."

I slipped around him and walked toward the cafeteria. His voice came after me. "Think about what I said."

When I felt he was no longer there, I paused, and looked behind me. He may have been gone, but the creepy feeling on the back of my neck lingered.

Doubling back, I left the graveled path and routed my way in front of the row of tents facing the jungle. I returned to the spot where I'd had my peculiar conversation with

153

Whitewater. No one was around, including him. But I wanted to know his whereabouts, just to be on the safe side.

I followed the cigar smell and hoped I wasn't somehow tailing Pedersen. Two cigar smokers. Who would have thought?

I lucked out and caught Whitewater going up the steps into his assigned bungalow. He closed the door behind him. I didn't come out from my hiding place but looked around me.

His bungalow was next to Dr. Lancaster's. Now knowing his predatory nature, maybe he and his boss were much closer than I thought. But what was more interesting was what he meant by "she's not the only one in control."

Chapter Twenty-Five

The end tent nearest the jungle was labeled "Carla Pérez, Administrative Assistant." Her tent was next to "Samantha Hernández, Classroom Instructor." I hadn't met this Hernández, as I understood she was on a two-week leave of absence. But if she was teaching the locals to read and write, she was okay in my book.

I knocked loudly on the prefab door of Carla's tent and waited. I called her name out several times and waited. I looked around for anyone in the vicinity. Nada. I barged in.

She wasn't there, and the lights were out. I took my phone out and switched on its light, flashing it around the room. Neat as a pin. Even little pillows placed just so on a cot with a dust ruffle. All in pink.

"Did you see something?"

Yikes! Carla Pérez's voice. Right outside the door.

Fer crying out loud, I thought, *doesn't anybody go to dinner around here?* I turned off my flashlight and did a swan dive under the cot. The door opened a split second later.

"See what? Like what?" asked a masculine voice.

"A light. I saw a light."

"Well," the man said reasonably, "there's nobody here. Must have been a lightning bug."

They were speaking in English, and the man sounded as American as my tax accountant, which, by the way, happens to be my CPA husband. My PI mind went racing. *What American male is working the site? I haven't had a chance to check*

155

out the male volunteers and assistants yet. It could be anybody. Rats.

"Maybe someone is hiding under the cot. I should look," Carla said.

Yikes!

"There's nobody under the cot," the male voice said. "Besides, I have other plans for that cot."

Double yikes!

She giggled. "Oh, Curtis."

He giggled. "Oh, Carla."

So, this is the comptroller. And I thought he was nothing but a dork.

Silence. Then heavy breathing. Then they both fell down on the cot. I was glad the cot was sturdily made. Otherwise — smashed PI.

But their combined weight did cause the cot to sink down in the middle, meeting my nose. I rolled back a little to get out of the way, and my hand ran into a small, metal container about the size of a cigar box. If I was stranded here for a while, I just might have to entertain myself, see what's inside. Meanwhile, I concentrated on the goings-on overhead.

"No, no, Curtis."

No, no? Thank God!

Carla went on. "Not now. I only returned for my notes. I promised Dr. Lancaster," Carla said, "I would bring her the up-to-date list of supplies, so she could look them over at dinner. I left the list in the pocket of my sweater."

"Come on, Carla." His voice was both seductive and pleading. "You can be five minutes late."

Five minutes? I was right the first time. He is a dork.

"No, I cannot. She will wonder what happened to me."

"Let the bitch wonder."

Well, at least he's spot-on in his assessment of Lancaster.

156

There was some movement, and one of them stood up. In any event, the depression in the cot lessened.

"Dr. Lancaster is my boss. I have to go." Carla's voice, sounding a little farther away, firm, and businesslike. Then she turned on a little seduction herself. "But later? Tonight? I will come to you."

He leapt to his feet almost overturning the cot in his enthusiasm. "Promise?"

"I promise. I bought you a present, Curtis," she cooed.

"You did?"

"Yes, a beautiful box of cigars. From Havana. I got them in Guatemala City last week. I'll bring them with me tonight. For afterward."

And yet another cigar smoker? Doesn't anybody pay attention to the surgeon general?

"Then I'll be smoking several, baby."

Yuk.

More silence, heavy breathing, then giggling.

"Let me get the list, and then I must go," Carla said in a husky tone. "Leave now. Make sure no one sees you."

Another silent moment followed by the sounds of a suction-filled, messy kiss.

"Oh, Carla," he whispered. The door opened but before it closed, he said, "You make my blood boil."

His blood may be boiling but mine ran cold. I wondered if she would search under the cot now that she was alone. Instead, there was some rustling. I saw the lights go out and heard the door open and close. I waited ten seconds and then came out, bringing the metal box with me.

Realizing I couldn't see well enough into the box without more light, I crawled under the cot again. I thanked whatever gods there may be for the stupid dust ruffle while I cursed canvas tents. I turned on my flashlight and opened the box.

157

It contained pieces of expensive-looking jewelry and a green-enameled cigar lighter. A gold locket caught my eye. I opened it up. JJ and Martín's smiling faces, small though they were, stared back at me. So here was JJ's missing locket. And did the rest of these things belong to other people, too?

After a brief hesitation, I returned the locket to the metal box and placed it exactly where I'd found it. I crawled out again, straightened my clothes, and leaned my ear against the door. Satisfied I didn't hear anything, I opened the door a crack, and looked out. No one.

Scooting out, I hurried down the path to the cafeteria, briefly wondering what Gurn was up to, why a boxful of jewelry was hidden under Carla's cot, and just how two people can make love in five minutes. Let's face it. Sometimes less is less.

Chapter Twenty-Six

I entered the cafeteria right behind Professor Felicity Adler. She sensed someone was behind her and stopped short, wheeling around.

To avoid crashing into her, I had to stop short myself. I tried to keep my voice light and breezy.

"Good evening, Professor Adler. How has your day been going?"

She gave me a haunted, almost terrified look. Really? Too much bran in our muffins?

After gaping at me, her lower lip trembled before she answered. "What? I... what?"

I became concerned. "Is everything all right? You look like you've seen a ghost."

"I did, I think. Outside. Behind the temple. There was a man."

"What man?"

"I don't know. I couldn't see him clearly. He was in the shadows. But please don't tell Dr. Lancaster. She thinks I'm seeing things and being hysterical. She'll fire me. Please don't tell her."

"Well, let's go take a look. See what we can find." I pivoted in the direction of the exit.

"No," she yelped, grabbing my arm to prevent me moving. She had a strong grip. People nearby stopped eating and looked at us. Adler lowered her voice instantly and dropped her hold on me.

"No, he's gone. I watched him leave. Back into the jungle. Only — "

"Only what?"

"He was dressed in a warrior costume like the one Alejandro had on. But he wasn't dead. I saw him. I'm not hysterical. I saw him."

Even though she normally had a good three inches over me in height, I watched her visibly shrink before my eyes.

"I think you've had a shock," I said. "Let me get you some hot tea or maybe a glass of wine. Why don't you sit — "

"No!" Her voice was sharp. Once again, everyone nearby turned and looked at us. She softened her voice and tried to smile. "No, thank you. I don't want anything. I think I should just go and lie down. I'll be all right. Thank you."

She started to pass by me for the exit. Now it was my turn to reach out and grab her by the arm.

"Are you sure you don't want to talk to someone about what you've seen? If not Dr. Lancaster or me, someone else?"

She didn't answer but shook her head. Out of nowhere, Dr. Abeba showed up. She wrapped a friendly arm around the trembling woman and spoke in low tones to her. Felicity Adler responded in kind. Together they left the cafeteria. I, along with Adler's spellbound audience, watched them exit.

Turning away from this, I searched the room for my mother. I felt a soft breeze from either the open windows or the overhead fans. Whichever, it was more than welcomed. A sudden rush of fatigue overcame me. Maybe the encounter with Professor Adler was the last straw of a long and hectic day.

Lila sat in a corner on the other side of the room. She was alone at a table for four and glued to her cell phone. She'd thrown her jacket on one chair and her pith helmet on another to ensure no one took them. I hurried over, removed her pith, and sat down.

"*There* you are." She looked up and smiled brightly at me. "Where's Gurn?"

"He should be here any minute." I deliberately kept it vague, hoping he would show up in a few. Lila would be upset if she knew we'd split up. She likes to think he takes care of me. I like to think I take care of him. Maybe we take care of each other. I decided not to mention my strange encounters with Lancaster's assistant or Whitewater until Gurn arrived. Then we could discuss it from different angles.

"Any updates on JJ and Martín, Mom?"

"Yes. Jacqueline says Martín is *awake* and doing *much* better, but his ankle is broken in *three* places. The delay of *so* many hours before *setting* the bones in place has made the procedure even *more* complicated. In all likelihood, his leg will have to be *elevated* and *immobile*, possibly for as long as a *week*. But they will know more after they operate this evening. They want to do it as *quickly* as possible. Jacqueline will, *of course*, remain at the hospital by his side throughout."

"So, she'll be there and not here for the next several days. That's good."

A puzzled look came to Lila's face. "*Why* do you say that? *Why* is her being *there* and not *here* a good thing? Liana, are you *keeping* something from me?"

"Not a thing, Mom. Just ramblings of the mind."

"Your mind does *many* things, Liana, but it does not *ramble*."

"Listen, Mom, when I know for sure what's going on around here, you will be the first I tell. Well, maybe the second. I might tell Gurn first. But what were you doing when I showed up? Texting someone on your phone?"

"You are *changing* the subject, young lady."

161

"Yes, ma'am."

She let out a deep sigh, which she often does around me. "Very well. You can *neither* phone *nor* text on cell phones in this locale, Liana. *Only* on satellite phones. Our phones are little more than a camera or an e-reader. Try to *remember* that." Chastising over, she went on. "I am rereading *Mayan Civilization: A History from Beginning to End*. I downloaded it to my phone *right* before we left. It's edifying."

"Is it?"

"It *reaffirms* many things. Did you know all archaeological materials can be grouped into *four* main categories?"

"No. But then no one ever tells me anything."

She either didn't hear what I said or chose to ignore me. "The four would be artifacts, ecofacts, structures, and features *associated* with human activity."

"What's an ecofact when it's at home?"

"Ecofacts are naturally organic or inorganic remains found in an archaeological site, *suggesting* they were deposited there as a result of human *activity*. Seeds, charcoal, minerals, and unmodified shell or bone are just some examples of ecofacts."

"So not something like pottery?"

"No. That's an *artifact*, an *object* made by a human being. An ecofact, or biofact, is any organic material that has cultural or historical significance."

I stared at my mother as if seeing her for the first time. "Mom, you really know your stuff. And you love it. I suspect that's the real reason you wanted to come along."

Then Lila Hamilton-Alvarez did something I rarely see her do. She blushed. "Well, certainly that's *one* of the reasons. But helping to find Martín was the *main* reason."

I reached out and covered her hand with mine. "Mom, under that Balenciaga wardrobe and Christian Louboutin shoes beats the heart of a caring, loving woman."

She glared at me. "I should *think* my *apparel* has little to do with my *finer* qualities. And since when is my *heart* in my *feet*?"

"Just expressing myself, Mom. Sorry. Maybe ill-put. Let me take it back. Oh, look," I practically shouted, "there's Gurn." I leapt up and raced to meet him as he crossed the room to us.

"Sorry I'm late," he said, gathering me in his arms.

Embracing him briefly, I broke free and said, "Boy, your timing couldn't have been more perfect. I've had foot-in-mouth disease again."

"With Mamá?"

"Who else?"

We arrived at the table where my mother sat, possibly seething. It's hard to tell with her. She removed her jacket from the chair and gave Gurn a ready smile. We both sat down. I turned to Lila.

"Mom, now that we're both here, I want to tell you that Gurn and I split up after we left you. He followed Mr. Machete—"

"Dr. Pedersen," Gurn interjected.

"Into the jungle. I found myself dallying inside Carla Pérez's tent."

"I see," she said in a noncommittal tone.

I turned to Gurn. "So where did Dr. Pedersen go?"

"Not far, maybe a hundred yards or so into the jungle. There, a man was waiting—looked like a native to me—and they had a serious conversation for a time. Then Pedersen gave him a fat envelope. The man opened it, took out money, and counted it. From where I stood, it looked like a payoff."

163

"A payoff?"

While I'd been touting something was going on around here, actually having it proven was sobering. My mind raced. Or given my fatigue, as well as it could race on fumes.

Gurn went on, "After they talked for a few more minutes, Pedersen returned to camp. How did you do, sweetheart?" He waited. "Honey? You there?"

"Huh? Oh, sorry. I was thinking. Nothing is as it seems." I shook off my mood, then gave a verbatim exchange of the recent conversation between Professor Adler and me. I'm able to repeat back conversations word for word, if only on a short-term basis. Eidetic memory. Very handy for a PI.

Gurn looked at me, perplexed. "She claims to have seen another person dressed as an ancient Mayan warrior and wandering the jungle? When was this?"

"Just a few minutes ago. And she was pretty freaked out about it. And loud. She drew quite an audience."

"Is it *possible*," Lila asked, "that she has allowed her emotions to get the *better* of her? I find her to be a woman with less and less *ability* to cope with her surroundings."

"No kidding," I said. "She could use lessons in how to deal with stress."

"You mentioned you also had a run-in with Dr. Whitewater. What happened?" Gurn asked.

I closed my eyes and did another literal recount.

"He actually said," Gurn asked at the end of my chronicle, "'This may be Dr. Lancaster's dig, but she's not the only one in control'?"

"Yes."

"This is *most* interesting," Lila said. "He invited me to come to his bungalow this *evening* for a nightcap and a discussion. The invitation took me *quite* by surprise."

"I hope you're not going, Mom."

"Don't be *insulting*, Liana," she replied. "But even as I said no, I couldn't tell *what* his intentions were."

"Whether business or romance? That seems to be a specialty of his, keeping you wondering."

"The man is a cad," Gurn said, disgust resonating from his very being.

"Darling, you are a gentleman and a scholar," I said. "Some guys are neither."

"To be *completely* fair," Lila said, "Dr. Whitewater *appears* to be a scholar, but he might be willing to sell his knowledge to the *highest* bidder."

"Look out, Netflix," I said. "But all this stuff about the missing relics has me wondering if he's responsible for any of the incidents taking place."

"Along the lines of, 'The best defense is a good offense,'" Gurn said.

"Exactly," I said. "Although how much goes on around here without the head honcho knowing about it?"

"Dr. Lancaster," Gurn said while nodding in agreement.

I went on. "So, is she in control or is he in control? Or someone else?"

"Or is it a *team* effort?" Lila added her thoughts into the mix.

"Whatever it is, we need to find out. And there's more," I said. "Romance blooms between Carla Pérez and the comptroller, Curtis somebody or other."

"Winston," both Gurn and Lila said in unison.

"Yeah, that dorky guy. And let me tell you, if he thinks that all it takes is five minutes to—" I broke off and looked at both of them. "Never mind. I got caught up in a loop. But here's an interesting sidenote. I found JJ's stolen locket in a small box hidden under Carla's cot. It was among several other items."

165

"Does that mean *Carla* took it?" Lila asked, shocked at the idea.

"I can't think of any other reason why it would be in a box under her cot," I said.

"What were you doing under her cot?" Gurn looked at me. "Searching?"

"Searching, hiding, whatever. The point is, either Carla is a thief or a klepto."

"A kleptomaniac? I haven't heard of *anyone* being that anymore," Lila said.

"You mean," I said, "it's gone out of fashion? Never mind, let's eat. I'm so tired, I could go to sleep right here and now. I'm done for the day."

"Me, too," Gurn said. "We should get to bed as early as we can."

"While I'm *thinking* about it," Lila said, reaching out her hand, "give *me* the locket, Liana. Jacqueline will be so *pleased* to have it returned to her."

"I couldn't risk taking it. We don't want Carla to know we know. Besides, if she's involved in what I suspect she is, kleptomania is the least of her sins."

Chapter Twenty-Seven

"Hi, Richard," I said, gulping in great gobs of air. "I need you to do me a favor. Actually, a couple. Well, maybe three. And sorry if I woke you. I know it's early."

"Well, good morning to you. You didn't wake me. I've been up since five. As you know, I like to give Steffi her morning cereal. How is it you are calling on your cell phone?" my brother asked. "I thought they didn't work in the jungle. That's why I gave you the satellite phone, even though you tend to lose them."

"I only lost one."

"Two."

"A bear stepped on the second. Wasn't my fault. Try telling a bear what or what not to do."

He burst out laughing. "Noted. But why are you out of breath?"

"I went to sleep at eight and woke up after nearly seven hours of sleep, raring to go. Gurn is still down, but he did the bulk of the manual labor yesterday. I decided nothing would be better than to start the day climbing the equivalent of ten stories in the heat and humidity."

"May I ask why?"

"JJ says cell phones work if you're standing on a mountaintop or on one of the taller temples." I paused, still trying to keep from panting.

"Which is it? A mountaintop or a temple?"

"I'm standing next to the sacrificial altar atop the El Cizin temple, to be precise. It's already hotter than blue blazes up here."

"That's probably more the humidity than anything else. But take some pictures for me, especially of the altar. I'll bet it's beautiful."

"In a way. There are channels cut into the stone allowing for the runoff of blood."

"Thanks for the reality check."

"You're welcome. But," I said as I pivoted a full 360 degrees, "the view of the jungle from here is spectacular, especially with the rising sun."

"So, you've become an appreciator of the Guatemalan jungle, eh?"

"Only from a distance, Richard. When I'm traipsing through it covered in mud, trying to avoid mosquitoes, pumas, and leeches, not so much. But to change subjects —"

"Changing."

"First, is there an update on JJ's father?"

"Yes, I spoke with Ida around ten o'clock last night. The doctors say her husband's out of danger. She plans on calling JJ sometime this evening with more details. Also, to get another update on Martín."

"Then we will let mother and daughter take care of themselves and move on to other business."

"What's up?"

"I just now texted you a list of names. Hopefully, you can run a check on them."

A ping sounded on Richard's end. "Got it. Let's see. Professor Felicity Adler, Dr. Joan Lancaster, Dr. Josefina Sanchez, Dr. Bjørn Pedersen, Dr. Phillip Whitewater, Dr. Benjamin Storrs, Professor Emilien Bernard, Dr. Kia Abeba, Curtis Winston, comptroller, and Carla Pérez, administrative assistant for the project. They are all in the field of archaeology, I take it?"

"Yes. From what I can tell, they seem to have the run of this place. Interesting characters."

"How deep do you want me to go?"

"Start with, are they who they say they are? And are they in any financial trouble?" I paused before asking, "Can you do it right away? This morning?"

"Doable. Just let me wipe the Pablum off my shirt."

"Then I have in my possession another sat phone belonging to two jóvenes from a nearby village."

"Modern civilization is everywhere."

"Can you trace it, or at least tell me who it's registered to?"

"Is it on?"

"Yes."

"You have it?"

"For the moment, yes."

"Sat phones emit a signal, which is traceable. What's the number?"

I took the phone out of my pocket and read, "It's 502 5555 7234 5668."

After a moment, Richard said, "Okay, I wrote it down. When I get back to the office, which should be in about a half an hour, I'll see if I can find the owner."

"I also want to know who's been called from it."

"You don't want much, do you?"

I blew some kisses over the phone. "Thank you, Richard. You are the best. By the way, how much has Lila filled you in on what's going on around here?" When we are in work mode, we call our mother Lila. Saves a lot of hassle.

"I talked to her last night. She, unlike a certain sister of mine, likes to keep me in the loop."

169

"Yeah, yeah, yeah." This time I blew a raspberry into the phone.

"So noisily demonstrative. And thanks for your sympathy." We both laughed before he went on. "But Lila called mainly to tell me JJ and party, which would include the deceased, arrived at the hospital and that Martín was getting the care he needed," he said. "And she also mentioned the Policia Nacional Civil arrived at the site around five or five thirty yesterday evening."

"Here are a few more tidbits," I said. "The police met JJ and party at the landing site. One officer accompanied the body on the chopper to the morgue. Sergeant Juárez and three of his men came here to interrogate us about Alejandro's death. They came as soon as they put out a logging fire about thirty miles away. They arrived a sooty lot."

"It can't be easy," Richard remarked, "to function as both the fire and the police department."

"They don't, normally. Turns out this fire was one of the largest in years. Illegal logging. It was a duty call for all available public servants no matter what their governmental position. They were exhausted by the time they arrived here."

I paused again, not sure whether or not to continue. I decided to reveal all. I don't pull any punches with my brother.

"Richard, they're out of their depth on this, especially the one in charge, Sergeant Juárez. I think he's a bit of an idiot."

"Are you alerting me that you are about to become Miss PI Buttinsky? I thought now that Martín was found, you'd be leaving this morning."

"Nope. Even if we wanted to, we can't. The police confiscated everyone's passports. I suspect more for show than anything else. We're here for the duration."

"The duration? What does that mean?"

"One or two days, whatever it takes for them to satisfy themselves they did what they could. They may even shut the site down. Unless —"

"Unless?"

"I find out what's going on."

"Uh-oh."

"Uh-oh all you will, but the police think Alejandro was probably killed by local Mayans who don't want their gods messed with."

"Couldn't that be it?"

"No. A native or two may be up to no good, but what's going on around here runs much deeper. Believe me, Richard, the game's afoot."

"There's trouble afoot when you start quoting Sherlock Holmes."

"Try to be philosophical about it, brother mine."

My brother's voice took on a warning edge. "Sister mine, solving this murder — if it is a murder — could take weeks if not months."

"I hope not. You should see my nails after only a couple of days. And I'm running out of sunscreen. But what needs to be done, needs to be done."

"Oh, great. More philosophy."

"But to change subjects —"

"Changing again," he said, letting out a martyred sigh. "You want something else besides the background checks. What is it?"

"I also uploaded a folder to the cloud. That's why I climbed this stupid temple in this stupid heat, because it's the one place where my stupid cell phone works."

"Having a stupid morning, are we?"

I ignored him. "JJ copied the folder from her cell phone to mine, and this is the only way I knew how to give you access to it."

"What's in the folder, Lee?"

"Documentation of the thefts and vandalisms that have taken place at the site for several weeks. Go through everything, but pay attention to an image. Number three-two-four-six. In fact, enlarge it if you can, enhance it if you have to, but I want to know what the pastel-colored blotches are in the background trees. Text me whatever you find out on the sat phone. I'll be back on the ground."

There was a pause. "You're kidding. You climbed to the top of a temple in a hundred and ten degrees to have me look at blotches?"

"I think it's important. And it's only ninety-five degrees right now. Another thing. Alejandro's autopsy will probably take place today if it already hasn't. Please break into the online medical examiner's files at the Hospital Regional de San Benito. I want to read the postmortem report on Alejandro Rios."

"Well, now I know you are so high in the stratosphere you need more oxygen. Do you have any idea how long it would take me to break into a hospital's security-protected files? It would be faster and easier to ask for them."

"I thought you were an IT genius," I teased.

"Only my wife and mother think so."

"So does *Wired* magazine," I protested. "And so do I. Well, never mind. Dr. Abeba is the physician who confirmed Alejandro's death. She'll get the information for her records. Maybe she'll pass the info on to me. If not, I'll steal the file from her office."

"That's my girl."

"You're off the hook on that one."

"Thank you."

"However, can you find out who Alejandro's next of kin is?"

"Not to continue in the uncooperative spirit, but don't they have that info in their on-site office records? Who do they contact in an emergency?"

"I bumped into Dr. Lancaster last night and asked her for the info. She categorically refused. Something about his privacy. And said in her haughtiest British accent."

"You don't like her," Richard observed.

"I don't," I said, not skipping a beat. "Among other things, she's a bully. Yes, I know most bullies are cowards at heart, but that doesn't prevent her from running roughshod over everyone who works for her. You should see the frazzle she's made of her assistant. And there's something else..." My voice petered out as I searched for the right word.

"Lila mentioned her condescending attitude," Richard offered.

"That's not it. Something far more dangerous. She's oblivious to what she does to people and how they react to it. She's like a ticking time bomb."

"Be careful, Sis. You never know about time bombs. They could go off at any minute."

Chapter Twenty-Eight

I made a quick call to Tío to find out how he and the cats were doing. I knew he would be up. He rises with the sun.

"Buenos días," he said. "It is good to hear from you, *sobrina.*"

When he calls me his niece in Spanish, the word is filled with total and unconditional love. I've said it before, and I'll say it again: Everyone should have a Tío in their lives. I wish it for the world at large.

"It's so good to hear your voice, Tío. I see you remembered to look at the name of the incoming call on your phone."

"You teach me and I learn."

"I am the one who is taught by you, but I do know a few technical things. How are you?"

"We are well."

It was not quite the royal we, for I knew he included the cats in the statement. I also knew my kitty kith and kin were probably not missing me one bit, thank you very much.

"I can hear Tugger in the background, yowling some sort of complaint."

"The sound of the phone wakes him up."

"He's such a prince, Tío."

"And you would have it no other way." We both laughed. He went on, "Your mother phones me last night to tell me you have found Martín. It is a mission accomplished."

"Yes, but I don't yet know why he was being held prisoner."

174

"He knows something someone does not want him to tell." Tío's response came quick and easily.

"Is it that simple?"

"Do you not say, often the simplest answer is the right one?"

"Do I? Well, good for me. I don't think whoever it is counted on his loss of memory from hitting his head on a rock, though."

"He remembers nada?"

"Nada. But following the logic, whatever he can't remember must be important."

"You often say that, too."

"You know, I've got to start listening to me, Tío."

"I would advise it. You are, how you say, one smart cookie."

Phone calls accomplished, I began my slow descent to the bottom of the temple. As I came down, this ancient city spread out before me. I did a fast history lesson in my head.

As far back as four thousand years ago, the ancient Mayans built two types of temples or pyramids. Either they were shrines to their gods or used in sacrificial rituals. For sacrifices, the temple was climbable on all four sides leading to the top. Each side of the temple had ninety-one steps, with the sacrificial, top platform completing the mandatory three hundred and sixty-fifth step, in honor of their calendar.

In this, El Cizin was typical. However, like many Mayan temples, El Cizin was unique in the executions of its design.

Either planned by local priests or at the whim of the king, it stood taller than most at one hundred feet. In front, the steps stopped three-quarters of the way up, exposing a recessed platform. There, a wide entrance was cut into the stones. It led into what was, for lack of a better word, a foyer.

This foyer connected to the internal parts of the temple. Externally, on both sides of the entrance, the outer steps continued to the top. Where, of course, rituals occurred between priests and victims I didn't care to think about.

The rising sun had shifted, and the front side was now in partial shade. I paused at the platform to cool off. Pulling out my water bottle, I drank deeply, and sat down cross-legged on the platform. I spun around and looked into the dimly lit interior. I'd paid little attention to it on my way up but found myself captivated. So much so, I rose and moved closer, staring into the relative coolness.

Dr. Lancaster told us visitors were forbidden access to the temple. It was still unknown and could be dangerous. She'd emphasized the word "dangerous" as if that would deter me. I never pay attention to claptrap like that. Drive the I-880 at rush hour. Now, there's danger.

My eyes adjusted to the dark. A stone relief came into focus, cut into the entirety of the back wall. It featured a pretty nasty-looking god surrounded by death and mayhem. Here must be El Cizin, I thought, in all his glory. Mayan earthquake god, god of death, ruler of the subterranean land of the dead, and yada yada.

Arms held high, El Cizin carried ancient weapons and writhing serpents in each hand. But it was his face that seized the imagination. The artist who carved this stone captured perfectly the expression of pure evil.

If I got my history right, in later years under the influence of the Spanish conquistadors, El Cizin would be depicted as a dancing skeleton, smoking a cigarette. Pretty watered down, I thought, compared to the guy I saw before me.

The relief was flanked on either side by two freestanding, squat statues, half man, half snake. Their faces looked as if they were experiencing a bad case of acid reflux. All in all,

Stephen King's novels have nothing on the Mayans. I stood, taking it all in.

"What are you doing, Liana?"

If catapulting yourself into the air qualifies as a sports category, Olympic gold, here I come. I must have jumped ten feet at hearing Lila's voice come out of nowhere. While airborne, I let out a yelp resembling an Austrian Alps yodel. The sound echoed back at us.

"My *apologies* if I frightened you, dear," she said mildly, giving me a regal but inquisitive smile.

Clutching at my chest with a shaking hand, I let out a small laugh. "That's all right, Mom. I got caught up in the PR spin the Mayan's gave El Cizin. He sure was one scary-looking dude."

"Yes, *indeed*," she said. "*Quite* impressive." She studied the stone relief.

Meanwhile, I studied her. She was dressed, of course, in another Grace Kelly safari outfit. Taking the curse off all the beige was a soft, silk organza scarf in Dresden Blue, nattily tied around her neck. The shade perfectly matched her eyes.

She looked cool, radiant, and not just ready for the day, but ready for her closeup, Mr. DeMille. Oh, wait. That was Norma Desmond in *Sunset Boulevard*, not *Mogambo*. Need to get my movies straight. For sure I looked like something pulled from the sea, maybe the *Creature From the Black Lagoon*.

"What are you doing here, Mom?"

"I might ask *you* the same question," she responded. "I *saw* you from below and thought I would *join* you."

"I was at the tippy-top talking on my phone to Richard and then to Tío. I sent Richard the folder JJ gave me."

"I hope you didn't ask him to *do* anything, Liana," she chided. "You *know* he has his hands full running the business alongside Peter. And then, of course, he *does* help with the care of our little Stephanie... " Her voice dropped off and a look of total joy covered her face at merely saying the name of her only grandchild.

"No, no, of course not," I lied. "I would never bother Richard. I just wanted him to have the folder." I changed the subject abruptly. "Did you come from our tent? Was Gurn still sleeping?"

"Yes, but breakfast *ends* in about an hour. It's six thirty now. We should *go* and wake him."

"So, we have an hour, do we?" I stepped deeper inside the foyer.

"*Liana!*" Mom's shocked voice resonated off the stones. "Dr. Lancaster *strictly* forbade us access to the temple."

"Did she? I don't remember." I walked to one of the statues, reached out, and patted it on its little squat head. "Besides, with a little luck, no one else is here. Something about personnel meetings and assignments starting first thing each morning. All I want to do is have a little look-see. After all, we have an hour."

"I *strongly* advise *against* it. We are not allowed any form of *exploration* within the temple. Dr. Lancaster was *explicit* in —
"

"Oh, piffle," I interrupted. "I don't give a rat's patootie what Dr. Lancaster says."

"Liana." Mom's tone was now double chastising. "*Open* hostility does *not* become a lady. *Nor* does that type of language."

"I'll try to keep it under wraps," I said, looking to the left and right. I was sure both sets of stairs led down into the innards of the temple.

"I choose the stairs on the left just because." I headed for it, pulling out my phone. I turned on its flashlight. "Joining me?"

She turned on her phone's light and moved forward but said, "I am *opposed* to this, Liana."

"Duly noted. Come on, Mom."

I shone the light up, down, and around the stairwell. It was surprisingly clean for being thousands of years old. I then settled the beam on the slightly worn treads of the stone and took my first step into the lower depths of this world. The air was cooler but smelled as if it had been hanging out in the place for several millennia. Which it had.

Eight steps down, we came to a small landing with a waist-high, narrow ledge, probably built for a statue. Sitting on the ledge were three electric lanterns, just begging to be used. I picked one up, found the on button, and pressed it.

Strong white light, almost football-stadium bright, shot out from the lantern. It took my eyes a moment or two to adjust to the brilliance. Once I did, it only stressed how oppressive it is to have solid stone overhead, underfoot, and on walls. You'd never see a staircase design like this on *Property Brothers*.

"Liana, I don't feel *comfortable* in doing this. I think we should go *back*."

"No way. But if you want to leave, go ahead," I said, turning off my phone's flashlight and taking the next step down.

"I'm not leaving *without* you," she said, following me.

Men's voices came from the bottom of the staircase, reverberating off the stones. There were also the slight sounds of movement. I stopped short.

"Shhhh! I hear something."

Lila banged into me and dropped her phone. It landed with a clatter on the stone tread below.

Whoever they were, they were nearby and heard us. Someone flashed a light up the staircase and yelled.

179

"Who is there? Identify yourself."

The accent was thickly French. Professor Emilien Bernard, the man who found Alejandro's body on the steps of the pyramid along with Gurn and me.

"Professor Bernard," I said, trying to keep my voice easy-breezy. "It's only me, Lee Alvarez, and my mother, Lila Alvarez."

I picked up Mom's phone and handed it to her.

"Professor Bernard," Lila called out, in her hostess-with-the-mostest voice. "So nice to meet you again."

Silence.

We continued down toward the man standing at the bottom of the staircase. Behind him, crouching down among the rubble, was an older Guatemalan man. Masonry trowel in hand, he looked startled at seeing us. A small bucket of what looked like mortar sat by his side.

Staring daggers at us, Professor Bernard said, "You cannot be in here. This is off limits to all but those contracted to do scientific study of the temple."

It was as if we'd crashed the famed *Le Lido Cabaret* in Paris and he was the bouncer. He looked ready to eject us physically from the premises.

180

Chapter Twenty-Nine

"We've been told that under ordinary circumstances that is true, absolutely," I chirped, smiling brightly at the professor. Making it up on the spot, I continued. "But as a reward for finding Martín, Dr. Lancaster said we could explore the temple as long as we didn't touch or take anything. I don't think this lantern counts." Wearing an impish grin, I held the light upward.

Bernard was not taken in by any impishness I might have thrown at him. Basically, he was not imped. But he didn't appear to want to call me an out-and-out liar, either.

"I do not understand." His reply was halting and uncertain.

"Would it make it *easier* if I *translated* what Liana said into French?" And without hesitation, Lila repeated it verbatim in flawless French. Then she gave him a smile, more regal than impish. She doesn't imp.

"I understood what your daughter said," Professor Bernard growled. "I do not understand why Dr. Lancaster would break her own rules."

"Then you should take that up with her," I said with sudden firmness, reversing my previous approach. "Because here we are, and here we intend to stay."

He and I stared one another down until he shrugged his shoulders in concession. Then he turned and muttered something to his helper who'd been watching our exchange as if it were a tennis match.

I looked around. Off the stairway going in several different directions were wide corridors. Large chunks of fallen stone and smaller pieces of plaster littered the floors. But a smattering of red- and mustard-colored paint on stones indicated the walls' past glory.

Professor Bernard seemed to be working on what looked like a former altar, broken and in sad need of repair. Whatever previously rested atop it was long gone.

He bent down to study a corner of the damaged altar. Picking up one particular chunk of stone from the floor, he fitted it into a missing section. He nodded to his helpmate, who took the piece and slathered on some mortar. Together and very exactingly, they set the stone in place. It was like putting together a giant puzzle.

Fascinating though this was, I knew Lila and I should get going while the going was good. I chose one of the three corridors and signaled to her to head for it.

On catlike feet, which is not easy to do in hiking boots, we tiptoed into another corridor. With the exception of no damaged altar, it looked exactly like the one we'd just left.

Lila whispered, "Liana, do you *know* where we are going? I suspect all these corridors look *alike*. How will we *find* anything? Or keep from getting *lost*?"

"I'll use the last map JJ made," I said, pulling my phone from my pocket. "As you know, I have Dad's knack for reading maps."

"I like to *think* you inherited that gift from me."

I gave Lila a broad smile. "I like to think I inherited my sense of style from you."

"This is no time for *levity*, Liana."

"Okay then."

After a small search on my phone, I found JJ's latest drawings of the guts of the temple. Enlarging the map, I turned to Mom. "See? We're right here on the seventh floor of the temple. The damaged altar is back that way." I pointed behind me.

"Is the hidden *staircase* on that map?"

"JJ said it was." I moved the cursor from point to point, found something, and enlarged it. "I remember her saying it was just past an archway at the north end of the lowest known corridor. Here it is, roughly drawn, but it's right below us!" I tapped the map with pride. "Easy peasy lemon squeezy. Now all we have to do is walk down seven floors and there we are."

"I don't know that we can do this in *under* an hour."

"Of course we can." I turned and looked at my mother with utter sincerity. "Mom, I have to see that blackened mural. It should take less than ten minutes to get there. Walking back up might take a little longer. We'll figure it out as we go along."

"Very well. I see this is *important* to you. I will try to think of this as an *adventure*, Liana."

"That's the spirit. You don't think we'll run into any snakes, do you? Forget I asked that. Bad karma."

I moved toward the end of the corridor. Lila followed. I came to another set of stairs, shone the light down a rubble-filled staircase, and hopped down in between stones. I heard Mom's voice behind me.

"Sometimes I wonder *why* I *listen* to you, Liana."

"Sometimes I wonder why you do too, Mom."

Chapter Thirty

It was slower going than I would have liked, but twenty minutes later found us on the floor, which, according to the map, led to where the hidden staircase was. Here the corridor was in much better shape and the air pretty breathable. I began to question if there weren't air passages built into the temple.

That was just one of the things I would ask when we exited the temple. That is, if anyone was still speaking to me, including my husband. While he was used to my independence, this may have pushed the boundaries.

We came to an archway with pictures painted above it. "Wow! This part of the temple looks like it was built only a few years back. It's in excellent condition." I turned to Lila and pointed to pictures over the arch. "Any idea what that says?"

She put her flashlight back on and aimed it at the glyphs. "I'm afraid not. But in making an *educated* guess, with the images of people in various stages of dying or being smitten down, I would *say* it's some sort of *warning*."

"You mean, 'Abandon all hope, all ye who enter here'?"

"More than *likely*."

"This is getting good, Mom," I said with a grin. I moved forward with more energy and excitement than before.

Ignoring me, Lila looked straight ahead. "There's a staircase."

"Yes, but," I said, searching the nearby walls, "the one we want is hidden from sight." I looked at JJ's rendering. "About here. I'm thinking," I drawled, patting the walls, "if we can find some sort of trigger that opens a hidden door..."

"You *mean* one of the many *pulleys* and *counterweights* often designed by the architects of the time?"

"Yeah. Those." I ran my hand across a section of relatively smooth plaster. A slight depression made me pause. "What have we here?"

I pushed at it. Nothing. I pushed harder. I felt rather than heard a click. A tall panel, the width of a door, slid open. I felt a whoosh of air.

"Why, Liana," Lila exclaimed. "*Look* what you've found!"

"I had a lot of help from JJ's map," I admitted.

I put down the lantern and pushed the panel open even more, as wide as it would go. Picking up the lantern again, I extended my arm as far as I could into the space. Here was a wide but steep staircase.

Jaguars, pumas, parrots, peacocks, and monkeys, painted in vibrant colors and larger than life, adorned the walls of the stairs leading down. Even riddled with centuries of cracks, you could still see their magnificence. I stood transfixed, trying to take it all in.

"*Move*, Liana," Lila ordered. "It's close to seven. We need to get *back*."

"Yes, ma'am. But I want to be respectful. We are stepping into a hidden world that until recently hasn't been seen in thousands of years."

"That's why they call it *exploration*, dear," she said, giving me a gentle shove.

We descended. After several steps, the panel behind us closed, again with the slight click you felt rather than heard.

185

Too late I wondered if I would be able to find the depression on this side of the staircase in order to get out.

Oh well, I thought, *JJ got out a few weeks back, so there has to be a way. I'll deal with it later.*

The clearance above was high, possibly to allow room for priests or servants to carry the king's coffin or sarcophagus above their heads. Running the length of the ceiling was a scene more ethereal in nature, done mostly in shades of greens and blues.

Showcased above was a river filled with linked lily pads, their white flowers floating serenely overhead. Halfway down, a small boat held a seated king dressed in his finest raiment. I was surprised all the jade he was wearing didn't sink the small boat.

At the end of the fresco near the bottom of the steps, a figure of a heavenly god beckoned. The lily pads seemed to guide the king to the cloud-bound god. Along the shoreline, his subjects bowed and scraped, looking on in awe.

"Isn't this *wondrous,* Liana?" Lila said, taking pictures with her phone. She paused for a moment and stared up at the ceiling with reverie. "In the Maya religion, virtually *everything* in the world was viewed as sacred, to be protected."

"Except their enemies. They usually got their hearts cut out."

"It is a *rare* culture that has *no* flaws. Take the *French* Revolution—"

"Oh *mon dieu,*" I interrupted, "not Great-Grandfather, to the ninth power, Jean-Christophe Baptiste, again."

"He was *merely* a wigmaker," she said smartly, still shooting images with her phone at every step. "He did not deserve to *die* under the guillotine."

"Right. Let's talk about the river you're taking so many pictures of."

Still in teacher mode, she said, "The river of *which* I am taking so many pictures."

"Whatever. The river seems to be front and center of the fresco. Why's that?"

She switched gears smoother than a race-car driver. "The Maya believed rivers and water-filled caves carried them to the underworld or afterlife. It's as if we're meant to *start* the journey into the underworld from this *glorious* staircase."

"Sorry, Mom, but when I look at this, all I can think of is a laundry chute with drawings all over it."

"You need to put yourself in the Mayan frame of *mind*, Liana."

"I'll give it a try."

I followed the overhead river to the bottom of the staircase and came to an abrupt halt. Not just because the stairs ended but because of what greeted me. Hello, Mayan frame of mind.

The stairs emptied at one end of a rectangular room, about thirty by sixty feet. The river, lilies, and gods continued overhead but turned to the left, leading to an intricately carved stone sarcophagus positioned on the far side of the room. It was enormous. There was no doubt this was the main focus of the burial chamber. The reason for it all. The body of the king.

Even with my Godzilla lantern, from that far away, his tomb looked cold, otherworldly, and out of place. I was drawn back to the surrounding walls and ceiling, alive with gorgeous colors and images. Aside from a few cracks here and there, it was as if they'd been painted yesterday. Here was a grandeur I never expected to see, not even in a museum.

I paused to make a remark along those lines when I felt something. A slight quiver. It was as if a heavy truck rolled by.

"Mom, did you feel —?"

But she'd zipped right by me, almost unconscious of my presence. She stopped dead center at the wall to the right of the staircase, aiming the light from her phone on the scene. She backed up a few feet to take it all in, then simply gaped. I hurried to her side and held the lantern up. The scene brightened before us. With a sharp intake of breath, I, too, was overwhelmed by what I saw.

Dozens of small, detailed scenes depicted all aspects of Maya daily life. Farmers, hunters, slaves, peasants, artisans, merchants, nobility, priests, warriors, and leaders went about their business before us.

These small tableaus acted as a picture frame for a much larger scene of life-sized figures of nobility: six men and women gathered around a seated king. Posed on an ornate jade throne, he extended his arms out to them. At his feet sat a young child, playing with a doll-like toy. The attitude of the people came off familiar and casual as if they were caught chitchatting.

"This must be the *family* the king left behind," Lila commented, with no small amount of reverence in her voice.

I didn't say anything but searched my phone for JJ's folder. Once found, I saw she had taken an image of this mural. It got lost in the translation. Painted on the walls was vibrancy and life, with small details that couldn't be captured by a camera, no matter what you paid for the phone.

I pulled myself away and turned once again to face the king's sarcophagus. Moving closer, I noticed the wall behind it was covered with yet another mural.

While the familial mural used mainly warmer tones — yellows, oranges, and reds — this wall was painted in cooler blues and greens. A vibrant blue sky filled with stark white stars held three gods. They gazed at the sarcophagus resting on a pedestal in front of the mural.

"I do not believe that slab of stone could have been *carried* down the staircase," Lila observed. She, too, had turned and came to my side, snapping images with her phone. "It must weigh five or six *tons*."

"That's what I was just wondering, Mom. How did they get that thing down those stairs?"

"Archaeologists *believe* Pakal the Great's sarcophagus was created *first*. It was placed where they *knew* they would build the temple in later years. It was done *decades* before he died."

"So maybe they did the same thing with this King Whatshisname."

"B'alaj Chan K'inich," Lila interjected.

"When he died," I went on as if she hadn't spoken, "they could have carried his coffin down the stairs and put it into the sarcophagus already here. Man, that slab is about the same size as a few nightclub dance floors I've been on."

Lila got antsy and returned her phone to her jacket pocket. "Have you seen *enough*, Liana? We really *should* go."

"Not quite." I turned away from the sarcophagus. "This is what I came for."

"For *what* you came."

Ignoring yet another of her English lessons, I crossed to the blackened mosaic-tiled mural. After setting the lantern on the floor, I searched the many pockets of my pants for a packet of facial tissues. Once found, I pulled out a tissue.

"And here's what I came to do."

I went to a lower corner of the mosaic fresco. In a circular motion, I wiped a small amount of what was purported to be black spray paint. It lifted right off.

I stepped back and studied what I'd achieved with great satisfaction. "Just what I thought."

Lila came closer, leaned down, and looked at the cleaned mosaic tiles. "I don't *understand*."

189

"Next you'll be saying it doesn't make any sense. But it does. It's a mixture of soot and mineral oil. An old trick. Completely covers, but easily wipes off. And no damage to the tiles."

"Why would anyone *do* that? It doesn't make— Never mind, I *won't* say it."

"Buying time, Mom. That's what was going on. As I suspected, whoever did this didn't want to destroy the fresco, just hide what was on it for as long as possible."

I felt a slight roll under my feet. I grabbed on to my mother's arm. Some dust fell from the ceiling. I looked up.

"I hope that wasn't what I think it was."

"Liana, I suggest we leave *right* now."

"Stellar idea."

We hurried across the room and headed for the stairs. Halfway there, the ground began to seriously shake. Sounds of a freight train surrounded us. Only it wasn't. It was an earthquake.

A strong jolt threw us to the floor. We clutched at one another, unable to do more than that. Plaster rained down from the ceiling. The earth shuddered and groaned. Thunder roared from the staircase.

We watched in horror as an avalanche of falling stones, mortar, and wood beams from the ceiling surged down the steps and filled the stairwell. In five more seconds, we would have been at that very spot. And probably crushed.

Somehow, I managed to get to my feet, then pulled my mother up. Nowhere else to go, we fled to a corner of the room hoping for a modicum of safety.

As quickly as it started, it stopped. The earthquake probably hadn't lasted more than ten seconds, but it was the longest ten seconds of my life.

An eerie silence descended, followed by a disquieting calm. All that remained was stirred-up dust, some still falling from new cracks in the ceiling.

"I think it's over," I said, turning to Lila. "Mom! Are you all right?"

"I *think* so. What about *you*? Are you *hurt*, Liana?" She looked me up and down.

"No, no, just shaken." I coughed. Fine particles of dust and grit coated the inside of my mouth. "I hope the dust settles soon. It's hard to breathe in here."

I looked at Lila and she looked at me. We didn't say it, but breathing might become a real problem real soon.

"We need to get out of here, Mom," I said, trying not to panic.

I headed for the rubble that was once a staircase. And our only exit. I stopped a foot or two away.

"Well, Dr. Lancaster was right about these walls being unstable." I turned to my mother, who was brushing dust off herself. "Mom, I hate to say it, but this doesn't look good. It's about twenty feet up those stairs to the door. And it's blocked by tons of debris."

"Do you think anyone *knows* we're *in* here, Liana?"

"I don't think so. It was a last-minute decision on my part, and we snuck around Professor Bernard and his helper."

My heart lurched. Gurn! I didn't even kiss him goodbye, just left a quick note. An ambiguous one, at that. I turned to Mom.

"Mom, let's check our phones to see if we can get a signal. It's a long shot, but maybe."

She reached inside her jacket pocket and pulled out both phones. I did the same.

After looking at one phone and then the other, Lila shook her head. I looked down at my phones. The words "no

191

service" stared back at me. I tried to look on the bright side. I was only down to 68 percent power on one and 81 percent on the other. Not bad.

Bright side. Suddenly I was aware we could still see. We should have been in total darkness. The lantern, of course!

I looked for the lantern I'd been holding when the earthquake struck. It lay on its side but was still working. I hurried over and picked it up. Undamaged.

I'll have to write a glowing review for Consumer Report, I thought, *should we ever get out of here.*

"We must *remain* calm, Liana." Coughing, Lila came to my side.

"I'll give it my best shot. But we need to get out of here and fast. Gurn doesn't know where we are, and he must be wondering."

"And if news of this earthquake reaches the internet, Richard will become worried about us."

I coughed again, my throat scratchy. I pulled out my water bottle. Half gone. I rinsed the grit out of my mouth and spit it on the floor anyway. Lila looked away, but didn't take a swig from her own bottle of water.

"Let's go back to where we were," I said. "The dust seems less there. We can wait for it to settle a little."

I crossed to the corner, sat down on the floor, and leaned back against the wall. Lila joined me. I looked at her. She looked at me. Then my mother, who really is the best, reached out, took my hand, and gave me an encouraging smile. Guilt overtook me. I nearly burst into tears.

"Mom, I am so sorry I got you into this mess."

"I would say these things *happen,* but that may be *gilding* the lily."

"I know! It's me! I never learn. I'm so sorry."

"I'm glad you're not down here *alone*, Liana, that's all. It would be *difficult* to be here all alone." She looked around her and coughed again. She took a delicate sip of water.

"We can't let too much more dust get into our lungs, Mom. I think I've got one of Gurn's bandannas on me. Maybe I can rip it in half for both of us."

I searched my pockets and found the red bandanna. It tore easily enough. I handed one piece to Lila. After I tied my half over my nose and mouth, I watched her do the same.

"You'll notice the air is already a little cleaner where we are," I said. "I wonder why?"

"Why, *indeed*?"

We sat for a few minutes. I would like to say in companionable silence, but nothing could be further from the truth. Trapped inside a king's tomb. There must be better ways to go. Out of nowhere, something burbled out of me, surprising even me.

"Mom, tell me about Mr. Dirk Goodman."

"Who?"

"Dirk Goodman. You were on your survival training with him. You said he was named well. What did you mean by that?"

"What on *earth* made you think of him *now*, Liana? Sometimes your *thought* processes take me aback."

"Aha! Classic avoidance. You don't want to talk about him."

"That's *ridiculous*. But I'm not comfortable with just sitting here, Liana."

"Don't want to shoot the breeze, eh?"

"We need to find a way *out*."

"I agree," I said, rising. "So, we will table Mr. Dirk Goodman for the moment and start looking."

Reaching out a hand, I helped pull Lila to her feet. We stood for a moment side by side surveying the tomb that had become our prison.

I turned back to Lila, about to say some words of reassurance, when I noticed the scarf around her neck. We were standing stock still, but one silky end fluttered ever so slightly.

"Mom! Do you see that?"

"What?"

"Don't move but look down at your scarf."

She did as commanded. We both stared at it for a split second.

"Yikes! Give me that." I snatched at the scarf and fairly ripped it from around her neck.

"Liana, what is the *matter* with you? That was rude."

"Air."

"What?"

"At the top of the stairs when I first opened the door, I heard a whooshing sound. Now I realize it was air escaping from this room into the hallway above. And now this." I held her scarf up. "Look at it. It's moving. Ever so slightly but it's moving. That means air is coming into this tomb from outside." I gestured to the wall, reached out, and tapped it. "If I read JJ's map right" — I tapped the wall again for emphasis — "this is an outside wall."

"It may be an outside wall of the temple, Liana, but we are about twenty feet *below* ground."

"But maybe the tunnel mentioned in one of those glyphs is here. A hidden tunnel meant for the king."

"A *distinct* possibility. It would provide a way for him to go to the underworld. But *how* do we find it?"

I extended the scarf the full length of my arm. "All we have to do is hold this puppy up, walk up and down along this wall, and watch the scarf for its strongest movements."

"How *clever* of you."

"Who would have thought a crappy piece of silk chiffon might save us."

"Watch your language, Liana. I'll have you *know* that's a Ferragamo."

Chapter Thirty-One

For nearly an hour, I crept back and forth near the wall. Unfortunately, the scarf floated at the slightest provocation. Then I found if I took a step, paused, held the scarf out, and waited to see if it moved, that was the way to go.

Meanwhile, I knew Gurn must be desperate to know where we were. And for sure the news of the earthquake must have hit the internet by that time. Richard was probably freaking out.

Lila had been following my every move. I turned toward her and handed off the scarf.

"Why don't you continue doing this? I'm going to get down on my hands and knees and sniff along the wall. It works for dogs so maybe it will work for me."

"I'm losing heart, Liana," she said out of the blue. "I may *never* see little Stephanie again." Her voice quivered.

"No, no, Mom. We can do this. The air is fresher than it should be if we were totally sealed in. It's coming in from somewhere, and I will find that somewhere."

I pulled the bandanna off my face and went to the far corner. Dropping down on all fours, I put my nose to the bottom of the wall. This time I was even more meticulous in my search than I had been with the scarf. Looking across the sixty feet of wall to the other side, I knew it would take hours. I had a thought and sat up on my haunches.

"Mom, if you were a Mayan and you were going to build a tunnel leading out of this room, where would you put it?"

She thought for a moment. "Dead center. The Mayans *loved* symmetry. In fact, in their culture, balance was *quite* important."

"Center it is," I said, standing up. I felt a twinge in the small of my back. "Ow. Well, that hurt. I should have done a barre this morning."

I moved to the approximate center of the room, dropped down again, and began to crawl along, my nose next to what in my world would have been the baseboard. It didn't take me long.

"Mom! Bring me that scarf!"

She ran over, dropped to her knees, and handed me the scarf. "What is it?"

"A current of air. Right here." I held the scarf against the wall and it fairly danced. I rose to my feet. After drawing the scarf up and down along the wall, I stood. "There's a crack running straight up for about six feet. You can hardly see it, but nature knows it's there. Look at that! It goes across, too, for about three feet. You can hardly see any of this, even from here. Look!"

She leaned in and studied the wall. "Their workmanship is *extraordinary*. How they managed to bring these two pieces of stone *so* close together is *astonishing*."

"Before you write a review, now what? Is there a lever that opens a door? Is this a secret panel that slides open? Now that we've found it, how do you suggest we get whatever it is to open?"

She didn't answer me but stood and backed up about a foot. After a minute or two of studying the crack and surrounding wall, she said, "I would *venture* to guess this is a door *not* a panel. And it is most *likely* controlled the same way the panel at the top of the stairs was controlled."

197

"You mean weights and pulleys are rigged to a trigger in one of the stones. Wait a minute. Let's back up more and look at the total mural. Maybe it contains a clue as to where that trigger is."

I picked up the electric lantern and held it high, studying the scene. Busier than the other murals, this painting was of a king sitting on an altar floating in the middle of space. He was surrounded by animals, fruits, and vegetation. Below him, in various poses of supplication, were worshiping priests. The background was a brilliant blue. One of the king's fingers reached out, extending right where the end of a door might be.

I moved closer. The extended finger wore a round, green ring, his only jewelry in this painting. I reached up and ran my hand over the ring. I pressed the ever-so-slight indentation.

A shudder came from behind the wall. Then the grating sound of stone rubbing against stone. The door pulled back and swung open on one side at the same time. The movement was so gradual it was as if it was shot by a slow-motion camera.

"Wow! Now there's a feat of engineering," I said as we stared at the ever-widening opening.

A cool breeze ruffled my hair, fresh and alive. But once the door was completely open, the six by three space seemed to be nothing more than a black hole. I stepped inside, again holding the lantern high. I could only see a few feet in, but the walls and ceiling appeared to be painted the same blue as the mural.

"Okay, this is the way out."

"And what if it *isn't*, Liana?"

"Then we're going down with kings, Mom."

Chapter Thirty-Two

"Let's *rest* for a minute, Liana. My ankle is starting to bother me."

It had been two hours, and still we advanced toward nothing but blackness. The tunnel, while dry and clean, did have stones and plaster scattered on the floor, especially after the latest shaking.

Lila had been busy looking up at paintings on the ceiling that led the king to his immortality. She hadn't seen a rock, stepped on it, lost her balance, and twisted her ankle not more than a few hundred yards in. She'd tightened the laces on her boot, but the sprain had become painful nonetheless.

"No problem, Mom. Let's rest."

I sat down cross-legged on the limestone floor. Her descent to the floor was slow, given her ankle.

"Boy, I can see," I joked, "the big danger in the jungle is not a fer-de-lance or jaguar, but twisted ankles."

She didn't laugh or chastise me. "Maybe you should go on *without* me, Liana. When you get out, you can *send* someone back."

"Mom, please. Martyrdom does not become you."

"I'm *just* saying, Liana—"

"Well, don't," I interrupted, more testy than not. "We can rest anytime you say. It's not a problem."

"How *far* have we traveled, Liana?"

"It's hard to keep track of, and we are on a bit of an incline, but maybe a mile, a mile and a half," I said.

"And still no *sign* of it ending." Her voice was thin and tired.

I didn't answer but found bile rising in my throat. This was all my fault. If I hadn't been so pigheaded and barged into the temple despite all caution thrown at me, we wouldn't be in the mess we were in.

Fifteen minutes later found us moving on and me wondering where a good coconut tree was when you needed one. But I was determined to make amends, to lead us to safety. If I had to carry Lila Hamilton-Alvarez on my back, that's what I would do.

The breeze increased. The air smelled sweeter with every step we took. My spirits rallied. I began to babble.

"We're getting close to the end. I can sense it. And let's look on the bright side about that earthquake. We're in a place where there should be a bat or two. Or maybe a hundred. But they probably got scared away by the earthquake and are off doing batty things. Or possibly the constant cold wind doesn't encourage hanging upside down and sleeping."

"You're *nattering*, Liana."

"Yes, ma'am. Wait! Mom, I think I see light at the end of the tunnel. Literally. We're almost free!"

I turned around and went back to Lila, who'd been lagging behind. She was exhausted, and her face registered pain.

"Come on, Mom. Let me help you."

"*Thank* you, dear."

I wrapped my arm around her waist, and she wrapped hers around my shoulder. I half carried, half walked her the last quarter of a mile to the ever-brightening light, protest though she did about being a burden. She's not heavy. She's my mother.

200

The breeze increased with every step, becoming more of a wind, often with a whippet-like howl. If I hadn't been working so hard, I might have even felt a bit of a chill.

Finally, we came to the end of the tunnel and stepped out onto a winding path. The wind noises died down only to be replaced by the sounds of rushing water. It felt chilly as well. Like standing in front of an open refrigerator door.

I couldn't see much because rocks of every size and height surrounded us. I helped Lila to one shaped almost like a chair. After sitting her down, I stepped clear of the rocks for a better view. What I saw looked like something you'd find at Disneyland. Only this was real.

We were in an enormous, globe-shaped cavern at least forty feel high and nearly a half a block wide. Prism-like stalactites overhead and stalagmites below sparkled like diamonds. Before us and cutting through the middle of the dry cavern floor was an underground river. On the other side of the river, cascading waterfalls fed into the opaque turquoise waters. The river itself seemed to start from somewhere beneath the earth, burbling up to the surface, and flowed I know not where. But I'll bet it took many a Mayan king with it.

I turned to my left, my eyes following the incoming rays of the sun. Directly below the vault of the cave was a wide entrance. Sunlight poured in, rays dancing magically on the undulating waters. But most important, there was a path that descended from the mouth of the cave to where we were. Freedom.

"Liana," Lila said, having hobbled to my side. Her voice took on the same reverence I was feeling. "I wonder if this is what *heaven* looks like."

"Maybe so, Mom. Because I've never had as much faith as I have now."

Chapter Thirty-Three

"Mom, why don't you stay here? I'll go up and call Gurn and ask him to come help us. Maybe he can even bring a mule for you to ride."

"I'm coming *with* you."

"It's not necess—"

"I'm coming *with* you."

"Mom."

"Liana!"

"Or you'll come with me." I looked up at the forty-foot path to the mouth of the cave, assessing it. "This path is pretty narrow. Why don't we rest here for a half an hour or so, and then we can—"

"We'll start *now*."

"Or we can start now."

"It's been at least three or four hours since the earthquake."

"More like five, Mom."

"*Precisely*. The family must be worried *sick* about us. We must leave *now*."

"And we're off."

Lila followed as I picked my way through the rocks, stalagmites, and debris. At the bottom of the path leading up and out, I turned back to see the tunnel entrance. I couldn't find it.

"This is weird," I said. "Where's the tunnel? I can't see it even from here." Then it occurred to me. "I'll bet the Mayans brought in those rocks and piled them in front of the entrance in such a way that no one would find the tunnel. I'll bet they built this path, too." Glancing up, I shook my head. "Amazing."

"The Mayans were *exquisite* thinkers. They had *very* inventive minds."

"Now if only they'd invented Uber, but no one can think of everything." I looked up at where we needed to go. "Okay, Mom. Last lap." I reached out for a small jutting rock and pulled myself onto the ascending path, calling back, "Stay away from the edge and as close to the wall as possible."

"There is no need to state the *obvious*."

"I'm just saying."

"There's no *need* to say."

"Mom, if I didn't know better, I would say you're getting a tad snarky. But who can blame you, with your ankle and all."

"Don't be *ridiculous*. *Ladies* are never snarky. Even *with* injuries."

"Okay then."

And it was like that all the way up. As we came to the pinnacle of the path, I looked to the other side. Sure enough, here the two paths converged, the other side descending to the waterfall. Rocks wet from the constant splashing from the waterfall glistened as the noonday sun hit them.

"What *are* you looking at, Liana?" Lila's voice held more than impatience. It held fatigue and enough. Enough of pain, enough of pushing yourself, enough of everything.

"Nothing, Mom. Sorry. Let's get out of here."

With a shiver, I stepped out into sunlight. Much brighter than inside the cave, I blinked and closed my eyes for a moment. It was cooler than I thought it would be. I looked around me. We were at a higher elevation somewhere at the foot of the mountains. Meanwhile, Lila reached inside her jacket for her sat phone. She nudged me.

"*Call* Gurn and let him *know* we're all right. I'm calling Richard now."

I pulled the sat phone from my pocket and looked at it. Service, finally. Six calls from Gurn and two messages and one call from Richard. I didn't listen or read them but hit Gurn's number. He answered in the middle of the first ring, his voice sounding just short of frantic.

"Sweetheart! It's you!"

"Darling! Yes, it's me."

"Are you all right? Where are you? Did you get caught in the earthquake? Why haven't you been answering my calls?"

"I'm so sorry. We're okay, darling. We're okay," I repeated. "We were in a place where the phones didn't work. Details later. What about you? Are you all right?"

"Better, now that I've heard from you."

"Are you alone?"

"Yes, I've been walking the perimeter of the temple looking for a trace of you. Professor Bernard said he last saw you inside, heading down a hallway. So that's where I was for the last couple of hours. But when I couldn't find you. I was hoping you'd gotten out."

"We're out, but it would be great if you could come get us. Just you. No one else."

"What's going on?"

"I'll tell you when I see you. But for now, we need your help. Mom has a twisted ankle. Nothing as serious as Martín, but it's hard for her to walk. Think you can you snag us a mule?"

"They've still got a couple hanging around here. I'll find Paco—"

205

"No! No Paco. No one. Just you. And if you can't bring a mule, find that palm frond that served us so well yesterday."

"I'm not sure what's going on, but as long as you're both okay, that's all that matters." He paused. "Listen, Lee, sweetheart" — he paused, letting out a deep breath — "there's been another development."

"You mean besides the earthquake?"

"I don't know how to tell you this, so I'll just come out with it. Dr. Lancaster is dead."

I froze. "What? What happened?"

"A fer-de-lance. In her bungalow. Bit her several times last night. Apparently, she didn't even try to get out, although I'd like to know why. They found her dead a while ago. The police are on their way back."

I could hardly breathe. "Oh my God. It's escalated."

"What's escalated? Never mind. Tell me in person. Do you know where you are?"

"Not really. But I think our GPS is still locked into one another's from yesterday."

"Just a minute," he said. There was a brief pause. "Okay, I've got you. You're under three miles away. I'll borrow one of the mules — "

"Darling, if you need to tell anyone, keep it simple," I interrupted. "We got lost in the jungle, had no phone reception, and Mom hurt her ankle. Don't say anything more."

"Right now, I don't know anything more."

"True enough."

"I'll be there as soon as I can. You're sure you are all right?"

"Yes, but a little hungry. I'll bet Mom is, too. Bring us a couple of bananas." Now it was my turn to pause. "Darling, I love you. And I'm sorry I worried you. I'll try not to let it happen again."

I could feel him smiling through the phone. "I suspect it goes with the territory, but thanks for the apology. And I love you, too."

Chapter Thirty-Four

Lila had finished her conversation with Richard and was looking at me, waiting for me to finish mine with Gurn.

"Liana, your brother was *quite* relieved to hear that we are all right."

"I'll bet."

"He told me to tell you he texted *important* information to your phone, and you should look at it as *soon* as possible."

"Okay, I will. Thanks. Gurn's on his way, hopefully, with a mule for you to ride back to camp. He shouldn't be much more than an hour. Meanwhile, let's find ourselves a place to wait. One more thing, Mom. Dr. Lancaster is dead. Gurn just told me. She was bit by a fer-de-lance. They found her in her bungalow this morning."

She sucked in breath. "This is *unbelievable*."

"Yes, it is."

"Why do you have that *look* on your face?"

"What look is that, Mom?"

"Like something happened you *thought* might happen but…"

"But hoped it wouldn't? Maybe so, but I sure didn't count on this. It has a ruthlessness to it I didn't suspect. And it's made me nervous."

I glanced at the sat phone, suddenly beat. A nearby rock beckoned to me and I sat down. After letting out a huge sigh, I said, "What a morning. I should have listened to you and gone to breakfast."

"You should *always* listen to me, Liana. I'm your *mother*."

After saying this brief lecture, she gave me one of her warmest smiles. Whatever mess I'd gotten her into that day, she'd forgiven me.

"And I am grateful to you, Mom, every day, for your wisdom and strength, even though I don't always show it. Now that I've got my Mother's Day card out of the way, let me read Richard's texts. Maybe he'll clear a few things up for me." I stood up abruptly. "Mom, why don't you come to this nice rock, sit down, and rest your ankle? I'll find another spot."

"Thank you, Liana," she said, again with a smile. I smiled back while vacating the rock. I leaned against an adjacent boulder, which felt surprisingly cool, reminding me of inside the cave. But everywhere felt a bit cooler, even comfortable, not like the jungle at all. Then I remembered having read the mountainous areas have days that are usually sunny with temperatures in the seventies, while the nights become quite cool.

Putting the weather report out of my mind, I turned to my brother's text. Richard is a big believer in talking his texts into the phone rather than typing. It makes for longish missives, but that's his way.

Lee, got the info on all the names you wanted except for one. Can't find anything on Dr. Bjørn Pedersen, archaeologist, other than his degree. After that, he seems to have disappeared from sight. Send me anything you have on him. Here's an interesting fact. Carla Pérez was arrested for shoplifting five years ago. Charges dropped in lieu of therapy. Comptroller Curtis Winston does the books for Supreme Organic Guatemalan Reserve Coffee as well as El Mirador. Winston flies to Guatemala City for the coffee company once a week. Two of your archaeologists are in trouble. Dr. Josefina Sanchez's latest paper has been challenged by the International Archaeological

209

Reporter. Professor Emilien Bernard hasn't published in three years and might not get tenure. They are both in a make it or break it situation on this dig. The rest check out. For the most part, they are rich in degrees but barely eking out a living. Except for Dr. Lancaster. She's loaded. About two and a half mil in cash and bonds. Inherited it when her parents died. There's no other immediate family. Even her ex-husband is dead. That's all for now.

Well, no wonder Dr. Lancaster had devoted herself to the dig. I felt a pang of sorrow for her. No family. I couldn't even imagine such a thing. It was a lot to digest, so I mulled things over for a moment or two. I then read his second text sent forty minutes later. Not as long or as illuminating.

Lee, just heard there's been a 6.1 earthquake in Guatemala. Epicenter, El Mirador. Are you all right? Called Huckster, but he doesn't know where you are, either. Get back to us ASAP. Haven't had a chance to check on the blobs in the image you sent me. Will get to it soon. Call me.

Out of the corner of my eye, I saw Lila take off her hat and fan herself with it. We were in direct sun with no nearby shade available. It had to be close to 1:00 p.m., and the temperature was climbing. I typed a return message to my brother as fast as I could.

Richard, sorry I worried you. Will try not to let that happen again. 3 more jobs, please. 1 - See if Pedersen works for anybody else. I am forwarding a picture I took of him last night. Can you use the face recognition program you carry on about to find him? 2 - Does Lancaster have no family at all? Please double check for any far-off relative or close friend. Lastly, check if Dr. Kia Abeba was in Antigua four days ago. If so, why was she there? Never mind about the blobs. I know what they are. Thanks. After a moment I added, **Lots of love.**

When returning my phone to its assigned pocket, I found a half-eaten bag of peanuts lingering at the bottom. Cargo pants. They may make you look like a sack of potatoes, but they can be a walking convenience store.

Barely able to keep from yelling out yippee doodlebugs, I poured out half the nuts in my hand and gave the remainder of the bag to my mother. Share and share alike.

After shoving my handful into my mouth all at one time, I managed to say, "Mom, you stay here. I'm going to see if I can find where it's best to meet up with Gurn, especially if he's bringing a mule."

"*Try* not to talk with your mouth *full*, Liana."

I swallowed hard. "Sorry. Should I repeat what I said?"

"That *won't* be necessary." She nibbled on one peanut at a time. Ever the lady.

Taking stock of where we were, I looked around me and saw we came out on top of a mound. Of course, forty feet beneath us was the cave and tunnel, but there was no indication of it on the surface. Not sure which way to go, I followed a sloped trail going down and around a large rock formation.

Once I rounded the rocks, I could do little more than gasp. Rooted to the spot, I stared at the view at the end of the trail. It was a small valley hidden by surrounding hills and basking in the sun. Almost as if lost in time, it seemed like Guatemala's version of Shangri-la. But most importantly, here was the real inspiration for the mural created so long ago in the king's tomb. And maybe why the mural had been blackened out.

To make sure, I pulled out my phone and found the image. Yup. In the background and to my left were the double-peaked mountains. To the right was a winding river. And in between were evenly spaced, well-groomed trees. Hanging on most of the trees were beautiful flowers, many in pastel colors but a few in a deep, rich burgundy. Exactly like in the mural. That made this idyllic spot thousands of years old.

I don't know how long I stood transfixed, trying to absorb the scene. I only came out of it when I heard Lila come up behind me. But I still couldn't move.

"Liana," she whispered, her voice containing a similar awe she'd shared in the cavern, "isn't that the *same* scene as the *mural* in the king's chamber?"

"Yes."

"And what you've been calling *blobs* are *flowers*, aren't they?"

"That's right, Mom."

"Only there doesn't *appear* to be as *many* of them as we saw in the *mural*."

"No there doesn't. Shhh!"

Three men appeared out of nowhere from in between the trees. I didn't recognize them as any of the workers at camp. These men were older, middle-aged. They wore gloves, and each carried a wooden box.

"Come on," I whispered. "I don't want them to see us."

I grabbed Lila by the hand and helped her back up the path to behind the cluster of rocks. We returned near the mouth of the cave. I tried to think of my next move.

"Mom, let's head down the other side of the mound to the edge of the jungle."

"You mean *east*?" She looked down at the small compass clipped to her lapel.

"You certainly get your money's worth out of that compass, Mom. East it is. We need to be far enough away from what we've just witnessed and to be lower. Gurn will find us. He's locked on to our coordinates."

This descending path was littered with rocks and uneven in many places. It was arduous helping Lila, even though it wasn't far nor a very steep grade.

212

As we slowly made our way down, Lila was thoughtful. "Liana, you don't seem to be *surprised* by what we just saw. Am I being *dense*? I have no *idea* what those men with the boxes were doing. Yet it seems to make *sense* to you."

"Yes, I'm afraid it does, Mom."

Chapter Thirty-Five

"How is she doing, Dr. Abeba?" I turned and looked at my mother resting on a cot in the first-aid tent. Dr. Abeba didn't answer but went to the other side of the room.

I followed her. "Doctor?"

While returning unused gauze and other paraphernalia to a cabinet, she said, "It is merely a mild sprain. She should return to normal in a few days." The doctor didn't or wouldn't look at me.

"I've never known my mother to be normal at anytime," I joked. "If this experience is going to normalize her, how refreshing."

The doctor paused, turned, and gave me a cold, blank stare. I rushed on.

"Doctor, I don't suppose you have a copy of Alejandro Rios's autopsy report? I sure would love to know the exact cause of death."

Her answer was brittle. "I haven't received anything from the medical examiner, but when I do, I will not be sharing details with you, Ms. Alvarez. It is not customary to share information of that nature with anyone outside of the authorities and family members. You are neither, correct?"

"No, I'm not. I just —"

"I thought not," she interrupted, closing the cabinet door with a clipped gesture, much as her words had been with me. Not done yet, she went on, "You are simply looking for a thrill."

"A thrill?" I was shocked by the statement.

"I've met people like you before. People who like to know the titillating details of other's lives. I will not be a party to that."

"Listen, I don't know the people you're hanging out with, but I'm trying to investigate a man's death. I get my titillation from other things," I added.

"I understand Alejandro's parents are dead and he was an only child. He had an uncle in Guatemala City. If that uncle should get in touch with me and ask for details, as the attending physician I will share them with him. Not you. I have been told about you."

I was thunderstruck. "What have you been told about me?"

"I have work to do. There will be no further discussion about this."

She turned and walked toward the small lab room. While crossing the room, she continued talking to me over her shoulder.

"Alfredo will return shortly with a set of crutches for your mother to use during her confinement and some ice packets. She should stay off her foot as much as possible: keep it iced, and elevated."

I didn't take to being dismissed so easily. "Can you at least tell me if you know what poison was on the blow dart shot at my husband? Surely, I am entitled to that information."

She wheeled around and looked at me with unhidden disgust. "According to forensics, the blow dart was dipped in a small amount of curare, derived from the Chondrodendron tomentosum plant. It wasn't enough to kill a human being but enough to paralyze for several minutes. Curare is a common poison used by the Indigenous people to hunt small game."

"So, it wasn't poison from a yellow dart frog?"

215

"As I said, no. I will answer no more questions. Good day."

Dr. Abeba exited into her lab. I stood for a moment letting what happened sink in. Dr. Abeba did everything but call me vermin and spit on me, while reciting the Hippocratic Oath. Most annoying.

Chapter Thirty-Six

Lila was asleep on her cot. I was laying in Gurn's arms on his cot and glad to be there. The cot was only meant for one, but after my episode under Carla Pérez's, I knew it could support two. Besides, I needed a good cuddle.

Freshly showered, the morning's escapade had been washed from my body but not my soul. Whoops! Another touch of William Somerset Maugham. Time to stop reading his books.

But it was the closest I'd come in a long time to losing my life. And I'd dragged my mother in on it. Bad PI, bad.

Once we got back to camp, I thought we'd be fending off a barrage of questions from everyone. Not so. Between Dr. Lancaster's death and the earthquake, no one had any interest in our whereabouts. Most didn't even know we were missing.

Sergeant Juárez and several officers arrived at camp shortly before we returned. Fortunately for me, he was busy interviewing the masses. He sent a message saying we were scheduled to see him later in the day. I did not look forward to having more stupid, Mickey Mouse questions thrown at me again. But I decided to deal with it when it happened.

So, in that moment, I snuggled into Gurn's chest and felt myself about to drop off. But I had a thought and my eyes opened wide.

"Gurn, darling," I whispered, careful not to disturb Lila, "who takes over now that Dr. Lancaster is no longer with us?"

"I've been told it's Benjamin Storrs, if only temporarily," he whispered back. "He's the project administrator, whatever that is."

"I thought it was him. According to Wikipedia, the project administrator has the task of dividing over a hundred people into a dozen different excavation site and campsite rotas."

"What's a rota?"

"A list showing when each of a number of people has to do a particular job. I looked it up."

"And memorized it. I love your eidetic memory."

"It can come in handy. But to continue, the project administrator is also the repository for all participant information such as indemnity forms, registration forms, health forms, and so forth. According to song and legend, the project administrator tends to know where everything is and is the backbone of the excavation."

"In other words, Bennie Storrs knows where the bodies are buried, figuratively and literally."

"And is only answerable to the project manager."

"The now dearly departed Dr. Lancaster."

"Bingo. Makes one think, doesn't it, darling? Speaking of Dr. Lancaster, unlike the tents, isn't her bungalow a permanent structure, built on a two-step-high foundation?"

"Yes, it is, sweetheart."

"So how did that fer-de-lance get up the steps and then inside the bungalow?"

"That's what I was wondering."

I tilted my head back looking into his face. "Hmmm. And you mentioned something about her being bitten three times?"

"That's what Dr. Abeba says."

"Why didn't she scream her head off after being bit the first time? Her bungalow is close to the tents. Everyone would have heard her if she had."

"That's what I was wondering."

"Who found her?"

"Her assistant, Felicity Adler. When Lancaster didn't turn up for the morning meeting, Adler went to her bungalow. The earthquake put everyone on edge, so after knocking and getting no answer, Adler barged right in. She found Lancaster dead on the sofa, saw the snake, and fled. Adler, by the way, did scream her head off. Everyone who heard her came running. I, unfortunately, wasn't one of them. I was taking a shower." He looked down and kissed me on the nose. "What does your detective mind say about all this?"

"It says to check out Lancaster's bungalow."

"Let's go," he said in a stage whisper, jumping off the cot.

He was so energetic about it, I was thrown off-balance and nearly landed on the floor. Sitting up, I picked up one of my boots and shook it out.

"Well, I can see you didn't need much convincing," I also said in a stage whisper. "Boy, I sure hope this trip doesn't take out of me what it's taken out of my boots. Just look at them."

"A good cleaning will fix that. But back to Dr. Lancaster. While I wasn't on the scene, I think her death is suspicious."

"And convenient for a lot of people," I said, lacing up a boot.

Gurn sat down beside me. I reached down for one of his boots and handed it to him. Shaking it out as well, he said, "If what you told me on the trip back is true —"

"I'll be surprised if it isn't. Shhh."

I put my finger to my lips when I saw Lila stir. We both stopped talking. Gurn continued to lace up his boots in silence. I stood and jotted a short note to my mother with the vague message we were going for a walk. I wasn't sure she'd wake up before we got back, but I didn't want to take any chances. I'd already gone over the limit in my communication skills, or lack of them, with my entire family. At least for the day.

We exited the tent as quietly as possible and didn't pass one single soul on our way to Lancaster's bungalow. I suspected people were laying low. Someone being bitten by a fer-de-lance in their own humble abode can give one the willies. If I wasn't a nosy sleuth who never minded her own business, I'd be lying low myself.

I ran up the steps of the bungalow and tried the door. Locked. Rats. Did that mean someone was inside? I knocked on the door, then put my ear to it. Not a sound. I rattled the door.

"It doesn't sound like anyone's in there, darling," I said.

Gurn went to a nearby window and peered inside. "It doesn't look like anyone's in there, either. And for the record, it looks like they've removed the body."

"Well, there's a relief. Then why don't we —"

"*Buenos tardes,* señora, señor."

We turned to see Sergeant Juárez coming up the graveled path followed by two police officers, one male and one female. Being a male-dominated culture, it surprised me to see a Guatemalan policewoman, even though she was bigger than the two men and looked like she could take a puma down.

I returned my focus back on Juárez. "Uh… hi," I said. "We were just—" I stopped midsentence. The rest of the sentence would have been "breaking in."

220

Chapter Thirty-Seven

"Please allow me, señora, to give you access to Dr. Lancaster's bungalow," Sergeant Juárez said. His tone was cordial and friendly, but he remained at the bottom on the steps. "I had to make certain no one else would disturb anything. Agenté López has been looking out for you and was told to notify me when you showed up at the bungalow."

"Agenté López?"

"Yes, she is most efficient."

"I see. Where is Dr. Lancaster's body? We don't see it inside."

"No, no. It has already arrived at the morgue. Two of my men escorted it there about an hour ago. Meanwhile, I have protected this bungalow from any intruders by having the door locked from the inside," Juárez said.

He turned to one of his male agentés. Juárez told him in Spanish to go around the back, crawl in through the unlocked window, and open the door. The officer did so, while Agenté López stood at the base of the stairs with her hand on her baton. She definitely looked efficient, if not a little threatening.

Juárez came up the two steps to the small landing and stood by my side. "I am glad to see you, Señora Alvarez. I was about to seek you out."

"You were?"

"Si." He turned to Gurn. "You do not mind, señor, if I call upon the talented mind of your wife in this situation?"

"Not at all," Gurn said graciously. "I often call upon her talented mind."

"She is not only trained—"

"But has a gift for putting seemingly unrelated facts together and making sense of them," Gurn completed the sentence.

"This is what I have come to understand." Juárez smiled at Gurn.

"Gentlemen," I said, "you do know I can hear you?"

A noise from inside the bungalow prevented either from replying. The door opened, and the young agenté moved aside to let us enter. We stepped into a square, open space, probably around twenty-five by twenty-five feet.

The kitchen, dining room, living room, and bedroom areas were sectioned off, but all abutted one another. Against one wall was a small room, closed off by a door. Probably the bathroom. On all four sides there was at least one window, so the room had a bright, airy look to it.

But it was surprisingly messy. Clothes and papers were tossed everywhere, and a few drawers were open. I turned to Juárez.

"Did your people do this?"

He shook his head. "No, we have done nothing but seal off the room."

Always one to get to the heart of things, Gurn asked, "Where's the snake?"

"Hacked to pieces," Juárez said. "It was sunning itself by the window when Dr. Lancaster's assistant came into the room. Several men came in soon after with machetes." He crossed to a nearby window and pointed. "You can still see the blood of the animal."

Gurn had yet to move from the front door. Neither had I. I looked around me.

222

"And there was only the one? Snake, I mean." I wasn't venturing inside until I knew for sure.

"Si. We did a thorough search of the bungalow. There were no other snakes."

Juárez smiled at me. I didn't smile back.

"Other than the snake, did any of the hackers touch anything in the room?"

"Not that I know of," Juárez said. "At least, they did not admit so to me. They said once they killed the snake, they left and called us."

"That doesn't mean that someone wasn't in here after the snake was killed," I said. "How long did it take you to arrive once you were called?"

"A little over an hour, señora. We came immediately."

"But still, it was an hour before you took the body away and locked the door. Not to mention that afterward, if someone wanted to, they could have crawled in the window as your man did."

"That is true," he acknowledged. "But what does that mean?"

"It means we can't be sure the crime scene hasn't been messed with." A cluster of papers laying on the floor caught my eye. I looked at the sergeant and gestured to them. "May I?"

"Of course." In a sweeping gesture, he stepped aside.

I whipped on my rubber gloves, went to the papers, bent down, and picked up several. A fast look told me what they were.

"Well, here could be our answer as to why Dr. Lancaster was dragging her heels about getting a crew in to shore up the walls of the king's tomb."

223

Gurn walked over to me but didn't reach out for the papers. I held one up for him to see. The sergeant stayed where he was. He seemed to be studying me.

"It looks like a thesis," Gurn said. "But she should have been long done with her thesis on archaeology."

"I think it's more of an academic paper." I read aloud, "*The Discovery of King B'alaj Chan K'inich's Tomb, One of the Greatest Finds of the Twenty-First Century*, by Dr. Joan Lancaster. This paper appears to document the find as hers and hers alone. Where's her computer?" I looked around me and, still holding the papers, crossed to a laptop and small printer on a desk in a corner. "The file is probably on here."

I studied the papers in my hand again. "Look at this. In the heading on each page is the name, Society of Latin American Archaeology."

Juárez asked, "What is this society of whatever you said?"

"Society of Latin American Archaeology. I'm not sure what it is, though. Why don't we look it up?"

"Allow me." Gurn pulled out his sat phone and did a search while Juárez and I waited. After a few strokes, Gurn began to read.

"The *Society of Latin American Archaeology* is a quarterly journal that publishes original papers on the archaeology, ethnohistory, and art history of Latin America, Caribbean, and all regions in the continental New World that are south of the current U.S.-Mexico border."

"Bingo," I exclaimed.

"There's more," he said, and continued reading. "Once accepted by the committee, the journal publishes articles, reports, and comments in method and theory, field research, and analysis using the Latin American database as a foundation for scientific study and research."

Realizing the significance of what he'd read, Gurn looked at me. "Does that mean she was writing this paper hoping to prove the king's tomb was her find before the big reveal was made public?"

"I guess she could make a claim for it," I said. "It happened on her watch, but from what JJ says, it was predominantly Bennie's find, and he should at least share in the glory."

"Dr. Lancaster says she made a discovery?" Juárez stopped talking and just stared at me.

"I think so. It certainly looks like she wanted this paper in and published beforehand so her name would be synonymous with the find."

"Meaning she would get all the credit," Juárez said, comprehending the academic mind.

"Exactly," I said. "If anyone else on the dig knew about this, especially Dr. Storrs, it might be a crackerjack reason to want her dead."

"You astonish me, Señora Alvarez," Juárez said. "I did not even think to look at those papers."

"Well, don't lose heart, Sergeant. I've been doing this type of thing a lot longer than you. But you must have learned other things, right? Are you willing to share?"

He smiled and crossed to the small, square table with its four wood chairs sitting around it. "I will tell you everything I know. But first, señora, let us sit down and talk. You, too, señor."

"We need to be careful not to touch anything else," I said, setting the papers in their original position on the floor and removing my gloves. "Not until your team can go through and check it out. This is a crime scene… of sorts."

Juárez smiled at us. "I do not know if charges can be brought against a snake. And it is already dead. Anyway, come. Sit. Please."

I hesitated. I can be like a dog with a bone when it comes to the integrity of my work. "Sergeant Juárez, I don't want to contaminate —"

"This will be my responsibility," the sergeant interrupted with more authority than he'd shown before. Then he relaxed and became more cordial. "Please. You will sit."

We crossed to the table. I reluctantly pulled out a chair and sat. Gurn did the same. Sergeant Juárez was the last to sit, and when he did, his attitude was one of a host.

"I have been thinking about you, señora, since I met you yesterday. And what you do for a living. Tell me why you believe this is a crime scene." He emphasized the word "why," then looked at me intently.

"Let me ask you this, Sergeant Juárez," I said. "How else do you think the snake could get into this room? Someone had to have brought it in."

He shrugged. "They have been known to inhabit human structures."

"That would be ground-level structures." Gurn entered into the conversation. "Such as barns and homes with no elevated foundation. This bungalow is a good thirty-six inches off the ground. I am assuming the fer-de-lance was an adult?" Juárez nodded. "They tend to lose the ability to climb when they mature."

"I did not know that," Juárez admitted.

"From what Gurn tells me," I said, "it is unlikely it came in under its own steam. But let's table that for the moment. What did you want to talk to me about?"

226

Juárez hesitated, then stared down at his folded hands on the table. He suddenly looked young and vulnerable, like not much more than a kid. "My father is not happy with me."

"That would be the capitán," Gurn said.

Juárez nodded, still looking down. "He has always expected me to follow in his footsteps. Become a respected member of the Policia Nacional Civil."

"Not to be rude," I said, "but I don't know if you have a leaning for this sort of thing."

He looked up at me with open, honest eyes. "I do not."

"How did you become a sergeant, then?"

"I take exams well. But that does not mean I can do it in real life. My father, he is a good policeman. But the Policia Nacional Civil has not always had a good reputation. He is trying to change that. When you told me the name of your detective agency, I knew it sounded familiar. So, I called my father last night and asked him about it. He told me he met Roberto Alvarez years ago. They worked together on a drug-trafficking case involving Guatemala and the States. They became friends. They even have the same first name, Roberto."

"Your father knew Dad?"

"Si. Even though he was not a policeman but a private detective, they found they had much in common. I understand he is no longer with us, your father, for which I am sincerely sorry."

The wound that never heals. "Yes, four years now."

"They both believed *honor sobre todo*."

My eyes grew misty. "Honor Above All. My family motto. How did you know that?"

"Because it is my family's motto, too. Honor Above All," Hector repeated in English. "We may have more in common than you think, Señora Alvarez. At least, that is my hope."

227

Chapter Thirty-Eight

"I had no idea we shared some sort of history."

My voice was soft and almost childlike. I felt ten years old again.

"I did not realize this myself, until we talked yesterday. You are lucky." Juárez's tone was wistful. "You wanted to follow in your father's footsteps. But as for me... " His voice dropped off.

"That's not what you want."

"No." He paused, possibly searching for the right words. He shrugged, then said simply, "I do not like this work. I do not like guns. I do not like knowing that every day I may get shot or not come home. Maria, my wife, she does not like it, either."

"Well, life is short," I commented, becoming an adult again. "You should do what you want with your life. At least, that's what I think."

"Until now, it did not matter so much. I wanted to make my father happy. But my father-in-law has an auto repair shop in Flores," Juárez said. "He wants me to come into the business with him. I like cars. Always, I have worked on cars. It is through my father-in-law I meet Maria when I worked for him. She is carrying our first child."

He stopped talking and looked down again. I picked up the conversation.

"What you're saying is, other things are more important now. More important than disappointing your father."

He looked down again at his hands and emitted a big sigh. "At the fixing of cars, I am good. I understand cars. But this. I do not know even where to begin." He hesitated, then turned to Gurn. "I do not mean to be disrespectful of you, señor. But the gift you spoke of earlier is what I seek. The señora's gift."

"No disrespect taken." Gurn leaned back in his chair. "She's the best investigator I know. No one appreciates her gifts more than me."

"Why, thank you, gentlemen," I said. "But as I'm feeling a little bit like a present from Macy's, let's drop the gift analogy." Both men laughed. I turned to the young sergeant. "Back to you. What specifically do you want of me?"

He took a deep breath, hesitated for a moment, then blurted out, "I want you to find out what is going on in this camp. There is something, but I cannot place it. On the phone, my father also says the snake should not have been in the room, for me to find out what happened. I do not know how to do this. But you..." He paused and looked into my face. "You do. Unlike me, you are good at this."

"Let me get this straight. Sergeant Juárez, you are asking for my help?"

"Yes, señora, and please call me Hector."

"You mean because you're bearing your soul to me? In that case, call me Lee."

He gave off a small, embarrassed giggle. "Lee, thank you. Earlier you used the words, crime scene. That means you believe a crime has been committed. As does my father."

"I do. In fact, several crimes have been committed and are being committed right now at this camp. The most serious is murder. And I believe what took place in this bungalow last night is very likely murder. Tell me, though, if your father also believes something is rotten in Denmark, why doesn't he come here and take charge of the investigation himself?"

230

"He would if he could, but he is in Guatemala City at a yearly conference that awards government funding for the war on drugs. This year, he says the chances are very good he will get one, but he must be there in person. He also says it is imperative this crime be solved as soon as possible. He does not want the trail to become cold."

"And you're caught in the middle," I said.

"Believe me, what he is doing is as important. Like so many other municipalities, Flores is much underfunded. We need up-to-date equipment, more personnel for this war on drugs. Many innocent people die yearly from gangs and drug wars. But there is little money for the fight. My father has not had a raise in years."

"I'll bet your mother doesn't like that," I commented.

"My mother is no longer with us, Lee. She passed away ten years ago when I was fifteen."

Gurn and I muttered our condolences, but Hector talked over our words.

"Since then, my father has devoted himself to making life safer for everyone. Not just in Flores, but in all Guatemala."

"He sounds like a good guy." A thought occurred to me. "Whoops! There's a fatal flaw in your logic, Hector. If *I* solve these crimes but *you* take the credit for it, your father will think you *are* good at it. What are you going to do, *then*?"

I'd emphasized chosen words just like Lila does, and I felt my stomach curdle. I'd have to think about that later. And take some Tums.

His eyebrows shot up, and his mouth dropped open. "But I did not intend for my father to think I solved these crimes. Quite the contrary. I want him to know the truth. You will be unconcealed, out in the open. I will do whatever you say. He will know that. Then he will realize..."

Again, he paused. Once again, I picked up the conversation.

"He will realize a policeman's life is not for you. And maybe he will let you go your own way."

"I have already told him of meeting you. And of your gif… uh… abilities. He is an accepting man, a fair man." He paused and showed me another embarrassed smile. "*Perdoname*, but as to the official version, in order for him to save face, it may have to be written that I did solve it."

"Bureaucracy is still bureaucracy. No need to ask for forgiveness," I said. "I don't want the credit. And it's probably a good idea if everyone thinks I am helping the police rather than taking over. But do I have your clout behind me?"

"You will have it fully. This I can promise."

I took a deep breath and pretended I hadn't made the decision to solve this mystery long before our little chitchat. With a magnanimous gesture, I said, "Okay, Hector, I'll do it."

"Thank you!" A look of relief flooded his face. "You will be doing me a great service. You will be helping me change my life."

I leaned in. "In that case, here are my terms: I want you to turn over every bit of information you have so far. Furthermore, I want all your facilities available to me. In short, your entire department has to be at my disposal. No questions asked. Are you agreeable?"

"Si."

"Good. I'll get you a list of things I need to know. Here's something right off the bat. I want a toxicology report done on Dr. Lancaster. I want it run ASAP. And I have Alejandro Rios' knapsack hidden in our tent. It has the word 'uayeb' written on it, supposedly in blood. If I give it to you, can you have the blood analyzed to see if it's human or not? Also, ASAP?"

"Si. Whatever you need. Where is it?"

"Hidden under the blanket on my bed."

"I will send one of my people for it right away."

He pulled out his phone and began texting. "I am sending a message to the *médico forense* in Flores for the urgent need for the toxicology report on Dr. Lancaster. Anything else?"

"Yes, back to Alejandro Rios. Did you get the autopsy report back on him yet?"

"Si. A copy was sent to my phone about an hour ago. I have not looked at it yet."

Shocked at his admission, I let out a soft laugh. "I must admit you are not so good at this sort of stuff. But on the plus side, you're very cooperative."

Hector blushed. After a quick search for the document, he turned his phone around to face me.

I took the phone from him, enlarged the document, and began to read. I was dumbfounded.

"I don't believe it! Alejandro had familial hypertrophic cardiomyopathy."

"What is that?" Gurn said, then stared at me.

Hector also had a perplexed look on his face.

"According to the pathologist or *médico forense's* report," I said, reading from the phone, "Familial hypertrophic cardio-myopathy is an inherited heart condition that can thicken part or all of the heart muscle. In extreme cases, it can even cause sudden death. The doctor wrote that, given the condition of Alejandro's heart, the combination of being chased and the anxiety level brought on by it is what killed him. According to this, even though Alejandro was a young man, he could have died at any time from anything. He was virtually a walking dead man."

"So, he wasn't poisoned by a dart," Gurn said.

"And the snake could have come into this room by itself," Hector said with a sigh. "Even though you say it was unlikely. This is why I do not see where any crimes have been committed."

"Hector, Hector, Hector," I said, tsk-tsking my disapproval each time I uttered his name. "Let's deal with just the two deaths. Even if Alejandro died of natural causes, who dressed him up as a fourteenth-century Mayan warrior? And why? Who put the yellow dart frog in his mouth? And why? Who put a deadly snake in Dr. Lancaster's bungalow? Why trash her place? And why kill her?"

"You don't think Dr. Lancaster was simply not a neat person?" Hector looked around him.

"There's clean underwear lying on the floor, Hector, some of it still folded," I said. "No, someone was looking for something. And once they found it, she had to die."

Chapter Thirty-Nine

The three of us, Gurn, Hector, and I, sat for a moment reflecting on my last statement. It sounded impressive, but I needed more time to back up what I knew to be true. Finally, the silence and non-activity got to me.

"Well, all will be made clear in the fullness of time," I said, rising to my feet.

"It will?" Hector stared at me in wonder.

"Let's just say, that's the plan. Right now, I'm in search mode. So, let's get to it. Where was Dr. Lancaster found?"

Hector rose and crossed to the small living room area. "Here. On the sofa."

I followed him to the sofa. Pillows and a small throw blanket were strewn around. "She was here?"

"Si."

"Did you take any pictures of the body before you moved it?"

"No, we thought it was merely an unfortunate accident. I did not think—"

"In that case," I interrupted, "You'll have to tell me what she looked like."

"Swollen."

"What else?"

"What do you mean?"

"How was she dressed? What was the position of the body? Was there any sign of a struggle? Stuff like that."

"Of course! Apologies. Let me think."

"All righty," I muttered.

He closed his eyes and thought. "She was laying on the sofa on her back. One leg dangled on the floor, the leg that was bitten. And she was dressed in one of those frilly, see-through nightgowns."

"Really? Dr. Lancaster?" I tried to contain my surprise. "How was her hair?"

"Her hair? What do you mean, her hair?"

"Was it fixed up? Like she was expecting somebody? Or messy, like she had finished with somebody?" I waggled my eyebrows in a suggestive manner.

"Ooooh," he said, getting into the spirit of the thing. "It was neat and combed, just so. And she was wearing perfume. A lot of it."

"Yeah, I can still smell it. And I can smell something else, too. A cigar."

Turning to the coffee table, I saw it had been wiped clean. I moved on to the bijou kitchen.

"She had company right before she died. There are two clean snifter glasses and an ashtray here on the drainboard. The other dishes are in the cupboard. These three must have been washed at the end of the evening. Maybe after she was dead or at least, incapacitated."

"You mean, by the killer?" Hector's tone was all agog.

"Possibly. Why don't you take these three items and see if there are any fingerprints? I doubt it. Everybody watches *CSI*, but it doesn't hurt to check. But here's something promising. Liquid spilled by the sink that wasn't wiped up. Look."

Both men came over as instructed. They stood on either side of me, watching. I leaned down and took a sniff.

"Smells like brandy. Maybe from that."

I pointed to the top shelf of the cupboard. A bottle of Remy Martin cognac looked back at me.

"We should dust that bottle for prints, too."

Hector nodded.

I looked around me. "I wonder where she kept the trash?"

"Check under the sink," Gurn said.

"Good idea." I opened the door to the cabinet beneath the minuscule sink and spied a small, black plastic trash can. Removing the lid, I rooted around inside.

"My, my, my, my, my. Ashes." I took another sniff. "Cigar ashes. Sometimes a PI's best friend is her nose."

Gurn took the trash can from me and continued rooting. "Here's a cigar band. Cohiba Robusto. One of Cuba's finest."

"And sometimes a PI's best friend is her hubby." I flashed Gurn a grateful smile, then turned to Hector. "Hmmm. At least two or three men that I know of smoke cigars in camp. Do you have any idea who her company might have been last night?"

He shook his head.

"Have you asked anyone about her having visitors last night?"

He shook his head.

"Have you done... anything? Let me rephrase that. What have you done so far?"

He shook his head, smiled, then spread his arms open wide. "I apologize, but I had hoped that you—"

He broke off and looked at me with a sheepish grin. I grinned back.

"That's quite all right. Let's see what else is in this trash can."

I emptied the rest of the contents on the table. Several used paper napkins and a balled-up, blue paper tumbled out. I smoothed the blue paper out as best I could and saw it was of a heavier grade and legal sized. One end was torn. Something had been ripped off.

"Well, lookee here. You don't need to be a mental giant to figure out this probably had a legal document of some sort stapled to it." I did some fast thinking. "Hector, I don't want anyone to leave this camp, no matter what. And if anyone tries to leave, let me know right away."

An alarmed expression came to Hector's face. "A man named Curtis Winston has asked permission to fly to Guatemala City. He says he goes once a week to take care of a coffee company's books. He is the comp—"

"Comptroller," I interrupted. "Yes, I know. When is he scheduled to leave?"

Hector looked at me. "Tomorrow morning."

"Don't say anything to him now. Let him think he's going as scheduled. But keep a watch on his tent, and when he tries to leave, stop him. Then let me know."

Hector asked, "You think Curtis Winston had something to do with her death?"

"Dr. Lancaster's? No, no. But he has a lot to do with what's been going on around here. In fact, you could almost call him pivotal."

238

Chapter Forty

It was a night of a lot of thinking and little sleeping. Before the sun rose, I was up and did a barre. Very centering. I may have been sleep deprived, but I was ready to take on the world.

Gurn by my side, we were drinking coffee standing outside the cafeteria watching the sunrise on the temple. Breathtaking. I'll bet you never tire of the view.

The phone rang, and it was Hector. The comptroller was about to depart any minute. Time to rendezvous. Five minutes later we caught up with Curtis Winston as he was exiting his tent. He was dressed in jeans and a red-white-and-black-striped polo shirt, both designer labels. Secured on his back was a large knapsack filled to capacity. An Australian bush hat completed his ensemble.

He seemed more than a little surprised to see Gurn and me, not to mention our entourage of police. But he recovered well and feigned a smile.

"Er… hello. I'm not sure what you want, but I'm in a hurry. I have a plane to catch in Flores for Guatemala City. And I first have to get to the helicopter, which should be arriving…"

He broke off and looked around him. He was surrounded on all sides. I stood in front, staring into his face.

Curtis Winston looked back with a slightly haunted look, then swallowed hard. "What's going on?"

"Your trip to Guatemala City is going to be delayed for a while," I said.

"Possibly a long while," Gurn put in, standing tall beside me.

Turning to Hector, I kept my tone businesslike and official. "Isn't that so, Sergeant Juárez?"

"Si, Señora Alvarez," he returned in kind. Hector was fast on the uptake. He glared at Winston. "You will come with us, if you please."

"Take his knapsack and his cell phone," I said to Hector on the sly. "Be sure he can't communicate with anyone."

Wordless, he grabbed Curtis's knapsack from him. Even though Hector had no idea what was going on, he did a surprisingly good job of pretending he did.

"Hey!" Curtis protested.

"Be quiet, you," Hector said. "Find his cell phone," Hector ordered of his subordinates. He gestured for his two agentés to go to each side of Curtis, which they did. Obeying, they searched his jacket and removed his phone.

"Hey!" Curtis said again, trying to move away. Each officer firmly locked arms with him. Agenté López went so far as to remove her baton from her belt and hold it in the air in an ominous manner. The two looked at Hector for further instructions.

Hector leaned into me and whispered. "Where are we going with Señor Winston, Lee?"

I said under my breath, "Take him to the conference tent and hold him there."

"Take him to the conference tent and hold him there," Hector repeated to his agentés in a much louder voice.

They marched Curtis away. I watched for a moment, pulled out a piece of paper, then turned to Hector again.

240

"Hector, collect the people on this list and take them there as well. You'll find most of them at breakfast. It's six a.m. now, a little too early for them to be starting the day's work."

I handed him the same list of names I'd given to Richard two days before. He gave the list a quick once-over, then said, "Si, Lee. Anything else?"

"Yes, when you have everyone assembled in the conference room, check their trash cans for a used laundry bag. They're made out of muslin or canvas, about so big, and have a drawstring." I demonstrated the size with hand gestures.

"Anything else?"

"Yes, look for anything odd or out of place in their rooms. If you don't want to remove it, just make a note and tell me what it is. But what I do want is a metal box from under Carla Pérez's cot. Try to take it without her knowing and bring it with you. Let's meet in the conference tent at seven thirty."

Hector smiled at me. "All will be as you wish. I have some answers back from forensics. They worked all night. I will send what I have to your phone."

"Thank you, Hector. It sounds like you've got a good team. Remember, don't let Curtis go into his knapsack. Not for anything. Keep it in a safe place. And don't let him speak to anyone, not in person and not on the phone. I don't want him alerting someone, understand?"

He nodded and smiled again. "And you will tell me why I am doing all of this, later? Or is this something that will become clear in the fullness of time?"

I returned his smile. "One of the two."

He gave me a shake of his head and a small laugh. I watched him leave.

Gurn asked, "What can I do, love?"

241

"Help me find Paco. I have no idea where he is, and I need to talk to him fast."

"Why don't you beep him?"

"You mean he has a beeper?"

"You didn't know that?"

"Nobody tells me anything," I said.

"So you keep saying, and yet you seem to know more than anybody else about what's going on around here. Care to enlighten me?"

"Of course I will, darling. When we have more time and I get it all sorted out in my head. How do I reach his beeper?"

"JJ gave me the number yesterday." He pulled out his phone and did a quick search. "Here it is, seven-eight-five-one-one. Just put in that number, and when you hear two beeps, text in a short message. She says he usually gets back to you in less than ten minutes." I did as instructed, while Gurn watched me intently. "What else do you need?"

"From you? Just your undying love." I blew him a kiss.

"You got it. What else?"

"Why don't you see if Lila's awake yet and if so, bring her up to date. Then give Richard a fast call and see what he found out about Pedersen, or at least, try to light a fire under him. I need those answers."

With a nod of his head, he started for our tent. My voice stopped him.

"Oh yes. Then meet me at the four-thousand-year-old eatery. I'm hoping to have a chat there with Paco before the showdown in the conference tent."

"It promises to be one big party," Gurn said with a chortle. Again, he turned to leave.

"Not for some people," I called out. "It's going to be one big jail sentence. One last thing, darling. Bring your gun. You never know."

His demeanor changed from playful to sober. "I have it on me. And you, sweetheart?"

"Same here," I said.

"Then I'll meet you at the eatery, with or without Lila," Gurn said, and was gone.

I muttered to myself, "You know, I kinda like this barking-orders thing. It's good to be queen."

Chapter Forty-One

"Thank you for meeting me, Paco, on such short notice. I appreciate it."

Gurn had been right. Barely ten minutes had passed since I'd sent the message and here Paco was.

I sat on one of the chair-high stones in front of the faded eatery signs. The goat, pig, and lamb stared down at me. Paco, hat in hand, stared down at me. His monkey stared down at me.

Afortunado also clung on to Paco's neck tighter than I'd seen him do. It seemed as if he were comforting the man. Paco did appear to be nervous. Very unlike the man, but animals can tell that sort of thing and react to it.

My take on Paco was he had one foot in two different worlds at all times and, for the most part, was comfortable with it. But I think he knew instinctively a rumble was coming.

"What is it you need, Señora Lee?"

"Sit down, won't you? Nobody can hear anything we say here, Paco. It's completely private."

I gestured to another chair-high stone opposite me. He sat, his body rigid. Staring at me, nervous fingers turned his hat around and around by the brim.

"I didn't know Alfredo was your son." I smiled before going on. "And he plans to be a doctor. You must be immensely proud."

244

Paco relaxed an infinitesimal amount. "Yes, he is a good boy, a smart boy. But you did not call me here to talk about my son."

"No, I didn't." I shook my head and leaned forward. "You and I, Paco, we're going to talk a few truths now. It's time."

He thought about my words, stopped working his hat, and nodded. I knew from the start here was a pragmatic man.

"You were born and raised in El Mirador. That's where your family is. And friends. But your livelihood comes from this job and has for some time. When this dig is finished, and the camp is disbanded, you might stay on in some capacity when it becomes a tourist site. But you might go back to living your old life. That's one of the reasons why I believe you have, and understandably so, developed a live-and-let-live attitude toward both sides."

He said nothing but offered a slight smile and a nod of the head.

"But there's been a development, a problem. And one I think you can identify with as you, too, have a son on the brink of manhood."

His smile vanished, and he gave me a look that neither agreed nor disagreed with me. Again, saying nothing, he waited. Afortunado began to chatter.

"Shhhh!" Paco said to him, his tone sharp. Then he stroked his pet reassuringly on the head. Afortunado settled down. Paco turned to face me again.

My heart thudded against my rib cage. I knew if I didn't word things right, the one person who could help might decide not to do so. I fought back my own set of nerves and took a deep breath, ready to go on.

Then I saw Gurn fast approaching and alone. Where Lila was I didn't know, but I raised my hand ever so slightly in a stay-back gesture. He got the message and paused. Backing

245

up, he went behind an ancient stone statue of a Mayan god standing under the protection of a recently constructed wood roof. The new protecting the old. As it should be.

Determined, I went on. "The two twins, Geraldo and Jorje, are in trouble. In about an hour the police and the muckety-mucks who run this place are going to convene in the conference tent. Accusations are going to be hurled. Heads will roll. Geraldo and Jorje's part in recent events is going to come out. Unless they are there to explain themselves, to tell us who the persons are really to blame, they just might go to jail."

"Jail! They did something so terrible they might go to jail?"

"It could be seen that way. Alejandro's death might be seen as manslaughter, at least for some. Kidnapping Martín and holding him prisoner are both serious offences. And those two boys could be used as the scapegoats for these crimes."

Paco was thrown. He gaped at me. "Juan Pedro's boys?"

"Yes. You've already said Juan Pedro Nacan has a reputation for being a man who doesn't always do things by the book, what is considered the right thing. Maybe the fruit doesn't fall far from the tree." I stared at him. Hard.

Paco shook his head. "No, no, no. Geraldo and Jorje are not bright, not like Alfredo. True, they are a little younger and can be foolish. But at heart, they are good boys. Whatever they did, they were made to do." He paused and thought. "Or they didn't realize the consequences."

"Maybe that's why they fled in such a panic when they saw Alejandro's body. They may have seen the handwriting on the wall. Do you know what that means, handwriting on the wall?"

"Misfortune comes," he said after a moment.

246

"Maybe it doesn't have to come, Paco. But it might if those two boys aren't there to defend themselves. It's also possible what's going on might take down Juan Pedro and his entire village. The police already believe all the vandalism, robberies, and trouble is because locals don't want their gods messed with. They're putting it down to local lore, superstitions. I don't think you can escape the law for long, not even in the jungles of Guatemala."

"No, you cannot." His voice held more solemnity than I'd ever heard from him.

"Because you are a good man, I am hoping you will find Geraldo and Jorje and bring them here to defend themselves. Maybe even their father."

"Why do you think they would listen to me?"

"You live in both worlds. They just might listen to you. And as Juan Pedro has been complicit in smaller things, this might not come out of the blue to him. But what may surprise him is that his sons might be taking the rap for everything that's gone down."

Paco stood. "What will surprise him is that I have become involved. We keep a respectful distance from one another's lives."

"But you are both fathers. He will understand that you are trying to help him protect his sons."

He thought for a moment. "Yes, he may understand that."

"Time is of the essence, Paco. You have only an hour, maybe two."

"I will try."

"Good. But you need to go now. Do you want to leave Afortunado here with me?"

He shook his head and chucked the monkey under the chin. "No, Afortunado is my good luck charm. And I will need all the good luck I can get."

247

Chapter Forty-Two

It was about fifteen minutes after sending Paco on his way. Gurn had come out of hiding and, as we walked toward the conference tent, I told him of the conversation between Paco and me. He, in turn, told me Lila would make her way there after seeing Richard's recent video of little Steffi playing with a new stuffed toy. Or rather, trying to eat the new stuffed toy. Grandparents live off that sort of thing.

If I remembered correctly, it was a toy baby rhino. One of the gifts sent by the International Rhino Foundation as a thank-you for Lila's latest donation, hoping to save these animals from extinction. I hope so, too.

We slowed down a little and lingered in the open courtyard of the dig. A new day in the jungle. The air felt warm and fresh on my skin. A soft breeze blew, almost caressing me. I closed my eyes, facing the rising sun.

Suddenly I didn't want to go to the conference tent. Like ever. Once I got there and went inside, everything was going to explode.

Gurn's voice interrupted ragged thoughts. "It looks like JJ is up early, too. I got a short text from her a moment ago. Martín is improving and she told him about the baby."

I opened my eyes, glad to be brought back from my downward mental spin. "Why don't we give her a call? There is a question or two I'd like to ask her."

Gurn pressed JJ's speed-dial number on his phone. She answered after several rings.

"Hi, JJ," I said into his sat phone.

"Hello, Lee," she said in surprise. "I thought it was Huckster, but I'm so happy to hear from you. Is he with you?"

It was good to hear JJ's voice. We moved to the center of the courtyard. No one around, Gurn put her on speakerphone.

"I'm here, and good morning, JJ," he said. "You're on speakerphone. I got your text, but we thought we'd talk in person and get a few more details on Martín's health."

"He's doing much, much better. The concussion turned out to be milder than the doctors first thought. His wooziness was due more to dehydration than anything else. You know about the pins they had to put in his ankle to keep it immobilized?"

"No," Gurn said, looking at me.

"Ouch," I said, returning his gaze. "That sounds painful."

"Well, not as painful as you'd think, considering how long the pins are, but he's on lots of pain pills. But that does mean he has to stay in the hospital for at least another three to four days."

"That's good," I said. I didn't want her affected anymore than she had been on what was going to go down soon.

"I had an ultrasound done yesterday afternoon. The baby is perfect." Her voice burbled over into a giggle. "I didn't want to know the sex. Or should I say gender? Whatever it is, we don't care. We are both beside ourselves."

Her happiness buoyed me. I saw it had the same effect on Gurn.

He asked, "And Uncle Samuel? How's he doing?"

"He goes home in two days. Mom is thrilled."

"So, all is well," I said.

"Yes. I can't tell you what it means to be able to say that. How are things going with you two?"

Gurn and I exchanged looks. There was a pause. "They're definitely moving along," I said, reluctant to unload a diatribe on her.

"Is something wrong?" She answered herself before either of us could speak. "There is. I can tell. Neither of you is your usual self."

"Everything's fine," I lied.

"It's just early in the day," Gurn added.

"No, it's not. Just a minute," she said. There was the sound of a rustle of movement. "I'm out in the hallway now. I don't want Martín to hear what we say. He's still upset by Alejandro's death. What's happened?"

"Well, we did call to give you an update, JJ," I said. "While this won't make Martín feel better, it might give him some closure. Alejandro died of a preexisting heart condition. Serious. According to the pathologist, he could have died at any time. Anything could have triggered it."

There was a sharp intake of breath on the other end of the line. "Does that mean he shouldn't have been working in the jungle at all?"

"Probably not," Gurn said. "But you can't stop people from doing what they love. Especially when they know their time is limited."

"No, you can't. Thanks for letting me know. I'll wait until the right moment to tell Martín. He was very fond of Alejandro, considered him like a kid brother. You know, he was only twenty-two." A small sob escaped her.

A thought occurred to me. "JJ, do you have any pictures on your phones of Alejandro? Something you wouldn't mind sharing with me?"

"Of course I do. Martín is not a picture taker, but I take them all the time. I have six or seven pictures of them together."

251

"Can you send them to me? All of them? Now?"

"Of course. I'll send them as soon as we hang up."

"Thank you," I said.

There was a moment or two of dead air before JJ asked, "Okay, you two. There's more. What is it?"

My new cuz was sharp. I looked at Gurn and he looked at me. He decided to be the bearer of bad news.

"There's been an accident. Dr. Lancaster is dead. Killed by a fer-de-lance."

Her intake of breath was loud and long. "Oh my God. How horrible. How did that happen?"

"It's too involved to go into now," he said. "But we'll call you back and fill you in on the details later today. Maybe we can do a video chat."

"Okay," she said, dragging out the word. "But I can tell that whatever you're not telling me is big."

Gurn shook his head at a loss for words and looked away. I took over.

"JJ, I promise we will have a long talk with all the explanations you want, this afternoon."

"I guess that will have to do," she said in a confused tone.

"Let me ask you one more thing before we hang up. If someone wanted to spread gossip or see to it a lot of people had information in the shortest amount of time, how would they do that? After all," I added, "this is like small-village life. There has to be a rumor mill."

I could feel her thinking on the other side of the line.

"Let's say someone wanted to spread something bad about me, for instance," I prompted. "Where would be the place to do it?"

"How could anybody say anything bad about you, Lee? You're wonderful."

252

"That she is, JJ." Gurn was quick to answer. "But let's say someone wanted to spread a rumor. How would they do it?"

"Well… I supposed the best way to do that is at one of our morning meetings. Most of the staff and heads of departments gather every morning at seven thirty in the conference tent to discuss the upcoming day. But beforehand, everybody talks about anything and everything. That's why I didn't go to Dr. Abeba when I thought I was pregnant. She's sweet but a major gossip. If I had, it might have been all over camp by noon."

"I wondered about that," I said.

With a guilty edge to her voice, she said, "I'm sure I'm giving you the wrong impression. When we officially start our meetings, we stick to business. But ahead of time, well, that's how I found out about Carla and Curtis."

I went on with the thought. "Anybody in particular spread that piece of gossip?"

She thought for a minute. "Oh, I'm sorry, Lee. I can't remember. I just overheard it when I was passing by someone. I can't remember who said it."

"Never mind," I said. "And thanks, JJ. We have to go now. Don't forget to send me the images."

"Wait a minute. I remember now. It was Consuela. She'd brought in more coffee and pastry for the meeting, like she does every morning. I don't know who she said it to, though. As I say, I was just passing by. Here's another piece of gossip about Consuela, for what it's worth. Now and then, a strange man has been seen sneaking in the back door of her kitchen late at night."

"Who'd you hear that bit of news from?"

"Bennie Storrs and Josefina Sanchez. They often walk around the premises together after dinner. I heard them whispering about it the other day. I don't know if it means anything or if I'm just further spreading gossip, which I hate."

"No, no, you're not. It's all for a good cause, believe me."

"You're still not going to tell me what's going on?"

"All will be made clear in the fullness of time," I said.

"That's her new motto," Gurn said, showing me a fetching version of his lopsided smile. "Give our love to Martín and save some for yourself."

"Will do." With a catch in her throat, she said, "I want you to know how grateful I am. I don't think Martín would be alive today if it hadn't been for you, Lee, and Lila."

JJ disconnected before we could reply.

Chapter Forty-Three

I couldn't speak for Gurn, but JJ's last words gave me the resolve I needed. I'd been starting to feel sorry for a few of the people involved in this, the ones I might have considered collateral damage. But not so. None of this was right. Two people had died and one nearly did, thanks to larcenous and greedy hearts. And they were going to have to pay.

I heard the ping of an incoming message, and as promised, eight pictures of Alejandro showed up on my phone.

I sent JJ a quick thank-you, and then we headed slowly to the conference tent. It was too early, still, but I had nothing else to do. On the way, I mulled things over. I stopped short.

"You know, I've got an idea."

"Just one?"

"Actually, two. And I'm really glad I asked JJ for her keys before she left, so we can get in and out of locked buildings around here. We have about a half an hour before the meeting. Maybe we can check out the Antiquities Room to see if anyone can get in without a key. And then we can head to the recycle room.

Yesterday the laundry bag might have been thrown into the trash and wound up in the recycling center. Why don't we go see?"

"Might be worth a look. But what say we split up? I'll take the recycle room. It's near the kitchens. I understand Consuela has a garden and she uses garbage scraps to fertilize it. The garbage and the trash are supposed to be kept in the recycle room."

"Unfortunately," I said, "I think they burn the trash daily."

"But yesterday's trash might not have been burned yet. It's early. And it's worth a try."

"Thank you, darling." He turned to leave. "Oh, and if you do find a laundry bag in the trash, try not to touch it by anything other than the drawstrings, okay?"

"Will do. I have my gloves with me, too."

"Good."

"You think the snake was transported to Lancaster's bungalow in one of the laundry bags, don't you?"

"A lot of these people know how to survive in a jungle. Some even know how to use tools to catch poisonous snakes."

"I would say most do. And they're easy enough to make. A long stick with a loop on the end. I've used one several times myself. When we were in the Amazon. When we wanted to save a snake from the fires but not get bitten ourselves."

"You've led a colorful life, Mr. Hanson."

"Backatcha, Ms. Alvarez."

He winked at me and was gone.

I was hurrying toward the Antiquities Room when my sat phone rang. I looked at the number of the incoming call.

"Finally! Richard! What have you got?"

"And a good morning to you, too."

"Never mind the pleasantries, although how is everyone?"

"We're good. Glad you and Mom are all right. She told me about her sprained ankle. Is it as minor as she makes out?"

"According to the doctor, she should be back to her lovely self in a day or two."

"I'll bet that was scary, Lee."

"It's not every day we go through an earthquake and get trapped in a temple's tomb. And then there's the underground river, but let's save that story for another time. Mom took all of it like a champ."

"That's Lila. Listen, while we're still talking personal, I sent you and Mom a video of Steffi playing with a new toy grandma sent her."

"Can't wait to see the little cutie patootie. Gurn said he left Mom watching it. You don't call her 'grandma' to her face, do you?"

"Not if I want to live to see another day. Mom will take being called Nana. And even that's a huge compromise." Our laugher rang out.

"So, on to business," I said after another chortle.

"On to business," he said, his voice sobering as well.

"What did you find out?"

"A lot, and some of it surprised me. But judging by the questions, I don't think you will be surprised."

"Did you text me the info yet?"

"Right this minute. That's why I'm calling. Read it, and let me know if you need any further explanation."

My phone gave off another ping. I looked at the incoming message. Sure enough, Richard's standard long and lengthy missive.

"Thanks, brother mine, it just came in. Listen, there's one more thing."

"Of course. There's always one more thing."

"I'll be texting you about it soon." My finger touched the disconnect button, but his voice stopped me from depressing it.

"Lee, be careful."

"I'm always careful."

257

"Extra careful. This has taken a much more dangerous turn than I thought it would. We're now talking about premeditated murder."

Chapter Forty-Four

Ten minutes later found me in front of the Antiquities Room. It should have been only two minutes, but I had taken time out to read Richard's massive missive. Nobody loves sending a boatload of facts and figures like my brother. He excels at it. Of course, I had asked for all the information, but it was a little overwhelming to see it all at one time.

Putting that aside, I stood in front of the Antiquities Room, wondering how the break-ins occurred. I stared at the only entrance, a thick, well-built metal door. Unless you had a key, you'd need a battering ram.

The building itself also looked solid. Short, single-storied, and made of stucco, it was no more than twelve or fourteen feet tall. A series of small, dirty windows ran directly under the roofline. I'd been told they didn't open.

Besides, no one could get into them unless they had a ladder and were on the small side. My hips and I would've had a hard time even with me being thinner than I'd been in years.

I walked around the building to see if the front door was the only way in or out. The hum of air-conditioning got louder as I neared the back. A large unit was built into the back wall, just chugging away. I couldn't wait to get inside.

I also noted there wasn't one single security camera, and a lot of the stuff inside was purported to be extremely valuable. I'd have to talk to the powers-that-be about that. Sometimes there's a little too much trust in the world.

Returning to the front, I inserted the key into the cylinder lock of the doorknob and gave it a turn. The lock was newish and well-oiled. No scratches or any other signs of tampering.

I pushed the door open and went inside, letting my eyes adjust to the lack of light. Meanwhile, the heavy door shut behind me of its own accord. Left in virtual darkness, I felt for the inside doorknob and pulled the door wide open. Then I let go. The door swung closed again, silent and fast. One more time, and I knew it could not be left ajar accidentally.

I went back outside and jiggled the doorknob to see if by using the key, I had permanently unlocked the door. Nope. Still locked. Again, using the key, I went in and checked to see if I could unlock the door manually from the other side. Nope.

There was no way of getting inside without using a key. And when you pulled the key out, the cylinder reverted automatically to the locked position. The door could not be left unlocked.

I stood in the dark, thinking. Whether there was an accomplice or not, whoever pilfered the relics had to be one of the higher-ups with a key.

Ten keys, ten suspects. Well, actually nine suspects. For my money, JJ was innocent of any wrongdoing. And I would think that even if she wasn't family. Call me a romantic, but she demonstrated repeatedly how much she loved Martín. She would never jeopardize his health the way someone else had.

I inhaled a sharp, icy breath. The air-conditioning felt good. The unit was pumping in cold air, stripped of much of the humidity. A double bonus.

Feeling for the light switch next to the door, I flipped it on. Florescent lights sputtered above me. The room took on an overall greenish hue, just like in the bathrooms. Only not as bright.

I looked up. Several of the light tubes weren't working. One flickered and died before my eyes. The scant lighting made the room look straight out of a 1940's horror movie. Maybe it's me, but if I were a four-thousand-year-old relic, I wouldn't put up with that for one minute. Shine a light on me, baby.

I pulled out my phone, turned on its flashlight, and scanned the square room. Possibly forty by forty, the center of the room was claimed by two long, side-by-side worktables. Shelves against four walls holding precious acquisitions climbed to just below the sealed windows. I wondered how the many statues, pottery, and vases sitting on the shelves, managed to stay undamaged after the shaking the morning before brought. It looked like all of them did, though.

Shrugging, I switched my attention to the tables. Standing on stilt-like legs, they were kitchen-counter height and held shards of pottery, broken statues, small clay thingamabobs, and a large box of earthquake putty, museum quality. Aha! My PI brain clicked in place. So that's how everything stayed in place on the shelves.

There was no other furniture save tall, backless stools scattered around the tables. Individual work lights and other tools were placed neatly at one end of each.

I crossed to the work lights and turned one on. A narrow but intense beam of circular light hit the table. Perfect for jewelry making, beading, or gluing clay pots back together. Absolutely no good for lighting a room. I turned it off.

I did a slow pivot, this time focusing on the shelves against the walls. Choosing a middle shelf, I toddled over and tried unsuccessfully to pick up a piece or two, forgetting about the putty.

Securely in place, pots, bowls, and whatever else sat evenly spaced apart, probably for better air circulation. Most were mended, glued together like 3-D puzzles. Others had parts missing, leaving you to guess what they were in their past life.

Regardless, all wore labels with details that pretty much screamed their value. Even a novice like me knew something that was thousands of years old either belonged in a museum or had private collectors drooling over it. And no interior security cameras that I could spot.

After tut-tutting for a moment, I concentrated on a lower shelf holding larger statues of people, gods, or animals. Many had varying degrees of time-honored damage, but a few were in near perfect condition.

As I walked by each statue, they stared back in a noncommittal manner. One fierce-looking large cat, however, had jade eyes that seemed to follow me around the room. Maybe he was guarding the lot. I could almost hear him growl.

I paused, no longer thinking about the puma. But, rather, what was behind him. The shelves looked deep, deeper than I thought. In this poor lighting, it was hard to tell the distance between the front of the shelf and the wall, but it had to be almost three feet.

An idea came to me, and not a pretty one. I stepped in between two shelving units. Against the wall and out of sight, a long row of what might be more antiquities lay hidden in the cool darkness, more shadows than not.

However, a stretch of one section of the back of the lower shelf was empty. I pulled out my phone and turned on its flashlight. Leaning in, I searched the shelf until I found something that should not have been there. Then I studied all eight of the images JJ sent me minutes before. Sure enough, a match.

I leaned on the shelf with all my weight. Solid. Solid and bolted to the wall. It didn't budge. The shelf was built to hold the weight of just about anything, including that of a dead man.

Chapter Forty-Five

Though I hurried, I was still a few minutes late in arriving to the conference tent. Two agentés stood on either side of the entrance. Gurn, who must have been waiting for me behind the tent across the path, stepped out.

"Hi, honey," he said, then looked around. Lifting up the end of a towel thrown over his arm, he showed me the hidden laundry bag. "Found it in the trash room, just like you thought. Numbers showing ownership. Don't worry, I've only handled it by the drawstrings, and I haven't looked inside. How did you do?"

"Found an answer or two, darling. What's going on in there?" I nodded my head toward the conference tent. "It sounds quieter than I expected."

"Hector's assembled everyone on the list. I watched them go in. They grumbled at first, but he told them to stop talking and be quiet. He can be forceful when necessary."

"Meaning he'll be good at getting people to pay their repair bills. Has Mom come through yet?"

"I haven't seen her. Maybe she's still in our tent with her ankle propped up. As for me, I've been staying out of sight until you got here."

"Thank you for the update, darling. You are so good."

Just as we both leaned into one another for a quick kiss, my phone chirped with an incoming message from Hector. I scanned through the long message knowing it had to be read before I went inside.

"Darling, here's a couple of things forensics sent to Hector, that he forwarded on to me. One, the blood on Alejandro's knapsack was goat's blood, not human. And two, Dr. Lancaster was given a strong narcotic, enough to knock her out for a couple of hours."

"And when she was under," Gurn said, "the killer released the fer-de-lance from the laundry bag. Probably a really pissed-off fer-de-lance."

"But only after searching the room."

"For what?"

"Her will and heir, I think. But I don't want to say anything more. I'm waiting for verification from Richard. I might jinx it or, if it's not true, sound like more of an idiot than I usually do."

"You never sound like an idiot, sweetheart. Well, hardly ever." He gave me one of his lopsided grins and we both laughed. His look became puzzled. "I wonder where the goat's blood came from?"

"I remember Consuela telling us she serves goat stew at least once a week," I said. "They're slaughtered on the premises. Consuela does that."

"So maybe she was the one who wrote those words of doom on Alejandro's knapsack in blood. Just one more thing in the ongoing game of terrorizing people."

"But, darling, that doesn't mean she's involved, simply because she has access to goat's blood. A lot of people could get ahold of some if they tried."

"But Consuela was the person JJ remembers spreading gossip about Curtis and Carla," Gurn protested. "And who is this strange man seen entering the back of the kitchen at all hours of the night?" He went on, ticking them off on his fingers. "And she can and does have access to practically anywhere in camp," he added. "She's a likely candidate."

"But does she have a key to the Antiquities Room, darling?"

"That's important?"

"All in all."

"Then you'll have to find that out, sweetheart."

"Just one more thing in a long list," I said with a sigh.

I shrugged my shoulders in a circular motion to release some of the tension in them. Then I inhaled and exhaled a deep breath, yoga style. It made me cough. Sometimes deep breathing does that to me.

"Okay. 'Once more unto the breach, dear friends, once more.'"

"King Henry in *Henry V*."

"Very good, darling," I said in surprise.

"I know my Shakespeare, pet. After all, my mother was an English teacher."

"I love your mom. In we go. Keep the laundry bag hidden under the towel."

Gurn nodded, and we entered the tent. As we passed the two agentés guarding the entrance, they nodded a greeting.

As before, the front of the tent held a long table with chairs facing the audience. Behind was a whiteboard for presentation purposes. A projector was off to the side.

An aisle separated the presentation table from the audience. As the audience always consisted of academics, small tables for writing or taking notes sat before uniformly spaced chairs. The first row was filled.

Reading from left to right were Professor Felicity Adler, Dr. Josefina Sanchez, Dr. Bjørn Pedersen, Dr. Benjamin Storrs, Professor Emilien Bernard, and Dr. Kia Abeba. Like most academics who never like to waste a moment, they were either reading or writing on notepaper.

In the second row, Dr. Phillip Whitewater sat, eyes closed as if contemplating a galaxy far, far away. Curtis Winston and Carla Pérez occupied two seats nearby. Carla kept flashing Curtis worried looks. Ignoring her, he stared straight ahead of him. His expression was blank, but he was picking at the bloody cuticle of one finger.

Paco wasn't there. I could only hope he would be bringing the white-sneaker twins and, if I was lucky, their father to reveal all. Or maybe he'd blown me off and was making tracks through the jungle never to be seen again. If so, it was too bad. I'd grown fond of Afortunado.

Hector sat alone at the presentation table. I was relieved to see Curtis's knapsack sitting on the floor next to his legs. Carla's metal box with all the stolen items lay hidden behind it. Hector faced the group, a slight smile playing on his lips. At seeing me, he rose.

"Buenos días, Señora Alvarez. Please, join me." He indicated the chair sitting next to him.

"Buenos días, Sergeant Juárez," I said.

Everyone stopped what they were doing and watched as I crossed to the front of the tent followed by Gurn. He set the towel-covered laundry bag at the end of the table, within my reach. He didn't take a chair but returned to the entrance and stood at attention.

I was about to sit when Consuela came in carrying refills for the half-eaten trays of pastry placed in the conference tent. On her heels was Lila. She maneuvered quite well on her crutches, which didn't surprise me. She does everything well.

"Just a sec," I said to Hector. I pulled out my phone and sent a quick text to my mother.

Mom, you're a part of this. Why don't you come up front and sit next to me?

267

I heard her phone ping, and she withdrew it from a small bag thrown over her shoulder. Shortly after, I received her text.

Don't be silly, Liana. This is your moment. Besides, I just got comfortable, and it would be something of an effort to get up and move.

Undaunted, I replied, **Come on, Mom. Don't be shy. Please come up and sit beside me.**

As she read my text, a look of annoyance came to her face. I've seen that look often. Within seconds, I received another text.

Liana, really. I am fine here. Please do what you need to do. Sergeant Juárez is waiting for you to begin. We all are. You are being rude.

"Yes, ma'am," I muttered to myself.

I exchanged looks with Gurn, who had been watching Lila and me texting. While he didn't know exactly what the exchange was between us, he knew I hadn't gotten what I wanted. He shrugged as if to say, mothers, what can you do with them?

Crutches resting on the chair beside her, Lila ignored all of us and began writing in her lavender leather journal. It was more stop and think, stop and think than steady writing.

Meanwhile, Consuela had refilled the pastry trays. She poured more steaming coffee into the carafes. All unobtrusive, all without looking at anyone. As she turned to leave, I said, "Consuela, won't you join us?"

It took the cook an instant to realize she was the one being spoken to. Startled or maybe embarrassed by my request, she shook her head shyly and headed for the exit.

"No, no, Consuela," I said. "I insist. Join us. I have a few questions for you. Please sit in the back row."

More wary than embarrassed now, she hesitated, then looked around her. It was almost as if she were looking for an escape route. Taking the end seat at the very back row, she sat down with reluctance.

Hector stood, cleared his throat, and addressed the group. "I think we can begin now." He turned to me. "Señora Alvarez, you have found what you were looking for?" His voice was loud, making more of a proclamation than a question.

"I have. In fact, I found several things."

I took a seat. Hector remained standing. Suddenly everyone seemed to come to life. An onslaught of questions flew to the front of the room, along with a few accusations and demands of knowing what was going on. Some even stood as they protested.

"Silencio!" Hector thundered. They were silent. "You will sit," he said, pointing to those few standing. "You will be quiet. This is an official police investigation. You will answer any questions asked of you by either me or the señora. Or I will take you to jail."

Stunned by his force, they did as he ordered. I was a little stunned myself. I had to give the young man credit. He may have wanted to be an auto mechanic, but the world would be missing one helluva showman.

Satisfied with the results, Hector sat down. He turned and whispered in my ear.

"Since I was a boy, that is a speech I heard my father give many times. I memorized it and was waiting until I could say it to suspects."

"Well, you hauled it out at the right time and did your father credit, Hector," I whispered back.

My turn to address the crowd. But I didn't stand.

"Ladies and gentlemen, thank you for your patience. I will make this as brief as possible. The troublesome things going on at camp for the past few months are more uncomplicated

269

than they've been made to look. It has been, in most cases, about misdirection.

"We were directed to look at the theft of artifacts. Not so. We were directed to think superstitious locals are responsible for acts of vandalism and destruction. Not so. We were directed to think a man was murdered. Not so. We were directed to think a woman died accidentally. Again, not so. It has been a world of misdirection. But one thing it has always been about is money."

Here I paused dramatically. I looked around me. Yup. I sure had everyone's attention.

"Let's go back to the beginning. Several months ago, small items of a personal nature began to disappear. There is in our midst a kleptomaniac. That's someone with a recurrent urge to steal, typically without need or profit."

While I was saying this, I deliberately did not look in Carla's direction. I heard a gasp, however, which seemed to come from Curtis.

"This gave someone an idea. Seeing how upset and thrown off-balance the group was from these small thefts, this someone decided to build on these incidents. Soon artifacts went missing. Ones with enough value the authorities had to be alerted, and troubling enough to keep people from looking at the real thefts."

There was a small disturbance outside the tent from people speaking in both Mayan and Spanish. Gurn rushed to the tent door as it was flung open.

Paco, complete with monkey, stepped forward. The two white-sneaker boys, Geraldo and Jorje, ill at ease, came to his side. They looked like they could bolt at any minute.

A man remained close by but stood behind the three. He was not quite as tall as Paco or the boys, but he was the one with presence. The first thing I noticed was his high

270

cheekbones and prominent nose. He absolutely looked like my idea of a Mayan warlord. This must be the father, Juan Pedro Nacan, I thought. And someone to be reckoned with.

"Please, come in," I said in Spanish, looking at the two jóvenes. "I just have one or two questions for you, Geraldo and Jorje."

But both boys stayed frozen in place, their eyes wide with terror. Their father uttered something to them I didn't hear. Whatever it was, it did the trick. They took a couple of steps inside the tent. It was a little crowded by the door, so Gurn gestured for Paco to go with him to the rear. I watched them move away, then turned my attention back to the sneaker boys. Again, I spoke in Spanish.

"If you two will sit down in the back row and wait a moment, I will get to you. I think you can help clear up a few things. And I thank you for joining us."

I tried to sound more gracious and kindly than I was feeling, hoping to relieve some of their fears. The boys knew they were in trouble, but I didn't want them fleeing the place or keeling over from fright. They crept to the back row and sat down next to one another. Their father stayed in the doorway. I turned back to the group.

"I think the bulk of you speak Spanish, enough for me to continue in the language. If you want me to repeat something in English, just let me know. I assume the man standing in the doorway is Señor Nacan, an important person in El Mirador. Is that correct?"

Juan Pedro Nacan acknowledged his status with one quick nod. He seemed quite sure of himself in a fairly tense setting.

"And you, Señor Nacan, you let me know if I say anything that is untrue."

Nodding again, his dark eyes took in everything. He was an intelligent man, which was no surprise. After all, he was

271

the well-known leader of a village. I suspected he knew full well the import of this meeting.

I turned to my captive audience. They sat staring at me, some nervous, some angry, some apprehensive – but all waiting.

"First, we're going to talk about what is being methodically pilfered from Guatemala. Not antiquities from the glorious past of the Mayan culture, but one of the country's rarest and most beautiful of treasures. Orchids."

A hubbub broke out.

"Silencio!" Hector banged the palm of his hand on the table top several times. As quickly as the exclamations started, they ended. I continued.

"Guatemala is known as the country of orchids. The national flower of Guatemala is the Lycaste Skinneri, a beautiful white orchid. Ironically, even the commonest of orchids, something you'd pay fifteen or sixteen bucks for at a garden center, is not allowed to be exported from the country.

"Several months ago, someone in this room made an amazing discovery, probably quite by accident. Nearby in the jungle, rare orchids are being cultivated as they have been for thousands of years. It started with... oh, what's his name... the king. The one who was in the mural that somebody deliberately blacked out."

"B'alaj Chan K'inich," Lila said, throwing her voice up to the front of the tent. "Maybe you should write it *down*, dear."

"Thanks, Mom. B'alaj Chan K'inich. As I say, starting with him, generations of villagers have toiled away to maintain these beautiful orchids. It was their sacred duty. The orchids were originally meant for the king and his court. But the demise of the empire meant little to the caregivers of the orchid garden. The nurturing and care for them remained, but the use has changed over the centuries. Now they are used by

272

the commoners in religious ceremonies. Village women wear them in their hair, or decorate their homes with them. But knowledge of their existence never left the village. No one other than the village knew the location of the garden. It was always kept secret. Until recently." I looked at Juan Pedro Nacan. "Isn't that true, Señor Nacan?"

He did not answer but nodded again.

"What prompted this change was the discovery of the El Cizin temple. Now hordes of people, strangers to the Mayan ways and culture, were on the scene. The nearby garden of orchids, no matter how hidden the caregivers tried to keep it, was in danger of being revealed. And that is exactly what happened when Alejandro accidentally came across it. But there was one more outsider who knew of its existence even before Alejandro. And its commercial possibilities.

"The people seated in this room have prestigious positions in the world of archaeology, but most of you don't make a lot of money. And suddenly here was the potential for making a great deal of money. It's easy to see how someone could give in to the temptation."

"I resent the implication that one of us would do such a thing."

The statement flew up from Dr. Josefina Sanchez. Hector pointed a finger at her but said nothing. She shut her mouth but leaned back in her chair with a scowl on her face.

"I am not implying anything," I said. "I am stating a fact. A thriving black-market industry exists, highly sophisticated, and quite good at what they do. Rare orchids, valued at thousands of dollars, are systematically being smuggled out of the country. Unfortunately, from right here at this camp."

More hubbub, more banging of Hector's palm on the tabletop, even though he looked as surprised as everyone else.

"You've got a lot of nerve," Dr. Storrs said, his pink face turning red from agitation. "You are accusing one of us — "

"You will be quiet," Hector interrupted, glaring at the man. The doctor gulped but was quiet.

"Please go on, Señora Alvarez," Hector said, now distributing his glare among the rest. "There will be no more interruptions."

"So, after the discovery of the orchid garden was made, this person went to Señor Nacan, the village leader, and more or less blackmailed him. He and the villagers could continue maintenance of the garden without any disturbance as long as they cooperated. Every week that someone would take just a few chosen orchids, paying the villagers probably ten or twenty bucks each for them. For the villagers, the blackmail was sweetened by the money, and they lost only a few orchids a week. I am certain they never knew the orchids were being smuggled out of the country and sold on the black market for thousands of dollars apiece." I looked at Juan Pedro Nacan. "Did you?"

He shook his head emphatically, a look of anger on his face. But he still didn't utter a word. I went on.

"But this someone needed more help to pull this venture off. Two other people, to be exact. A person who could keep records of the transactions. And, of course, there had to be another person with connections to the black-market world. But our someone was the person in control, staying on top of things, serving as the go-between for the business and the caregivers. But most importantly, this someone had the keys to the kingdom, access to everything in camp, free to move about anywhere they chose. That would be you, Professor Felicity Adler."

Chapter Forty-Six

A look of astonishment came to Felicity Adler's face. Dr. Lancaster's assistant stared at me, then half rose from her seat only to fall back into it again. She drew her hand to her heart before speaking. A soap opera heroine couldn't have done it better. Her voice even fluttered as she spoke.

"Me? That's absurd. Completely absurd. How dare you? I could never do anything like that. You're just making this up. That's what you're doing." Then she burst into tears.

"You're talking a lot of bull-cocky," a defensive Professor Emilien Bernard ejaculated, his French accent thick and sputtering. "Leave it to the Americans to have such fantasies going around in their heads. You should all be put away."

Chivalry may not be dead, but it can certainly be misplaced. I gave a quick glance to Hector. He was enjoying this immensely. I ignored the outraged Frenchman and raised my voice over the sound of Felicity Adler's crocodile tears.

"Professor Adler would be, as we say in the vernacular, the ringleader."

"I can't believe you are accusing me of this," she sobbed. "Someone, make her stop."

I was unmoved. "You're the one who struck a deal with the good señor over there."

I gestured with my head to Juan Pedro Nacan. Again, he nodded, but it went unseen by the rest of the people in the room. They were too busy becoming incensed, outraged, making noises of insurrection. It was the French Revolution all over again. Only I was the one heading for the guillotine. Even Hector looked alarmed.

I stood up. "Everybody, please! Calm down. Give me a chance to prove what I say is true."

They quieted down somewhat. I turned to Señor Nacan while I pointed to Felicity Adler.

"Señor, is this the woman who has been taking your orchids? Is this the woman from whom you have been receiving instructions and money?"

Before he could open his mouth to answer, Adler stopped crying and shouted, "He's lying. And it's his word against mine. You have nothing that proves what you are saying. It's all a lie."

Juan Pedro Nacan gaped at her. I was sure he had never been called a liar or spoken to like that in his life.

"Well, why don't we just see who's lying?" I turned to Geraldo and Jorje in the back row. "This is your phone, boys, right?"

I pulled the twins' phone from my pocket and held it up. The boys looked at one another and shrugged. Actually, it was more of a twitch.

Thanks for the help boys, I thought. *Typical teenagers*. I took a deep breath and persevered.

"Well, it was taken off these two by the man who rescued Martín and it's registered to Professor Felicity Adler. So the answer is, yes. All the calls and messages on this phone have been gone over by our office. Most are pretty innocent. But let's just call one particular number, one that shows up repeatedly, and see who answers, okay?"

I pressed a button. Everyone waited in tense silence for nearly ten seconds. It can take time for a number to be transferred by the satellite in the sky to a phone on Earth.

The sounds of the Abba song, "Money, Money, Money" filled the room. Felicity Adler looked down at her pocket, a frown on her face.

"Answer the phone, Professor Adler," Gurn said, moving closer. "Or I will answer it for you."

Felicity Adler pulled her phone out as ordered. Without answering it, though, she tossed it on the table. She looked straight ahead of her with no expression whatsoever on her face, her breaths coming quick and fast.

Her entire persona changed. She was no longer the overwhelmed, weak woman sobbing her heart out as before. She sat sullen and tall. After a split second, she turned and glared at me. If looks could kill, I'd be dead ten times over.

"You know, I have been listening to you talk nonsense long enough. You are one crazy lady, Ms. Alvarez, and you should watch who you slander."

"The definition of slander, Professor Adler, is someone who makes a false statement about a person that damages that person's reputation. I haven't done that."

"You think you're so smart, you interfering bitch," she screamed.

She was close enough to me I could see the spittle from her mouth. Charming. Then she picked up her phone and hurled it at me.

Fortunately, I was catcher for my softball team in high school. Some things you never forget. Automatically, I caught the phone right before it hit me in the chest. Although my hand burned from the impact, I casually set the phone down on the table next to the boys' phone.

But her action caused Hector to stand, hand on the gun at his hip. Two officers rushed toward her but not before Gurn was there. He grabbed her throwing hand and held on tight.

"You okay, sweetheart?" he asked me while never taking his eyes off the professor or relaxing his grip.

"Yes, thank you."

"You are under arrest, *Professora*," Hector said. His voice was terse and accusing. "I arrest you for the trafficking of stolen goods, the kidnapping of Martín Rodriguez, and the murder of Alejandro Rios."

"Not so fast, Hector. Let me finish," I murmured to him.

"I didn't kill anyone," Felicity Adler screamed, struggling to free her wrist from Gurn's hold.

She managed to stand up, knocking her chair over, but couldn't pull free. She reached up with her free hand and tried to scratch Gurn's face. Unruffled by her behavior, Gurn grabbed both her arms and pinned them behind her back.

However, the room gasped as a whole, some close to her even rising and trying to move away. Agentés went to each one and made them sit down again.

Within moments, Felicity Adler stopped struggling. A form of order descended, and the room calmed down. But the professor's peers and coworkers stared as if seeing her for the first time. I think they were.

Adler suddenly shouted, "He was dead! He was already dead. All I did was dress him in the warrior's costume and put him on the steps of the temple."

"Yes, it's true."

I deliberately spoke in a soft tone. I wanted people to concentrate, even strain to hear my voice.

"You didn't kill him. He died of a genetic heart condition brought on by being chased through the jungle. It could be deemed as manslaughter rather than murder, but that's up to the courts to decide. Regardless, you took advantage of his death. You stored his body in the Antiquities Room for two days waiting for the optimum opportunity to display it, probably timing it for after we arrived. Then you dressed Alejandro like an ancient Mayan warrior, put the poisonous frog in his mouth, and laid him out on the steps of the temple."

Some of the fight went out of Adler. "I just wanted to frighten everyone, feed into the legends and myths, hoping I could make the locals go away. Stop the progress. I didn't want them working here."

"And you kept at it. Like the other warrior you invented the other night that didn't exist. Playing up to supernatural fears. All in an effort to close the camp down so there would be no discovery of your lucrative business. Or, at least, until the garden was moved to another place."

"I didn't do it alone. He helped me," she spat, pointing an accusing finger at Curtis.

Hot dang, Andy Griffith's *Matlock* never had better courtroom drama. Heads turned, and everyone stared at the comptroller. The room became hushed again. Curtis Winston continued to look straight ahead but stopped picking at his bloody cuticle.

"Curtis," Carla said in barely a whisper. "You?"

He turned on her. "Like you're one to talk. Stealing everyone's jewelry and whatever else strikes your fancy."

Carla looked as if she'd been struck across the face. Her eyes glistened with tears.

"You said you'd never tell anybody."

"I said a lot of things, Carla. It doesn't mean I meant them."

Felicity Adler again tried in vain to pull free of Gurn. I stood and directed my comments to her.

"You stop behaving like a madwoman, or the sergeant is going to tack disorderly conduct on to an already long list of grievances. Aren't you, Sergeant?"

279

Hector, not expecting me to address him, looked like he had no idea what to say. After a brief hesitation, he recovered. "I will do more! I will toss you in jail and throw away the key." He gave me a self-satisfied grin.

Felicity Adler stopped struggling and sat down again, crossing her arms against her chest. Gurn stood over her, ready for any future disturbances.

"Okay, Curtis," I said. "Time for you." I turned to Hector. "May I have the knapsack?"

On hearing the word "knapsack," Curtis made more of an indication of a lunge in my direction rather than an actual one, but it didn't matter. Agenté López, the usual look of menace on her face, removed her baton from her belt. She waved it in the air, moving toward him. Curtis shrank back in his chair and was still.

Hector bent down and retrieved the knapsack. Before he could put it on the table, I said, "Gently, Sergeant. It has some very valuable items inside."

Once on the table, I unzipped the sack and removed several shirts and a pair of jeans from the top. Below, were 4 one-pound, silver-and-black coffee bags with the Supreme Organic Guatemalan Reserve Coffee logo on them.

"Be careful," Curtis said instinctively, before glancing at the intimidating Agenté Lopez.

"Don't worry," I said. "I know what's in them."

With exceeding care, I pulled out one bag and set it on the table. I undid the clear tape that sealed the bag, then opened it wide. Scooping out a handful of coffee beans from the top and sides, I drew out clear Bubble Wrap containing a stunning orchid, down to its bare roots.

Chapter Forty-Seven

Gold-and-wine-colored striped wings and a deep-ruby stigmata lip lay perfectly protected. I didn't bother to unwrap it. I didn't need to.

The room gasped almost as one as I laid it down on the table. Once again, with exceeding care.

"If I am not wrong," I said, "this orchid is a Paphiopedilum Rothschildianum. The Rothschild's orchid is one of the rarest and most expensive flowers on the planet. It was thought to be found only in the Kinabalu National Park in Malaysia, but here it is, in the jungles of Guatemala. Nature can be tricky that way.

"Those familiar with the black market say the plant, which only blooms once every seventeen years, can fetch up to five thousand dollars a stem. There are four orchids in this knapsack, probably commanding a similar sum. And these, or something as valuable, go out once a week."

I looked at the village leader still standing in the doorway. "I'm sure the amount of money being spent in the black market on these orchids surprises you, Juan Pedro Nacan." Possibly speechless, he simply stared, openmouthed.

"But these are the sums commanded these days. Are they not, Dr. Pedersen?"

I turned and looked at the man sitting in the first row, who had been so quiet yet so observant through all of this.

"Or should I say Inspector Pedersen, of the Convention of the International Trade in Endangered Species of Wild Flora and Fauna? You have not exactly been living a lie, as you have a degree in archaeology, but that is who you really are."

A shocked Bjørn Pedersen looked down with a small laugh and then up at me again. "Caught," he said, good naturedly.

"For those of you who do not know," I said, taking in the group, "The Convention of the International Trade in Endangered Species or CITES is a worldwide organization with a reputation for saving many species from extinction. Thank you for that, Inspector."

"Yes, saving endangered plants has become my life's work. I was sent here to find out how the orchids were getting out of the country. While I suspected who the perpetrators were, I could never figure out how they did it. None of my informants knew, either."

"It was quite ingenious," I said. "Once a week, Felicity Adler would visit the garden and make her selections. Curtis would then wrap the orchids in protective Bubble Wrap and hide them in specifically marked coffee bags. He would deliver them to the Supreme Organic Guatemalan Reserve Coffee, under the guise of being there to do the accounts. The bags were sent with other, legitimate coffee bags by a delivery service to the buyers from mainly Europe and the States."

"So, they not only got a rare orchid," Pedersen said, "but a great cup of coffee."

I looked at the inspector with new appreciation. Now that the real man had come to light, he had a sense of humor.

"Yes," I said with a smile. "They arrived within days and in near perfect condition. I'll leave you to unwrap the remaining three orchids that are in the other coffee bags, shall I?"

"Thank you. I will do so with great care," he said. "On behalf of the Guatemalan government and CITES, thank you, Ms. Alvarez."

Hector, still standing, looked at me with confusion in his eyes. "But who is it that sends the orchids out of the country once they are put in the coffee bags?"

"The woman who co-owns the Supreme Organic Guatemalan Reserve Coffee Company. She has the connections and makes sure the goods get to the buyers. Margarita Winston, Curtis's wife."

"Wife?" Both Carla and Felicity Adler exploded with the word.

"Being a Don Juan is the least of his problems, ladies," I said to the two stunned women.

"Filly," Curtis said, turning and addressing Felicity Adler, "they mean nothing to me. You are the only one that—"

Felicity Adler turned her back on him in an exaggerated and marked manner. Not done yet, Curtis turned to Carla.

"Carla, baby," he crooned but got no further. Carla threw a glass of water in his face.

A few of the academics fought a losing battle to hold back their laughter, although it was probably more nerves than anything else. Even Lila tried to keep from smiling.

"Okay, to continue," I said, talking over the snickers. "Curtis has been a busy man. On top of everything else, he's also been cooking the books for his business to cover the monies from the orchids." I turned to Hector in an aside. "You didn't let him make a phone call or text, did you? Alert his wife?"

Hector shook his head. "Absolutely not. We took his phone away from him as you instructed. I will notify my father, and she will be arrested imminently."

"Perfect. I don't think she expects Curtis for another hour or two. Oh, by the way," I said, interrupting myself, "the missing artifacts are on the lower shelf of the Antiquities Room, next to the walls. Hidden from sight, the way Alejandro's body was for two days. You know, word to the wise. That room should be cleaned out every now and then."

"That's right," Felicity Adler yelped. "They were never stolen. Only misplaced. And you can't prove otherwise. And you can't prove I had anything to do with smuggling black-market orchids or with Alejandro's death, either. You haven't got a thing against me."

"You mean other than the Mayan warrior's costume missing from the Museo Miraflores in Guatemala City shortly after your visit there? As an archaeologist, you had access to their archives, and you are listed as a recent visitor, and I'm sure we'll find your fingerprints on the leather belt, sandals, and headdress when you dressed and carried Alejandro up the steps of the temple, aided, of course, by Curtis."

I took a deep breath after my long, run-on sentence. Reaching for her phone, I held it up.

"And thanks for throwing me this. I'm sure we'll find calls and text messages to Geraldo and Jorje, including threats and intimidations to underage teenagers.

"That is a crime we in Guatemala do not take lightly, Professora," Hector said with severity.

"And I'll bet your exchanges with Curtis are also on your phone," I said. I was beginning to enjoy myself.

"He will also be facing similar charges. We have you both dead to rights," Hector added, then leaned into me and whispered. "I heard my father say that once."

"It's possible he may have watched a bit too much *CSI* back in the day," I whispered back. "But it is impressive."

284

Felicity Adler reverted once again to the role of the sobbing, overwhelmed, and innocent victim. This time, though, Professor Bernard did not rise to her defense but averted his eyes. Some people can learn.

Then out of the blue, Adler jumped to her feet and pointed an accusing finger at Curtis Winston. I have to say, this was the most volatile woman I'd ever met.

"He did it," she screamed. "I just did what he told me. He threatened me. I was afraid of him."

Curtis, who had been strangely quiet after his water bath, jumped to his feet as well. Shouting loud enough to be heard in Honduras, he protested her accusation.

"Afraid of me? As Frenchy said over there, bull cocky! This was all her idea. I just did what she told me to do. And I will testify to that."

"So will I, you liar," Adler shouted back. "See you in court!"

I turned to Hector. "I think the conviction of these two is going to be a piece of cake."

Chapter Forty-Eight

"Maybe you should remove those two and take them somewhere else," I said under my breath to Hector, "or it's going to be nothing but more of their histrionics. Suggestion – handcuff them and have your people take them to the supply tent. But watch them, though."

Hector nodded and, gesturing to his agentés, repeated with great authority, "Handcuff them, and take them to the supply tent. But watch them, though."

After a few feeble attempts to resist, both Adler and Curtis were dragged away. I waited until the room settled down before I turned again to Hector.

"I would like to stress that I don't believe any of the villagers were involved in smuggling the orchids out of the country. Or the sale of orchids, either."

I looked to Señor Nacan. He emphatically shook his head.

Before I could go on, my phone pinged with an incoming message. I glanced at the screen. Not one of his lengthy texts, Richard only wrote these three words: **You were right.**

Relief flooded through me. With a little effort, I picked up the thread of the conversation and hoped my distraction hadn't shown.

"The local people are not killers. They were protecting their culture and their way of life. Is there anything you would like to add in your or their defense, Señor Nacan?"

He nodded, looking a little embarrassed. He finally spoke up, his voice a deeper baritone than I would have thought.

"When I called Professora Adler about the young man's death, she threatened me. She told me to bring the body of the dead man to her late that night. She said if I didn't, she would tell the authorities my sons had killed him. And that they would believe her over me."

"In essence, she again blackmailed you," I said.

He held his head high but addressed me. "Yes, but I am responsible. My sons had nothing to do with any of this, other than obeying my orders as their father to take care of the wounded man."

"Which each one thought the other one was doing. That's right, isn't it?"

I looked to the back of the room at both Geraldo and Jorje for confirmation. I didn't know which one was which. They glanced at one another and then at their father. With a look of shame, both jóvenes nodded, then lowered their heads.

I turned to their father again, "Señor Nacan. Two nights ago, I believe you had help knowing when to come to the camp. It was through your friendship with Consuela, wasn't it? She would call you—apparently, everyone around here has a sat phone—and let you know when it was safe to visit the camp."

Consuela and the village leader exchanged quick looks. Señor Nacan rose to her defense.

"Yes, we are friends. But Consuela knew nothing of what the professora and I did that night. Consuela would often call me when she was done for the day, and it was safe for me to come play segura-lo with her. We play the game many nights when others sleep."

"Segura-lo. That's a card game equivalent to Texas hold 'em. A form of poker, right?"

They looked at one another. She nodded and he shrugged.

"I do not know this Texas hold 'em," he admitted.

287

"Nonetheless," I said to him, "you played the card game after you delivered the body to the professor and Curtis at the Antiquities Room?" He nodded. "That was around what time?"

"Ten o'clock," he said. "Then I played cards with Consuela for about two hours and returned to my village."

I turned to Consuela. She looked a little ashamed.

"I'm afraid I'm a bit of an addict. We don't play every night, but maybe two or three times a week. I can't help myself. It's a lot of fun, and I enjoy… well… the company."

"I, too, am an addict," he said. His face lost some of its hardness, the dictatorial edge, as he smiled at her. She returned his smile.

"Let me get this straight," I said. "Consuela, you know nothing about the death of Alejandro, the stolen artifacts, or the orchids?"

She looked bewildered. "No, I don't understand. We only play cards at night. He is my friend. He never…" She stopped speaking, befuddled. I suspected they were more than friends.

Señor Nacan turned to me. "Señora Alvarez, Consuela knew nothing about the garden or my business with the professora. And only that one night did I call Consuela to ask her if everyone had gone to bed. I didn't know what else to do. We had to bring the body to the camp or suffer the consequences. Consuela is my friend. She never would do anything dishonest. I swear."

He paused and stared at her. She stared back.

Okay, they were in love. And hopefully, it was not love behind the eight ball.

"Whatever you did, Consuela," I said, "maybe it was unwise, but I'm sure it wasn't illegal. You can sort it out with

288

your new bosses later on. For now, I wanted to just dot my i's and cross my t's regarding your part in all this."

"She had none," Señor Nacan insisted. "You have my word on this."

"Thank you, señor. And I take you at your word. Let's move on to the acts of vandalism and destruction, laid on the locals. Professor Felicity Adler and Curtis Winston were completely responsible for that. They not only wanted to frighten away the workers, but they were also trying to delay further investigation into the king's tomb, until they had time to move the orchid garden."

"The *mural!*" Lila said, her voice animated and alive.

"Exactly," I agreed. "The mural. When I discovered the so-called defacing was nothing more than sooty mineral oil, I knew it had to be someone devoted to archaeology. Felicity Adler could not bring herself to permanently destroy such a find. I originally thought Dr. Lancaster was in on it because she made the room off limits, declaring it unsafe. She may have had other reasons, but Dr. Lancaster turned out to be right about the unsafe conditions of the king's tomb. I learned that the hard way."

I paused, reached for a nearby bottle of water, and unscrewed the lid. Taking a fast drink, I steeled myself for the last round of events.

"Now we come to the most serious event in all of this: Dr. Lancaster's death. Premeditated murder designed to look like an accident."

Everyone in the room became silent. Following the old adage, if I'd dropped a pin, it could have been heard. I took a deep breath and plunged in.

"The killer tried to make it look as if it was somehow linked to the death of Alejandro and what was going on at camp. But it had nothing to do with any of it. Once again, misdirection. The fact is, the project manager, personally, had a lot of money. And she'd made a will. Even though it appeared she had no one left in the world — she'd even lost her ex-husband a few years back — that wasn't quite true. You can consider a lot of people family, especially when most of yours have passed on."

I reached over and pulled the towel covering the laundry bag toward me. I picked up a pencil from the table, whipped the towel off the laundry bag, and using the pencil, lifted the bag in the air.

"Here's how her murder was committed. This bag contained the fer-de-lance snake captured by the killer and brought to Dr. Lancaster's bungalow. The bag was probably left outside the door until she was knocked out from the narcotic put in her cognac. When she passed out, the killer searched for the will that verified the name of the beneficiary. Otherwise, why go through all of this? Once the will was found, the snake was released into the room, our killer fast departing. It was only a matter of time before the snake found Dr. Lancaster and bit her. She wouldn't have felt a thing, as she was unconscious. The fact it bit her three times ensuring her death was just the killer's good luck.

"How do you know all of this?" Dr. Josefina Sanchez spoke up again. "Can you prove anything you say is true?"

"That's my job, finding out how people commit crimes. It's usually cybercrimes, but it's done pretty much the same way. Follow the clues, find evidence. For instance, this bag has the killer's fingerprints all over it. And I'm sure traces of the DNA of a fer-de-lance snake are inside. And then, of course, there's the will. Dr. Lancaster's solicitor at Oxford agreed to share the contents of her latest will with the Guatemalan Police who have shared it with me. Her beneficiary and killer is her former brother-in-law."

Before I could continue, Dr. Whitewater leapt up, pulled my mother to her feet, withdrew a gun, and put it to her head. All in a matter of a split second. Everyone froze in terror.

"You don't have to say any more, lovely lady," he said. "Your mother and I will be taking our leave."

Hector half rose, his hand on the gun in his holster. Gurn and the agentés moved forward.

"Uh, uh, uh," Whitewater warned them. "Don't do anything rash. I've killed once. I don't have anything to lose. Everyone should retreat from the door, or I will be forced to shoot the charming Mrs. Alvarez."

I looked at Gurn in horror. Both of us were armed, but that didn't rule out Whitewater shooting Mom before either of us got to our weapons.

As if knowing what was going on in my mind, Gurn shook his head at me ever so slightly. He'd been trained as a hostage negotiator and knew to do whatever the man with the gun wanted. Maybe that way, nobody would get hurt.

Hector raised his hands in the air to show he wouldn't pull his gun. He gestured for his people to back away. Señor Nacan moved away from the door and joined Gurn and Paco in the back. Several agentés retreated to the rear of the tent as well.

Wrapping his arm around my mother's neck, Whitewater held on tight and pushed her toward the exit. But all I could focus on was the gun at her temple.

They advanced several feet, Lila limping all the while, when she said, "Wait, I need my crutches. I can't walk without my crutches."

Her voice shook with pain and fear. I'd never heard her sound more pathetic. As for me, I was having trouble breathing. I just couldn't take in any air.

291

Whitewater paused, then backed up to where the crutches were leaning against the chair, pulling Lila along with him. He took his gun away from her temple and allowed her to reach for the crutches.

But instead of putting them under her arms for support, she dropped one to the ground, swung the other crutch under the hand holding the gun, and pushed upward. The gun discharged into the ceiling with a mighty blast, then flew out of his hand and tumbled to the ground.

But Lila was not done yet. Using the crutch like a baseball bat, Lila slammed a home run into Whitewater's diaphragm. With an oomph, he bent over, expelling any air he might have had in his lungs. The third and final blow came when Lila whacked him over the head with the top of the crutch. As the sound echoed throughout the tent, Whitewater went down like an anvil. As far as I was concerned, Lila Hamilton-Alvarez won the game for the home team.

Chapter Forty-Nine

It was an hour later. Lila, Gurn, Hector, and I sat in our tent talking over a few things, with me still trying to take in enough air. Hector pulled out a bottle of Remy Martin from his bag.

"Is that—? I stopped midsentence.

"Si, Lee. This is the bottle of cognac from Dr. Lancaster's bungalow slated for the trash. I thought we would have a celebratory drink. And I thought we could use something after this morning," he added.

"There were no fingerprints on it?" Lila asked.

"None at all. Besides," Hector said, "Dr. Whitewater confessed, and we caught him taking a hostage." He looked at Lila. "You, Señora Alvarez."

"I *remember*," Lila said in a serious tone.

We all burst out laughing.

"I don't usually drink in the morning," I said, "and if I did, it would be a gin martini. Two olives. Severely shaken. But right now, I'm severely shaken at seeing my mother held at gunpoint. So, I will get some glasses."

"No need," said Hector, reaching into his bag again. "I have also commandeered the snifter glasses."

He tugged at the cork and poured a little in each of the four glasses. As he poured, I couldn't help but notice his hands were still shaking. As were mine, as were Gurn's. Not surprisingly, Lila's hands matched the steadiness of a neurosurgeon.

Gurn took his glass and said, "Well, as Theodore Roosevelt said, 'Do what you can, with what you have, where you are,' and this cognac is what we have."

"Yes, a toast." I lifted my glass high and looked at Hector. "To new beginnings. May you be swimming in motor oil for the rest of your life."

"Not *exactly* the perfect toast, Liana," Lila said.

"Please feel free to jump in with one, Mom," I said, and I hoped, graciously.

"Then let me *add*, Hector," she said, "may you have a *long* and *happy* life."

"Gracias, señora. You have all made that possible."

We each took a sip of the amber liquid. I inhaled a deep breath and tried to relax.

"So, Hector, before you head back to Flores with your three criminals, tell me what you think is going to happen to the sneaker boys, their father, and the village. Do you see any charges being made?"

He shook his head, looking down, and swirling the cognac in the glass. "No, Lee. I spoke with my father a few minutes ago, shortly after he arrested Margarita Winston. He says Juan Pedro will be put on probation for not telling us of the professora's blackmail demands. He feels there is no need to punish the village further. However, the orchid garden will be monitored by the government from now on to make sure this doesn't happen again."

"But it will be *allowed* to stay where it's been all these *centuries* and tended to by the *same* caretakers," Lila asked, "will it *not?*"

"Yes," he said. "I believe Dr. Pedersen will manage the garden until someone can be officially hired."

"And that means," I said with a smile, "Señor Nacan and Consuela will be able to continue playing cards together."

294

Everyone chuckled. In that moment, the notion of mature love was heartwarming.

"You are so very *clever*, Liana," Lila said after a moment's silence. "What made you *suspect* that Drs. Lancaster and Whitewater were related, if *only* by marriage? No one *else* seemed to know."

"The night we arrived. Whitewater said he was from Cambridge, the same as Dr. Lancaster. They were around the same age and in the same field. That got me thinking. But I didn't know he was her ex-brother-in-law for certain until Richard sent me a text confirming it right in the middle of everything."

"I want to know," Hector said with impatience, "how you managed to obtain the contents of Dr. Lancaster's will so quickly. Who gave it to you? You said it was shared with you by the Guatemalan Police, but I knew nothing about it. We only found a copy of the will hidden on Dr. Whitewater's person after we arrested him."

"Oh, that. I made it up. To see how he'd react."

"You made it up?" Hector stared at me, his eyes blinking rapidly.

"There's no way the information could have been subpoenaed from her solicitor, passed on to the Guatemalan Police, and then on to me in time. Something like that could take weeks. But what I did find out pretty fast, or Richard did, was Whitewater was her ex-brother-in-law. And wherever she went, she took him along. I just put the rest together. What I didn't expect was for him to be carrying a weapon."

Hector's face turned beet red. "That is my fault. I should have had everyone searched as they came in the conference tent."

"Now you know for the next time," Gurn said, his eyes twinkling. "If there's going to be a next time. Is there, my friend?"

Hector shook his head solemnly. "No. When he pulled that gun on your mother, my heart was beating so fast, I thought I would have a heart attack. I find this all too stressful. I do not care to go through it again. And my father has finally accepted that." He turned to Lila. "And you, Señora Alvarez, I cannot believe you were so cool under heat."

"Cool under fire." My response was automatic, something I always did when Tío made a malaprop. Suddenly I missed my uncle more than I can say. And the cats. "Sorry, Hector, that was rude."

"Lee," Hector said, "After solving this case and helping my father to understand what I wish to do with my life, you can say anything you want. I am forever in your debt."

"Thank you. But we all worked together to solve the case, including you." I turned to Lila. "I have to say, Mom, you were incredible. And you missed your calling. You should have been a professional baseball player. What a swing!"

Everyone laughed again. The tension lifted, and I reached another level of relaxation, which was to say, no longer hysterical.

"Well, I *certainly* wasn't going anywhere with *that* man," Lila said with dignity. "I merely *did* what I *had* to do. And Liana, I'm *quite* proud of you. Your summation skills have *markedly* improved."

"Thank you, Mom... I think. And thank you, Gurn, for taking on that wild woman back there. Felicity Adler's weirdness could have brought everything to a screeching halt. I think she's bipolar or something."

"She's something, all right, sweetheart," he said.

"And while we're giving out kudos, here's a toast to Richard's research skills," I said, lifting my glass again. "Once he told me he found out Dr. Lancaster married and divorced Whitewater's brother before she began her career in archaeology, it all fell into place for me. I decided to bluff the rest."

Gurn said, "I guess the two of them didn't want the smell of nepotism following them around, so they kept their past history a secret."

"She became a success in the field," I said, "but Phil Whitewater's career was little more than mediocre. Nonetheless, she took her former brother-in-law with her on whatever jobs she had."

"And this is how he *rewarded* her," Lila said. "As Oscar Wilde said, 'No good deed goes unpunished.'"

"I'm sure Whitewater resented her," I said. "I hope this doesn't sound too judgmental, but he is as vain, pompous, and narcissistic as she was. When he had the opportunity for his own success, a television show, and needed money to initiate the project, he didn't hesitate to do whatever was necessary to get it. Especially after he found out he was the beneficiary of her will. He was the only one at camp with any real motive for killing her."

"And all the ruckus going on around here fitted right into his plans," Gurn said.

"I suspect they became lovers some time ago, too, once again keeping it a secret," I said.

"Did that come from when I told you of the frilly nightgown she was wearing when she died?" Hector asked.

"See? You're getting the hang of it," I said with a laugh. "Sometimes it's just putting things together."

"Not for me, Lee. I'd rather put motors together."

We laughed again. A momentary silence descended on our little party.

"I must leave now," Hector announced and stood. "The station is on high alert waiting for the transport of these criminals. And this is my last official act before I put in my resignation. I am going out, as one would say, on a high." He gave us a broad smile.

"If you don't watch out, you're going to make a name for yourself, Hector, and they'll beg you to stay," Gurn teased. "Three criminals in one day."

"No, no, no," he replied with a laugh. "My father knows the truth. I have seen to that."

"And it's time for us to pack and head home," I said, rising.

Hector looked surprised. "You are leaving so soon?"

"We're not leaving at this *moment*, Liana," Lila said, still sitting. "We are *leaving* tomorrow morning. We have the whole *afternoon* ahead of us. Say goodbye to the sergeant *properly*."

"Sorry for jumping the gun," I said, smiling at Hector. "I guess I'm just anxious to get home. Let me wash these glasses so you can take them with you," I said.

"I leave the cognac and the snifters with you, Lee. I am not, as a rule, a man who drinks. But today, this was unprecedented."

"It was *indeed*, Hector," Lila said. "*I* will take care of all of this, Liana. Why don't you walk Hector *out*?"

When we three were at the door, Hector turned to us. "My friends, thank you for all you have done. Not just for Guatemala but for me, personally. You have changed my life."

"Let's not lose touch, Hector," I said, reaching out for his hand. "Our families have ties."

298

He grasped my hand and held it for a moment before he returned my handshake. Never taking his eyes off mine, he said, "Friendship often comes when you least expect it. I have spoken to my wife and told her if we have a girl, we will name her Liana." He reached out for a handshake from Gurn. "If we have a boy, we will call him Gurn."

Gurn jumped right in with, "Don't do that, man. Liana's a beautiful name, but you have no idea how many problems my name has caused me. No one can say it, spell it, or remember it. If you're looking for a boy's name, how about Roberto? That was Lee's father's name, and I believe is your father's as well."

"Yes, it is." Hector's face broke out in a smile. "To be honest, my wife was not happy with the boy's name. She feels it is not Latino enough."

"Hector, let me give you a tip," Gurn said, putting his arm around the younger man's shoulders. "That is the A-number-one reason not to use it. Remember, happy wife, happy life. It's true in any language."

Chapter Fifty

It was going to take time for the dust to settle after the happenings of the day. Call me paranoid, but historically it's the messenger who usually gets it in the neck when bad news is delivered. And we did that big time. There were probably a few who saw what we did as outside interference, no matter what was going on internally.

I could understand it was a lot for the staff and workers to take in. For months, two of their coworkers had been stealing as well as playing mental and emotional head games with them. Embarrassing secrets were revealed. A young man tragically died. The leader of the dig was murdered by one of their peers.

Things were never going to be the same. Consequently, we decided to make ourselves scarce and stay inside our tent for a while.

My stomach rumbled and I felt a little dizzy. That's what a glass of booze, even a small one, will do to you on an empty stomach. With a martyred sigh, I unbraided my hair for what I hoped was the last time. Then I looked in my hand mirror. Thanks to the humidity, my hair immediately took on a life of its own. What didn't coil into tight little ringlets exploded into frizz. I looked like a puli dog I once met on his way to the dog groomers. Bow-wow.

"I'm so hungry," I whined, "I could eat my own cooking." I threw myself on the cot like Sarah Bernhardt doing a death scene.

"I'll go to the cafeteria and bring us back some lunch," Gurn offered.

"Are you kidding? Someone might start throwing pots and pans at you."

"You're tired and burned out, sweetheart. I don't think people blame us for any of this."

"Liana could be *right*, Gurn," Lila said.

This was a first.

"Emotions could be *high* right now," she went on. "Why don't I *text* Consuela and ask if just this *once*, lunch can be brought to our tent?"

Before we could offer an opinion one way or the other, Lila typed in a message. Consuela was quick to agree, and soon after there was a knock on the tent door. Gurn opened it to see a smiling Consuela with a tray laden with her usual delicious dishes.

"I'll take that, Consuela, and thank you so much," he said, lifting the tray from her hands.

Still, she stood in the doorway. "May I speak with your wife?"

I got up from the cot with an internal groan. Lead-footed, I came to the door, expecting what, I did not know, but nothing good.

"Yes, Consuela?"

"Muchas gracias, señora, for what you have done." Consuela reverted to Spanish. "You have brought my friendship with Juan Pedro out in the open, and because of this — and other things — he has asked me to marry him."

My jaw dropped. For one of the few times in my life, I was speechless. "I… uh… er… What?"

"Si! I am a widow; he is a widower. We are both alone, and now we will not be. All because of you."

"I… uh… er… Really?"

301

"Liana," Lila chided. "Merely *say* 'you're *welcome*' to Consuela." My mother moved forward and pushed me out of the way with a gentle but firm shove. "My *dear* Consuela, the *best* wishes to both of you from *all* of us. May you have a *long* and *happy* life together."

"Gracias." Consuela gave us a bashful look. "I will be forever grateful to you. Thank you," she said again, but this time in English.

"You're more than welcome," Gurn said. "We're glad everything worked out for you both."

Consuela smiled and waved a goodbye before shutting the door. I grabbed a half a turkey club sandwich from the pile and threw myself down on the cot again. I was in mental lockdown but pretty noisy in my attack of the food.

"Liana," my mother said, giving me the once-over, "I fear *you* need a nap."

"I think I do, Mom," I said, chomping away. "I don't think I've had a full night's sleep since we arrived. The job is done and so am I. We have a couple of hours before we do our video chat with JJ and Martín." I crammed the last of the sandwich in my mouth. "Maybe I can get a little sleep before then."

I checked the batteries in my fan and turned it on. The room became silent but for the hum. I closed my eyes.

Consuela hadn't been gone but five minutes when there was another knock on the door. My eyes flew open. I sat up. Gurn looked at Lila and me before going to the door and opening it.

There stood Drs. Storrs and Abeba. I groaned again under my breath but got up and came forward to face the firing squad, if I may be allowed a moment's exaggeration. I couldn't, in good conscience, leave Gurn to face it alone even though I did stand directly behind him.

"Dr. Storrs, Dr. Abeba," Gurn said, placing himself in the doorway and blocking any entrance into the tent. "To what do we owe the pleasure?"

"Bennie, please, Gurn. Enough already with the Dr. Storrs stuff," the man said.

"Bennie." Gurn sounded friendly enough but did not move. "What can I do for you?"

"I hope I didn't..." Bennie threw a quick glance to Dr. Abeba, who stood beside him. He then corrected himself. "I hope we didn't disturb you, but when we didn't see you at lunch, we thought we would come here. We wanted to thank you before you left, for all you've done. Personally, and on behalf of the dig. I will, of course, be sending you a formal letter of appreciation in due course."

Still, I hung back, as did Lila. Gurn was doing a crackerjack job of being our spokesperson, so *have at it*, I thought. Bennie went on.

"Without your insight and diligence, the site might have been closed down permanently. What was going on might have never come to light. It was very edifying the way all of you, particularly Lee, uncovered the guilty."

Again, the word, edifying. Lila used it at dinner one night and now Bennie Storrs. Never heard it used before in a sentence. Must be an archaeological thing.

"Well," Gurn said politely, "Lee was just doing her job, at which she is quite good."

"Yes. A job well done." Bennie coughed nervously, then went on. "We have not fallen down on our side, either. Replacements for Dr. Whitewater, Curtis Winston, and Professor Adler are in the works. I've been made the acting project manager until the VIPs in DC come up with a permanent appointee. With a little luck, it will be me."

"Good luck to you, then. Anything else?"

303

"Yes," he said. "In case you may have noticed my behavior, I would like to explain why I have been trailing behind you these past few days. In particular, Lee. I was studying what she did and making notes. I have a feeling it might have looked suspicious."

Before Gurn could reply, I stepped around him. Time to put on my big-girl panties.

"Trailing behind us? Why, no," I lied. "We hadn't noticed. Are you writing a book?"

Astonishment covered his face. "Why, yes. That's what I was going to tell you." He coughed again, maybe nerves or to cover his embarrassment. "I've been trying my hand at writing a suspense novel. I... ah... er... I was trying to use you as... well... my muse."

"Your muse? A muse is a source of inspiration for a writing project, right? How flattering."

"Right. When I found out we were being visited by a real, live shamus, I had to find out what you did." His face darkened. "I'm not sure I will be able to continue with the book, though, what with my new duties. Writing a book takes a lot of time. And it's much more difficult than I thought it would be."

"That's what many of my writer friends say."

"Yes... well... I hope you will forgive any intrusion I may have made into your life."

"All is forgiven," I said with a wave of my hand.

"Thanks a lot," he said, obviously relieved. He turned to Dr. Abeba. "Before we go, Dr. Abeba has something else she wanted to talk to you about, Lee."

I turned, faced her, and waited. She looked down for a moment, then up at me, meeting my gaze.

"I wanted to apologize for what I said the other day in the first-aid tent. I shouldn't have listened to Felicity. But I

304

thought she was my friend. So, when she told me you were nothing more than a gossipmonger, looking for ways to trash people's reputations, I believed her. I am terribly sorry."

I sucked in a breath, feeling something. Relief? Vindication? Fatigue? I'm going with the latter. But suddenly a huge smile came to my face, unbidden. Let's face it. I'm a Pollyanna at heart. I do like it when things turn out well.

"That's okay. These things happen. I'm glad it's all been straightened out."

"Thank you for forgiving me," she said, returning my smile. "And for revealing the truth about Felicity. Although it is a sad day when people deceive one another under the guise of friendship. It should be a better world."

"Yes, it should. But it's people like you that help make it better. I understand twice a month you go to an orphanage in Antiqua and give free healthcare to the children."

"How did you know about that?" Her startled look changed to all-knowing. "I don't know why it should surprise me. You are good at what you do."

"A little birdie named Richard told me. But why the secrecy? You're doing a good turn."

She blushed and looked down again. "My daughter is a pediatrician at the local hospital. That's why I came to Guatemala. She is a good doctor and donates time to the orphanage as well," she added hastily. "But there are many children, and her days are long. I am helping her out."

"And it is a *chance* for you to *share* in your daughter's life," Lila said, coming into the conversation. "I *understand* that."

"Yes, but I couldn't let anyone here know, because Dr. Lancaster made it clear I was supposed to devote myself totally to the El Cizin site." She shot a guilty look at her new, if only temporary, boss.

305

"For crying out loud," Bennie said with a smile, "two days a month is not too much to ask, especially for such a worthy cause."

"Thank you, Dr. Storrs," she said.

"Stop with the Dr. Storrs," he said with a smile. "It's Bennie. I think we've had too much unnecessary formality around here, Kia. Gums up the works. We'll be on a first-name basis from now on, at least while I'm running things." He turned back to us. "We're gonna leave now and let you people rest. Once again, thanks for all you did."

After they left, I turned to my mother and Gurn. "You know, they could do worse than choose him to be the permanent project manager."

"And you gotta love that New York City accent," Gurn said, doing a fair imitation of Dr. Storrs.

JJ came on the line about two and a half hours later. Like most families, we babbled greetings all at the same time with no sense of propriety.

Looking well rested, JJ stood at Martín's bedside. He lay propped up on pillows, his injured right ankle suspended by something I couldn't quite make out in the picture. Despite his apparent incapacitation, he seemed alert and happy to see us, waving into JJ's phone. Martín was one of those rare people who had a million-dollar smile. And when he bestowed it on you, you felt every dollar of it.

"Before we get started," he said, beaming at us, "I think JJ should come lie down beside me for a few minutes. We promise no hanky-panky."

We all laughed. Martín's voice was strong and filled with humor.

"He's getting back to normal, folks," she retorted. She thought for a moment, breaking out into her own smile. "But putting my feet up sounds good."

"I will scoot over as much as possible," Martín laughed, looking down at his thick cast.

He did so, then reached out an arm for his wife. JJ sat down on the edge of the hospital bed, swung her legs over, and snuggled into his arms.

Lila, the ever-vigilant matriarch, took over. "This is a *time* when *Lila* knows best. We will keep this visit as *short* as possible so you both get some much-needed rest. Liana will *try* to cover only the *salient* points. How does *that* sound to everyone?"

"Whatever you want," JJ said with a laugh. "But we're happy to talk to you all for as long as we can."

"No, Mom is right," I said. "So, in twenty-five words or less, here goes."

True to my word, I did keep it as short as possible, aided by Gurn and Lila's input upon occasion. Taking in a deep breath when finished, I said, "And that's more or less what happened this morning."

"Of course," Martín said. "I remember now. Trees filled with orchids. I'd never seen anything like it in my life."

"And that's exactly why the villagers were told to keep you under wraps until the garden could be moved," I said. "Adler was afraid you'd spoil everything."

"I see." A look of reflection crossed Martín's face. "I only wish Alejandro had told me of his heart condition."

"Would it have made a difference?" Gurn asked.

Martín thought for a moment. During that time, several emotions seemed to cross his face, regret, understanding, and finally, acceptance. Then he shook his head. "No, I suppose it doesn't make a difference. We do what we need to do."

A sense of melancholy fell over the group. Then JJ picked up the conversation.

"So, Phil Whitewater killed Dr. Lancaster for her money. It's hard to believe."

"I know," I said.

"I didn't like her very much," Martín said. "But no one deserves to die like that."

"I can't find any other word for it besides despicable," JJ said. "All for money. Doesn't the Bible say money is the root of all evil?"

"Not quite," Lila said. *"For the love of money is the root of all evil: which while some coveted after, they have erred from the faith, and pierced themselves through with many sorrows. Timothy 6:10."* She realized we were all silent, gaping at her. Head held high, she added, *"Sometimes* the things you learn in *Sunday* school stay with you. Or *should."*

Before any of us could reply, Lila turned to me. "Liana, don't you *think* it's time for you to *tell* Jacqueline about her *locket?"*

"Of course. Sorry. With all that's been going on, I forgot about your locket, JJ. How I came across it is a long story, but it doesn't have too happy an ending for Carla Pérez. I found it among some other things she pilfered."

I reached inside a small pocket of my shirt and pulled out the round locket dangling from a gold chain. I held it in front of the phone's camera.

"My locket!" JJ instinctively reached out a hand to her own phone's screen, then pulled back. She closed her eyes. "You found it, Lee. You're just a… a… well, there's no other word for it, a miracle worker."

"Not really. I came across your locket more or less by accident. And not to worry, Bennie Storrs says he'll keep it locked up in his safe until you return."

"I can't believe I have it back," JJ said. "I think I'm going to cry."

"*Hormones*," Lila said with a smile.

"Then I must have hormones as well," Martín said, "because I think I am going to cry, too."

Chapter Fifty-One

I was stretched out in my usual spot on the chaise lounge on the back deck reading yet another of W. Somerset Maugham's books. It wasn't a Sunday, my usual reading day, but late Friday afternoon. One of those lazy days when the sparkling Palo Alto weather and the novel, *Of Human Bondage,* called out to me.

Tugger was sleeping, perched more off than on my chest, but managing to stay there. Baba snuggled on top of both my knees, her fluffy tail tickling one of my calves. Since our return from El Mirador the week before, the cats hadn't left my side. And I include bathroom visits in that statement.

Gurn appeared in the doorway. He took a deep breath as if to say something. I jumped right in.

"Uh-oh. I know that look."

"What look?"

"The look that says you have something to tell me."

"How about I love and adore you and can't wait to show you?"

He waggled his eyebrows. There was a sincerity about them I hadn't seen in the jungle.

"As you have been for the past week," I said, waggling my own eyebrows. "This has been fun, hasn't it? Too bad our home vacation is almost over, and we have to go back to work Monday."

He laughed and came outside, crossing to me. Leaning down, he gave me a quick kiss on the lips before he sat on the adjacent chaise lounge. "It's been nice to be just the two of us—"

"Plus the cats," I interjected.

"Not quite the same as a threesome with your mother, love Lila though I do. Tugger and Baba are much more cooperative. But that's not why I am disturbing you, beloved."

"You never disturb me, darling. Well, hardly ever."

"Good. Because I want to read you the letter we got in the mail from JJ."

"A letter? An actual, bona fide letter? I didn't think people wrote letters anymore."

"Well, apparently JJ does. Not only is it several pages long, but she has included a few visual aids."

"Visual aids! Now you intrigue me." I laid my e-reader down beside me. "What's up with JJ?"

Gurn cleared his throat and began to read. "*Dear Lee and Huckster, hope this letter finds you well. It's the first time I've written a letter in a coon's age.*"

"A coon's age?"

Gurn guffawed for a moment, a look of nostalgia coming to his face. "Our Uncle Bob used that expression. He was a hoot." He glanced at the letter and said, "Look, she says it right here." He pointed at a spot on the paper I couldn't see. Clearing his throat again, he picked up where he left off.

"*Remember how Uncle Bob used to say that all the time? I know it's only been a week, but I miss you three and wish you were here.*"

"Me too," I exclaimed. "Actually, no, I don't. I wish they were here. I don't want to be there. I am jungled out. Say, I've got an idea. Let's invite them for Thanksgiving. Maybe she can still take a plane by then. Here's another idea. You can fly

311

down, pick them up, and bring them here. What do you think?"

"I think you're very sweet. We can certainly invite them. We'll work out the details a little later. Let me go on with the letter."

"Absolutely. Continue, my good man," I said with a flourish.

Finding his place, Gurn read on. *"Mother says Dad is up and around and the doctors are saying he should make a full recovery. He and Mother are planning to make a long visit once the baby is born. Martin and I are doing well. He's spending a few hours at the clinic every day. Dr. Abeba is taking good care of both of us and even helps out with some of his patients until he can return full-time. Now that she is no longer swayed by Felicity Adler's lies, I find it easy to be friends with her."*

"Aw, that's so nice," I interjected. "I always liked Dr. Abeba."

"You said you didn't like her."

"Did I? Well, I like her now. What else does the letter say?"

"Alfredo is also helping out at the clinic until Martin finds a replacement for Alejandro. Martin says it's valuable experience for Alfredo and will look good on his college resume. I'm not sure if you know, but Alfredo got the scholarship and goes to university in the fall. We are all so proud. Paco sends his warmest regards and can't wait for you two to visit again."

"Fat chance," I said under my breath.

Gurn went on, possibly not hearing me. *"I included a picture I took of him yesterday. Afortunado is, as usual, on Paco's shoulder. Proud Papa."*

"Oh, let me see," I said, reaching out my hand for the photo. "Oh, look at that. Proud papa, indeed. And Paco looks good, too." We both laughed. "Seriously, Paco must be over the moon about Alfredo getting that scholarship. Well, go on, go on."

Gurn found his place. Again. *"I spoke with Aunt Lila the other day."*

Once more, I had to interrupt. "She calls Mom Aunt Lila? Does that mean I have to call Ida Aunt Ida?"

"Couldn't hurt. She's into that sort of thing." He repeated, *"I spoke with Aunt Lila the other day, and she says she's off crutches and went out dancing with a man called Dirk Goodman."*

"I told you something was up with that. Not that she's ready for anything serious."

"And if she is?" Gurn turned to me with a look of challenge in his eyes.

"Listen, that's between her and her conscience. Or is it she and her conscience? Whatever; Mom will do what's right."

He stared at me. "All right. Who are you, and what have you done with my wife?" He paused dramatically, then let out a loud cackle.

I chose to rise above the unspoken criticism of my relationship with my mother. "Ha ha. I will grant you sometimes Mom and I get caught up in each other's lives, but we had a long talk about it. She's just dating now and then. Nothing serious."

"Whatever you say. May I go on with the letter?"

"Please do."

"Let's see. Blah, blah, blah. Oh, yes. *I can't tell you how enthused the staff was when Aunt Lila forwarded all the images she took of the ceiling and entrance to the king's tomb right before the earthquake. Now they can try to reconstruct the ceiling the way it was before it fell in. And—"* He broke off after emphasizing the last word.

Then he repeated it. "*And they want me to thank you, Lee, for discovering the tunnel leading into the tomb from near the orchid garden. Using the tunnel, they are now able to get into the room without waiting for the debris to be cleared from the entrance. Bennie Storrs is beside himself. He wants to name two of the murals after you and Aunt Lila.*"

Gurn took a deep breath. Before he could go on, I began to ruminate. And out loud.

"All those gorgeous murals. Centuries old. I'm so glad they're going to be restored. You know, my favorite one was the—"

"I am never going to get this letter finished if you keep interrupting me, sweetheart."

"Sorry, darling. I shall try my best to stuff a sock in it."

My husband laughed. He's my best audience.

"That's all right. I don't like to cramp your style. But let's see if I can finish this before we have to go back to work on Monday. *I am including a hand-engraved invitation to Consuela and Juan Pedro's wedding ceremony.*"

"A hand-engraved wedding invitation? To Consuela and Juan Pedro's wedding? How sweet is that? Whoops, sorry, darling. Tick a lock," I said, mimicking a key locking my mouth shut.

This time he didn't even look up. "*The invitation is in both Spanish and Mayan. They are having a traditional Mayan ceremony, however. Consuela says it will be spiritual and interactive, in balance with nature and the four basic elements, fire, earth, water, and air. The ceremony will take place in the village and be officiated by a native priest, called a shaman. The bride and groom enter, playing a musical instrument or singing a Mayan song. Consuela has a beautiful singing*

314

voice, so I know it will be memorable. Then the ceremony ends with guests showering the newly married couple with flower petals."

"Wow! That sounds incredible," I exclaimed.

Once again, Gurn went on as if I hadn't said anything. "We were thrilled to be invited. Neither Martin nor I have been to an authentic Mayan wedding before, and I understand they're not to be missed! Of course, the entire Alvarez Clan is invited as Consuela and Juan Pedro's honored guests. Not that you're expected. I told them you said you'd never step foot in the jungle again, but they wanted me to send you an invitation anyway."

"Really?" I sat bolt upright. Tugger went flying off my chest. Baba was seriously jostled. "We're invited? We would be their honored guests?" I looked at the displaced cats. "Oh, sorry, kids."

Baba settled down again on my knees. Practically harrumphing, Tugger leapt up on Gurn's chaise and sat beside him. Gurn handed me the enclosed invitation with one hand, while absentmindedly stroking a put-out Tugger with the other. He had a puzzled look on his face. Gurn, not the cat.

"You sound like you want to go."

"Of course I want to go."

"But—"

"An authentic Mayan wedding. How exciting!"

"But—"

"I wonder what you wear to a Mayan wedding in the middle of the jungle? It's still rainy season there. One thing's for sure, no cargo pants. I'm going to burn those in effigy."

"But—"

"Let's see when this glorious wedding takes place."

315

I studied the invitation with excitement. Gurn watched me in stunned silence. I blathered on.

"Oh, goody. It's Saturday, two weeks from tomorrow. Wow! That was fast. But I guess when you run your own village, you can get things done. There's still plenty of time for us to prepare. We have sunscreen and insect repellent to use into the next millennium. And tons of quinine tablets. Mustn't forget those. What will I wear? I know! I'll get a Grace Kelly *Mogambo* safari outfit, only in turquoise. I look good in turquoise. Although I wonder if Abercrombie and Fitch make them in any other color besides boring beige? No matter. If there's one out there, I'll track it down. After all, I am a detective."

Laughing at my own joke, I caught Gurn still gawking at me.

"What is it, darling? Don't you want to go? Can't you fire up the jet in two weeks' time?"

"Of course I can. But I don't understand," he spluttered. "What about not wanting to ever step foot in the jungle again?"

"Oh, that," I said, giving him my brightest smile. "Don't be silly, darling. In hindsight, it was a valuable experience. Enriching, even. And remember, what doesn't kill you makes you stronger."

"I'll try to keep that in mind."

"And I spent two hours polishing up those stupid hiking boots. No point in letting all that hard work go to waste."

"Anything else you care to add?"

"Absolutely! To misquote Will Rogers, I never met a wedding I didn't like."

~

Afterword by Josie Thompson
Director of Planning FARES

Following the fall of El Mirador, during the preclassic apogee, its inhabitants never reoccupied the Ancient City. Why did it collapse? Where did the inhabitants go? What were their secrets? These inherently mysterious people, the preclassic ancient Mayans, have yet to reveal most of their enigmatic past. But every day through hard work and tenacity, the truth of their ways has unfolded to members of Mirador's Multidisciplinary team. I am proud to be a member of this team.

The FARES Leadership team is led by Dr. Richard D. Hansen, Ph.D, President and visionary of the Foundation for Anthropological Research and Environmental Studies (FARES), a non-profit scientific research institution based in Idaho. He has led the project for over thirty years. Dr. Hansen is a specialist on the early Maya and is the Director of the Mirador Basin Project in northern Guatemala. Other board members besides me include Kerry Arritt, CPA PA; Jody Lynn Hansen; Leland S. McCullough, Director, Legal Counsel; Francois Berger, Director and President, FARES-Guatemala; Dr. Nancy Swift Furlotti, Director; Dr. Glenna Nielsen-Grimm, Director; and Dr. Landon J. Hansen, Director.

I was taught in preschool that the Mayans were peaceful yet many of the recent discoveries show sacrifices and traditional bloodletting. They cut down trees to burn limestone and to create the building material to coat the famous pyramids and roadways. We have also found many remnants from battle scenes on the pyramids and it is known that the Mayans fought with soldiers from Teotihuacan, Mexico. Mirador and its wilderness hold the secrets of the

317

ancient preclassic Mayan. Preserving this unique landscape will allow future generations of archaeologists, biologists, and environmentalists to uncover its truths.

It is my hope the world will fight to preserve what remains of this cultural and natural gem. So many people throughout the world identify with Mayan heritage. The expansive wilderness provides habitat for the BIG CATS like Jaguars, Ocelots, Margays, Leopards and Pumas, and each year, new species are discovered. It is believed the Guatemalan jungle's botany also holds the recipes for cures for cancer. Can we abandon all that?

Increasingly and becoming more important, is the use of advanced technology to solve Earth's problems. We want to protect nature and culture so as to not repeat the mistakes that the Ancient Mayans did. Resource consumption contributed to the demise of the ancient preclassic Mayas. We, as a collective, global human race, are repeating these same mistakes of over-consumption and ruining our environment.

The biggest impediment to visiting Mirador is its limited access. But this remoteness catapults the area into the adventure traveler's dream list. Over the last fifteen years, I have made over twenty-five trips by foot, slogging through the mud to make the seven-day round trip. I will never forget any one of them.

Like many important topics this day and age, El Mirador has been recently politicized and misunderstood by several stake-holders. We need to move beyond this. Please help us preserve this last remaining contiguous cultural and natural landscape in Central America of the Ancient Mayans and all they have to offer. It is our human legacy.

https://www.fares-foundation.org/

Books by Heather Haven

The Alvarez Family Murder Mysteries
Murder is a Family Business, Book 1
A Wedding to Die For, Book 2
Death Runs in the Family, Book 3
DEAD...If Only, Book 4
The CEO Came DOA, Book 5
The Culinary Art of Murder, Book 6
Casting Call for a Corpse, Book 7
The Drop-Dead Temple of Doom, Book 8

Love Can Be Murder Novellas
Honeymoons Can Be Murder, Book 1
Marriage Can Be Murder, Book 2

The Persephone Cole Vintage Mysteries
The Dagger Before Me, Book 1
Iced Diamonds, Book 2
The Chocolate Kiss-Off, Book 3

The Snow Lake Romantic Suspense Novels
Christmas Trifle, Book 1

Docu-fiction/Mystery Stand-Alone
Murder under the Big Top

Collection of Short Stories
Corliss and Other Award-Winning Stories

About Heather Haven

After studying drama at the University of Miami in Miami, Florida, Heather went to Manhattan to pursue a career. There she wrote short stories, novels, comedy acts, television treatments, ad copy, commercials, and two one-act plays, produced at several places, such as Playwrights Horizon. Once she even ghostwrote a book on how to run an employment agency. She was unemployed at the time.

One of her first paying jobs was writing a love story for a book published by Bantam called *Moments of Love*. She had a deadline of one week but promptly came down with the flu. Heather wrote "The Sands of Time" with a raging temperature, and delivered some pretty hot stuff because of it. Her stint at New York City's No Soap Radio — where she wrote comedic ad copy — help develop her longtime love affair with comedy.

She has won many awards for the humorous Alvarez Family Murder Mysteries, Persephone Cole Vintage Mysteries, and *Corliss and Other Award Winning Stories*. However, her proudest achievement is winning the Independent Publisher Book Awards (IPPY) Silver Medal for her stand-alone noir mystery, **Murder Under the Big Top**.

As the real-life daughter of Ringling Brothers and Barnum and Bailey circus folk, she was inspired by stories told throughout her childhood by her mother, a trapeze artist and performer. The book cover even has a picture of her mother sitting atop an elephant from that time. Her father trained elephants. Heather brings the daily existence of the Big Top to life during World War II, embellished by her own murderous imagination.

Connect with Heather at the
following sites:

Website: www.heatherhavenstories.com
http://heatherhavenstories.com/blog/
https://www.facebook.com/HeatherHavenStories
https://www.twitter.com/Twitter@HeatherHaven

Sign up for Heather's newsletter at:
http://heatherhavenstories.com/subscribe-via-email/

Email: heather@heatherhavenstories.com.

She'd love to hear from you. Thanks so much!

The Wives of Bath Press

The Wife of Bath was a woman of a certain age, with opinions, who was on a journey. Writer and publisher Heather Haven is a modern-day Wife of Bath.

www.heatherhavenstories.com

Made in the USA
Middletown, DE
01 October 2021